PRAISE FOR
THE ALCHEMY OF STONE

A *Los Angeles Times* Summer Reading Selection

"*The Alchemy of Stone* may be ostensibly rooted in genre fiction and indeed be quite appealing to the genre fiction audience . . . But such is the alchemy of literary invention that it's quite clear *The Alchemy of Stone* explores our world within the confines of a world created with language alone."—*The Agony Column*

"The tale of a clockwork woman named Mattie whose heart is literally kept locked up by her maker, *The Alchemy of Stone* is set in a spy-ridden world of intrigue and class warfare. As a scientific revolution sweeps through the city of Ayona, Mattie discovers a secret that could help her lead a coup. If only she could figure out who to trust, and regain the key to her own heart. Written by the author of *The Secret History of Moscow*, this novel is beautifully strange."—*io9.com*

"Sedia's evocative third novel, a steampunk fable about the price of industrial development, deliberately skewers familiar ideas, leaving readers to reach their own conclusions about the proper balance of tradition and progress and what it means to be alive."—*Publishers Weekly*, starred

THE ALCHEMY OF STONE

Ekaterina Sedia

PRIME BOOKS

THE ALCHEMY OF STONE

Prime Books

www.prime-books.com

For more information, contact Prime.

ISBN: 978-0-8095-7284-7

ACKNOWLEDGEMENTS

I owe a debt of gratitude to the many writers and first readers who helped me with their advice, support and friendship: Paul Tremblay, Jay Lake, Catherynne Valente, Nick Mamatas, Paul Jessup, Paul Abbamondi, Sarah Prineas, Hannah Wolf Bowen, Mike Allen, Jessica Paige Wick, Darin Bradley, Ivona Elenton, David Schwartz, Jenn Reese, Forrest Aguirre, Barth Anderson, Jonathan Wood, K. Tempest Bradford, Darby Harn and Amal al Mohtar.

Many thanks to the wonderful folks at Prime—to Sean Wallace for having faith in this book and to Stephen Segal for his graphic design.

I am grateful to Jennifer Jackson, for being the best agent ever.

Finally, I am forever grateful to my family—Chris, my wonderful husband, and to my mom, dad, my sister Natasha, my dad-in-law, and Connie for their encouragement and love.

Thank you all for being in my life.

To my sister

Chapter 1

WE SCALE THE ROUGH BRICKS OF THE BUILDING'S FACADE. *Their crumbling edges soften under our claw-like fingers; they jut out of the flat, adenoid face of the wall to provide easy footholds. We could've used fire escapes, we could've climbed up, up, past the indifferent faces of the walls, their windows cataracted with shutters; we could've bounded up in the joyful cacophony of corrugated metal and barely audible whispers of the falling rust shaken loose by our ascent. We could've flown.*

But instead we hug the wall, press our cheeks against the warm bricks; the filigree of age and weather covering their surface imprints on our skin, steely-gray like the thunderous skies above us. We rest, clinging to the wall, our fingertips nestled in snug depressions in the brick, like they were made especially for that, clinging. We are almost all the way to the steep roof red with shingles shaped like fish scales.

We look into the lone window lit with a warm glow, the only one with open shutters and smells of sage, lamb, and chlorine wafting outside. We look at the long bench decorated with alembics and retorts and colored powders and bunches of dried herbs and bowls of watery sheep's eyes from the butcher's shop down the alleyway. We look at the girl.

Her porcelain face has cracked—a recent fall, an accident?—and we worry as we count the cracks cobwebbing her cheek and her forehead, radiating from the point of impact like sunrays. Yes, we remember the sun. Her blue eyes, facets of expensive glass colored with copper salts, look into the darkness, and we do not know if she can see us at all.

But she smiles and waves at us, and the bronzed wheel-bearings of her joints squeak their mechanical greeting. She pushes the lock of dark, dark hair (she doesn't know, but it used to belong to a dead boy) behind her delicate ear, a perfect and pink seashell. Her deft hands, designed for grinding and mixing and measuring, smooth the front of her fashionably wide skirt, and she motions to us. "Come in," she says.

We creep inside through the window, grudgingly, gingerly, we creep (we could've flown). We grow aware of our not-belonging, of the grayness of our skin, of our stench—we smell like pigeon-shit, and we wonder if she notices; we fill her entire room with our rough awkward sour bodies. "We seek your help," we say.

Her cracked porcelain face remains as expressionless as ours. "I am honored," she says. Her blue eyes bulge a little from their sockets, taking us in. Her frame clicks as she leans forward, curious about us. Her dress is low-cut, and we see that there is a small transparent window in her chest, where a clockwork heart is ticking along steadily, and we cannot help but feel resentful of the sound and—by extension—of her, the sound of time falling away grain by grain, the time that dulls our senses and hardens our skins, the time that is in too short supply. "I will do everything I can," she says, and our resentment falls away too, giving way to gratitude—falls like dead skin. We bow and leap out of the window, one by one by one, and we fly, hopeful for the first time in centuries.

———

LOHARRI'S ROOM SMELLED OF INCENSE AND SMOKE, THE AIR thick like taffy. Mattie tasted it on her lips, and squinted through the thick haze concealing its denizen.

"Mattie," Loharri said from the chaise by the fireplace where he sprawled in his habitual languor, a half-empty glass on the floor. A fat black cat sniffed at its contents prissily, found them not to her liking, but knocked the glass over nonetheless, adding the smell of flat beer to the already overwhelming concoction that was barely air. "So glad to see you."

"You should open the window," she said.

"You don't need air," Loharri said, petulant. He was in one of his moods again.

"But you do," she pointed out. "You are one fart away from death by suffocation. Fresh air won't kill you."

"It might," he said, still sulking.

"Only one way to find out." She glided past him, the whirring of her gears muffled by the room—it was so full of draperies and old rugs rolled up in the corners, so cluttered with bits of machinery and empty dishes. Mattie reached up and swung open the shutters, admitting a wave of air sweet with lilac blooms and rich river mud and roasted nuts from the market square down the street. "Alive still?"

"Just barely." Loharri sat up and stretched, his long spine crackling like flywheels. He then yawned, his mouth gaping dark in his pale face. "What brings you here, my dear love?"

She extended her hand, the slender copper springs of

her fingers grasping a phial of blue glass. "One of your admirers sent for me—she said you were ailing. I made you a potion."

Loharri uncorked the phial and sniffed at the contents with suspicion. "A woman? Which one?" he asked. "Because if it was a jilted lover, I am not drinking this."

"Amelia," Mattie said. "I do not suppose she wishes you dead."

"Not yet," Loharri said darkly, and drank. "What does it do?"

"Not yet," Mattie agreed. "It's just a tonic. It'll dispel your ennui, although I imagine a fresh breeze might do just as well."

Loharri made a face; he was not a handsome man to begin with, and a grimace of disgust did not improve his appearance.

Mattie smiled. "If an angel passes over you, your face will be stuck like that."

Loharri scoffed. "Dear love, if only it could make matters worse. But speaking of faces . . . yours has been bothering me lately. What did you do to it?"

Mattie touched the cracks, feeling their familiar swelling on the smooth porcelain surface. "Accident," she said.

Loharri arched his left eyebrow—the right one was para-lyzed by the scar and the knotted mottled tissue that ruined half of his face; it was a miracle his eye had been spared. Mattie heard that some women found scars attractive in a romantic sort of way, but she was pretty certain that Loharri's were quite a long way past romantic and into disfiguring. "Another accident," he said. "You are a very clumsy automaton, do you know that?"

"I am not clumsy," Mattie said. "Not with my hands."

He scowled at the phial in his hand. "I guess not, although my taste buds beg to differ. Still, I made you a little something."

"A new face," Mattie guessed.

Loharri smiled lopsidedly and stood, and stretched his long, lanky frame again. He searched through the cluttered room until he came upon a workbench that somehow got hidden and lost under the pile of springs, coils, wood shavings, and half-finished suits of armor that appeared decorative rather than functional in their coppery, glistening glory. There were cogs and parts of engines and things that seemed neither animate nor entirely dead, and for a short while Mattie worried that the chaotic pile would consume Loharri; however, he soon emerged with a triumphant cry, a round white object in his hand.

It looked like a mask and Mattie averted her eyes—she did not like looking at her faces like that, as they hovered, blind and disembodied. She closed her eyes and extended her neck toward Loharri in a habitual gesture. His strong, practiced fingers brushed the hair from her forehead, lingering just a second too long, and felt around her jaw line, looking for the tiny cogs and pistons that attached her face to the rest of her head. She felt her face pop off, and the brief moment when she felt exposed, naked, seemed to last an eternity. She whirred her relief when she felt the touch of the new concave surface as it enveloped her, hid her from the world.

Loharri affixed the new face in place, and she opened her eyes. Her eyes took a moment to adjust to the new sockets.

"How does it fit?" Loharri asked.

"Well enough," she said. "Let me see how I look." She extended one of the flexible joints that held her eyes and tilted it, to see the white porcelain mask. Loharri had not painted this one—he remembered her complaints about the previous face, that it was too bright, too garish (this is why she broke it in the first place), and he left this one plain, suffused with the natural bluish tint that reminded her of the pale skies over the city during July and its heat spells. Only the lips, lined with pitted smell and taste sensors, were tinted pale red, same as the rooftops in the merchants' district.

"It is nice," Mattie said. "Thank you."

Loharri nodded. "Don't mention it. No matter how emancipated, you're still mine." His voice lost its usual acidity as he studied her new face with a serious expression. There were things Mattie and Loharri didn't talk about—one of them was Mattie's features, which remained constant from one mask to the next, no matter how much he experimented with colors and other elaborations. "Looks good," he finally concluded. "Now, tell me the real reason for your visit—surely, you don't rush over every time someone tells you I might be ill."

"The gargoyles," Mattie said. "They want to hire me, and I want your permission to make them my priority, at the expense of your project."

Loharri nodded. "It's a good one," he said. "I guess our gray overlords have grown tired of being turned into stone?"

"Yes," Mattie answered. "They feel that their life spans are too short and their fate is too cruel; I cannot say that I disagree. Only . . . I really do not know where to start. I thought of vitality potions and the mixes to soften the leather, of the elixirs to loosen the calcified joints . . . only they all seem lacking."

Loharri smiled and drummed his fingers on his knee. "I see your problem, and yes, you can work on it to your little clockwork heart's content."

"Thank you," Mattie said. If she had been able to smile, she would have. "I brought you what I have so far—a list of chemicals that change color when exposed to light."

Loharri took the proffered piece of paper with two long fingers, and opened it absentmindedly. "I know little of alchemy," he said. "I'm not friends with any of your colleagues, but I suppose I could find a replacement for you nonetheless, although I doubt there's anyone who knows more on the matter than you do. Meanwhile, I do have one bit of advice regarding the gargoyles."

Mattie tilted her head to the shoulder, expectant. She had learned expressive poses, and knew that they amused her creator; she wondered if she was supposed to feel shame at being manipulative.

As expected, he snickered. "Aren't you just the sweetest machine in the city? And oh, you listen so well. Heed my words then: I remember a woman who worked on the gargoyle problem some years back. Beresta was her name, a foreigner; Beresta from the eastern district. But she died—a sad, sad thing."

"Oh," Mattie said, disappointed. "Did she leave any papers behind?"

Loharri shook his head. "No papers. But, lucky for you, she was a restless spirit, a sneaky little ghost who hid in the rafters of her old home. And you know what they do with naughty ghosts."

Mattie inclined her head in agreement. "They call for the Soul-Smoker."

"Indeed. And if there's anyone who still knows Beresta's secrets, it's him. You're not afraid of the Soul-Smokers, are you?"

"Of course not," Mattie said mildly. "I have no soul; to fear him would be a mere superstition." She stood and smoothed her skirts, feeling the stiff whalebone stays that held her skirts full and round under the thin fabric. "Thank you, Loharri. You've been kind."

"Thank you for the tonic," he said. "But please, do visit me occasionally, even if there's nothing you want. I am a sentimental man."

"I shall," Mattie answered, and took her leave. As she walked out of the door, it occurred to her that if she wanted to be kind to Loharri she could offer him things she knew he wanted but would never ask for—she could invite him to touch her hair, or let him listen to the ticking of her heart. To sit with him in the darkness, in the dead hours between night and morning when the demons tormented him more than usual, and then perhaps he would talk of things they did not talk about otherwise—perhaps then he would tell her why he had made her and why he grew so despondent when she wanted to live on her own and to study, to become something other than a part of him. The problem was, those were the things she preferred not to know.

MATTIE TOOK A LONG WAY HOME, WEAVING THROUGH THE market among the many stalls selling food and fabric and spices; she lingered by a booth that sold imported herbs and chemicals, and picked up a bunch of dried salamanders and a bottle of copper salts. She then continued east to the river, and she stood a while on the embankment watching the steamboats huff across, carrying marble for the new construction on the northern bank. There were talks of the new parliament building, and Mattie supposed that it signaled an even bigger change than gossip at Loharri's parties suggested. Ever since the mechanics won a majority, the renovations in the city acquired a feverish pace, and the streets themselves seemed to shift daily, accommodating new roads and more and more factories that belched smoke and steam and manufactured new and frightening machines.

Still, Mattie tried not to think of politics too much. She thought about gargoyles and of Loharri's words. He called them their overlords, even though the city owed its existence to the gargoyles, and they had been nothing but benefactors to the people. Did he know something she didn't? And if he were so disdainful of gargoyles, why did he offer to help?

Mattie walked leisurely along the river. It was a nice day, and many people strolled along the embankment, enjoying the first spring warmth and the sweet, dank smell of the river. She received a few curious looks, but overall people paid her no mind. She passed a paper factory that squatted over the river like an ugly toad, disgorging a stream of white foam into the water; a strong smell of bleach surrounded it like a cloud.

From the factory she turned into the twisty streets of the eastern district, where narrow three-storied buildings clung close together like swallows' nests on the face of a cliff. The sea of red tiled roofs flowed and ebbed as far as the eye could see, and Mattie smiled—she liked her neighborhood the way it was, full of people and small shops occupying the lower stories, without any factories and with the streets too narrow for any mechanized conveyances. She turned into her street and headed home, the ticking of her heart keeping pace with her thoughts filled with gargoyles and Loharri's strange relationship to them.

Mattie's room and laboratory were located above an apothecary's, which she occasionally supplied with elixirs and ointments. Less mainstream remedies remained in her laboratory, and those who sought them knew to visit her rooms upstairs; they usually used the back entrance and the rickety stairs that led past the apothecary.

When Mattie got home to her garret, she found a visitor waiting on the steps. She had met this woman before at one of Loharri's gatherings—her name was Iolanda; she stood out from the crowd, Mattie remembered—she moved energetically and laughed loudly, and looked Mattie straight in the eye when they were introduced. And now Iolanda's gaze did not waver. "May I come in?" she said as soon as she saw Mattie, and smiled.

"Of course," Mattie said and unlocked the door. The

corridor was narrow and led directly into her room, which contained a roll-top desk and her few books; Mattie led her visitor through and into the laboratory, where there was space to sit and talk.

"Would you like a drink?" Mattie asked. "I have a lovely jasmine-flavored liqueur."

Iolanda nodded. "I would love that. How considerate of you to keep refreshments."

Mattie poured her a drink. "Of course," she said. "How kind of you to notice."

Iolanda took the proffered glass from Mattie's copper fingers, studying them as she did so, and took a long swallow. "Indeed, it is divine," she said. "Now, if you don't mind, I would like to dispense with the pleasantries and state my business."

Mattie inclined her head and sat on a stool by her workbench, offering the other one to Iolanda with a gesture.

"You are not wealthy," Iolanda said. Not a question but a statement.

"Not really," Mattie agreed. "But I do not need much."

"Mmmm," Iolanda said. "One might suspect that a well-off alchemist is a successful alchemist—you do need to buy your ingredients, and some are more expensive than others."

"That is true," Mattie said. "Now, how does this relate to your business?"

"I can make you rich," Iolanda said. "I have need of an alchemist, of one who is discreet and skillful. But before I explain my needs, let me ask you this: do you consider yourself a woman?"

"Of course," Mattie said, taken aback and puzzled. "What else would I consider myself?"

"Perhaps I did not phrase it well," Iolanda said, and tossed back the remainder of her drink with an unexpectedly habitual and abrupt gesture. "What I meant was, why do you consider yourself a woman? Because you were created as one?"

"Yes," Mattie replied, although she grew increasingly uncomfortable with the conversation. "And because of the clothes I wear."

"So if you changed your clothes . . . "

"But I can't," Mattie said. "The shape of them is built into me—I know that you have to wear corsets and hoops and stays to give your clothes a proper shape. But I was created with all of those already in place, they are as much as part of me as my eyes. So I ask you: what else would you consider me?"

"I sought not to offend," Iolanda said. "I do confess to my prejudice: I will not do business nor would I employ a person or an automaton of a gender different from mine, and I simply had to know if your gender was coincidental."

"I understand," Mattie said. "And I assure you that my femaleness is as ingrained as your own."

Iolanda sighed. Mattie supposed that Iolanda was beautiful, with her shining dark curls cascading onto her full shoulders and chest, and heavy, languid eyelids half-concealing her dark eyes. "Fair enough. And Loharri . . . can you keep secrets from him?"

"I can and I do," Mattie said.

"In this case, I will appreciate it if you keep our business private," Iolanda said.

"I will, once you tell me what it is," Mattie replied. She shot an involuntary look toward her bench, where the ingredients waited for her to grind and mix and vaporize them, where the aludel yawned empty as if hungry; she grew restless sitting for too long, empty-handed and motionless.

Iolanda raised her eyebrows, as if unsure whether she understood Mattie. She seemed one of those people who rarely encountered anything but abject agreement, and she was not used to being hurried. "Well, I want you to be available for the times I have a need of you, and to fulfill my orders on a short notice. Potions, perfumes, tonics . . . that sort of thing. I will pay you a retainer, so you will be receiving money even when I do not have a need of you."

"I have other clients and projects," Mattie said.

Iolanda waved her hand dismissively. "It doesn't matter. As long as I can find you when I need you."

"It sounds reasonable," Mattie agreed. "I will endeavor to fulfill simple orders within a day, and complex ones— from two days to a week. You won't have them done faster anywhere."

"It is acceptable," Iolanda said. "And for your first order, I need you to create me a fragrance that would cause regret."

"Come back tomorrow," Mattie said. "Or leave me your address, I'll have a courier bring it over."

"No need," Iolanda said. "I will send someone to pick it up. And here's your first week's pay." She rose from her stool and placed a small pouch of stones on the bench. "And if anyone asks, we are casual acquaintances, nothing more."

Iolanda left, and Mattie felt too preoccupied to even look

at the stones that were her payment. She almost regretted agreeing to Iolanda's requests—while they seemed straightforward and it was not that uncommon for courtiers to employ alchemists or any other artisans on a contract basis, something about Iolanda seemed off. Most puzzling, if she wanted to keep a secret from Loharri, she could do better than hire the automaton made by his hands. Mattie was not so vain as to presuppose that her reputation outweighed common good sense.

But there was work to do, and perfume certainly seemed less daunting than granting gargoyles a lifespan extension, and she mixed ambergris and sage, blended myrrh and the bark of grave cypress, and sublimated dry camphor. The smell she obtained was pleasing and sad, and yet she was not certain that this was enough to evoke regret—something seemed missing. She closed her eyes and smelled-tasted the mixture with her sensors, trying hard to remember the last time she felt regret.

Chapter 2

MICE FLED FROM A TALL HOUSE PERCHED OVER THE GRACKLE Pond, and Mattie nodded to herself. The Soul-Smoker could not be far now, and Mattie quickened her step, her fine wooden heels clacking on the cobbles of the pavement and then the embankment, as the stream of mice fleeing in the opposite direction parted around her feet. The house stood wrapped in mourning wreaths, dark cypress branches wound in liquid smoke, with windows dark and shuttered. The exodus of mice was almost over, and the family, clad in their mourning whites, huddled on the porch fearful to go back inside until the reluctant soul was evicted.

Mattie wondered about the souls left behind like this, those little bodiless entities made of glassy, transparent fog that liked curling up inside the secret places of houses—behind wainscots, between the wooden planks of paneling, in mouse holes, in cupboards. She wondered why they and not the others lingered where they did not belong, where even mice fled from their watery, weak touch. What did they want? She supposed the Soul-Smoker would know.

She curtsied to the family—two young girls and a small boy, clustered around a withered old woman, their grandmother by all appearances. "I'm sorry for your loss," she said.

They nodded to her, respectful through their grief. Emancipated automata were not numerous, and even the wealthy (and Mattie assumed the wealth of the family based on the size of their abode and its desirable location next to water) treated them with reverence for their presumed merit. "We put the opium out," they said. "The Soul-Smoker should be by soon."

"I'll wait with you by your leave," Mattie said. "I have business with him."

They said nothing, but Mattie deduced from their lowered eyelids—shot through with delicate veins branching like naked winter trees—that they were not comfortable discussing the matter. She moved away from the porch and stood, erect and still, by an old tree burdened with ivy and long garlands of lichen. She waited for the Soul-Smoker in suitable silence and calm.

She caught sight of him as soon as he turned onto the embankment, making his slow way along the edge of the black pond. The man was small and thin, black-and-white in his black suit and a shock of white hair. His cane drummed a steady rhythm along the cobbles, and his blind eyes, white in his white face, stared upward into the darkening sky. Those who were taking the evening air by the pond scattered at his approach, getting out of his way with almost unseemly haste, risking stepping into the spring mud and staining their ornate shoes and brocade gowns rather than meeting the gaze of his eyes, empty like clouds.

When he approached the house, the family stepped off the porch and retreated into the depths of the garden, leaving the door open for him. His cane tapped on the steps and flicked from side to side, like a tongue of a venomous snake. He was about to put his foot onto the first step, but then he turned to Mattie, undoubtedly alerted to her presence by the loud ticking of her heart.

"Kind sir," Mattie said politely. "A word at your pleasure."

"Call me Ilmarekh," he said in a soft, almost feminine voice that lilted with some slight unidentifiable accent. "It's been a while since anyone wanted a word with me."

"I am Mattie," she said, and softly touched her hand to the blind man's.

He started at her touch. "Dear girl, are you an automaton?"

"Yes, sir," Mattie said. "I am an alchemist, and I'm in need of your help. Do you mind if I watch you while you do your work?"

"Not at all," he said. "Come inside."

The hallway was subsumed by the twilight, long fingers of shadows stretching from the hollow of the cupped ceiling, reaching all the way down the walls, and only retreating by the western windows, which admitted the last of the sunlight. Ilmarekh sniffed the air, and Mattie tasted it too; both followed the sweet cloying perfume of opium to the kitchen.

The soul of the deceased had already found it—there was a faint shimmer in the bowl of brown powder left on the kitchen table, and a strange watery halo surrounded it, as, Mattie imagined, through a veil of tears.

The blind man carefully patted the pockets of his severe jacket and extracted a long-stemmed pipe with a small shallow bowl cut from ancient knotted wood, silvery with age. Without any ceremony, he stuffed the bowl of his pipe with the opium and lit it with a thick sulfurous match. Sweet smoke filled the kitchen, and the liquid shadow danced in the rising puffs and writhed under the ceiling, becoming smoke, becoming shadow and disappearing, sucked through Ilmarekh's narrow, lipless mouth. His chest rose and fell in breaths that seemed too great for his narrow frame, and every last wisp of smoke was sucked into his chest and consumed.

When there was no opium left, Ilmarekh sighed and collapsed on the stool by the kitchen table. Bronzed pans reflected his white face and hair, and he seemed a ghost himself. The opium washed away the last color from his lips, and his white eyes were half-hidden under heavy eyelids.

"Are you all right?" Mattie asked. "I have tonics with me, if you're feeling weak."

He sat up, as if remembering her presence. "I am fine, I assure you," he said. "A new soul takes a while to settle."

"How many do you contain?" Mattie asked.

"Hundreds," he answered, without any pride or remorse. "I imagine you came to ask me about one of them?"

"Yes," Mattie said. "There was a woman, some years back, an alchemist . . . she used to live by the river, in the eastern district. Her name was Beresta."

The blind man remained silent, chewing the air as if tasting something in it. "Yes," he said after a while. "I know her."

ILMAREKH SAID THAT HE WISHED THE WORLD WERE SIMPLER; he had been blind since birth, and he tried to imagine seeing, from the vague and distant memories of the souls that lived inside him. His favorite things to imagine were reflections and shadows, and reflections of shadows running along a long, unending pane of glass. This is what he imagined the souls he consumed were like, and he fancied himself a mere reflecting surface—and instead of wandering alone through the world that was not kind to shadows, they found solace in seeing their reflection in Ilmarekh's soul, and the reflection gave them substance and contentment.

Among the hundreds of reflections he knew by feel and by their thoughts and memories twining with his own, he could locate Beresta with ease. He told Mattie that she was a shy, retiring soul that would rather remain unnoticed than communicate with him. "But I can coax her," he said.

Mattie tried to imagine what it was like, having someone else's soul sloshing inside one, silvery and elusive like a small fast fish that one could cradle in an open palm full of water but could never grasp without inflicting injury and distress. This is probably what it would be like to have any soul, she thought.

"She says she knows you," Ilmarekh said after a protracted silence. "Rather, she knows the man who made you."

"He sent me," Mattie said. Sitting in someone else's kitchen like that, not letting the worry about the owners intrude upon her communion with this small, strange man felt almost criminal and yet giddy. The slanted red rays of the setting sun set the pans afire and spilled thick amber puddles across the floor. The air smelled of cedar and amber.

"She says she knows your teacher," Ilmarekh said. "She says she'll tell you what you want to know if you tell her why you became an alchemist and why you chose the teacher you had."

BOTH QUESTIONS HAD THE SAME ANSWER. MATTIE remembered when she had been a simple automaton with sturdy metal hands designed for gripping broom handles and handling saucepans; she was intelligent enough for conversation, for Loharri did not like being bored. She used to bustle through the house crammed full of spare mechanical parts and sweep the workshop floors, raising angry clouds of dust full of tiny stings of metal particles, she cooked meals heavy with red, steaming meat designed to enliven her master's pale complexion and melancholy disposition. She waged protracted wars with small mice who were reluctant to leave the house and insisted on partaking of the food she brought from the market. Sometimes she went out with Loharri when he needed to run errands and wanted company or someone to carry things for him. She asked for nothing else and had not even heard about emancipation, even though an occasional twinge of dissatisfaction came unbidden every now and again.

This changed one day in June when Loharri, contrary to his complaints about the sweltering heat and repeated reassurances that he would not leave the house until the weather changed to something halfway sane, called her to go out with him. He gave her a machine to carry—a simple device, consisting of a bronze receptacle for water and a narrow nozzle; Mattie knew enough about Loharri's contrivances to guess that when the water boiled, the steam would be forced through the nozzle onto the blades of a fan above it, spinning them and the platform mounted over it. There were deep depressions in the platform, currently empty, and Mattie guessed that they were meant for something—probably small things that needed spinning.

She puzzled over the machine as they walked, turning it this way and that, and never noticed that they were walking all the way to the eastern district, a place populated by those who were not as wealthy as her master but not entirely poor. Apartments clustered on top of each other, wisely avoiding contact with expensive land underneath, and the air smelled of bleach and smoked fish, of old flowers and laundry drying in the sun.

They headed to one of the tenement buildings, no different from the others under their roofs of overlapping red tiles. They walked up the rickety stairs; Loharri's face was pale, and he sweated more than usual in his dark clothes; still no complaint escaped his tightly closed bloodless lips.

Mattie followed him, counting the creaking steps, and wondering about the reason for such uncharacteristic silence—usually, her creator was eager to offer his views on the weather, people populating any given area, and the latest election, whether she listened or not. That went doubly for any bodily discomfort he was experiencing, and his lack of complaining seemed downright ominous by the time they reached their destination—a narrow garret at the very top of the building, where all the heat of the day and every drop of fish smell had curled up comfortably and refused to leave.

Loharri knocked on the door upholstered with narrow

strips of pounded bark, and listened to the slow steps inside. Mattie listened too, her head cocked to her shoulder, the thing in her hands whirring softly in the leisurely tepid breeze.

A wild-eyed human servant, a small wiry girl with pimples and chipped teeth, opened the door, peering cautiously. She smiled at Loharri and opened the door wider, bidding him to come in. "Wait in the living room," she said. "Mistress Ogdela will be with you shortly."

"Living room" was too grand a name for the narrow part of the hallway separated from the rest of the tiny apartment by a folding partition decorated with butterflies. A long and lumpy settee covered by a checkered white and yellow throw left only a narrow passage leading to the rest of the apartment; a candy dish with several dusty marzipans rested on the stained table by the settee. Loharri sat and drummed his fingers on the surface of the table, unconsciously following the pattern of circular stains left by glasses of assorted sizes. His gaze would not meet Mattie's, and his mouth twisted especially tortuously.

Mattie remained standing, the machine in her hands held primly in front of her chest. Beneath the lifeless demeanor of an automaton she assumed every time Loharri had company—by appearing inanimate she remained inconspicuous, and people talked like they would if she weren't there—she wondered what it was about him today, why he was so different. The answer came to her when light, sprightly footfalls came from beyond the partition, and Loharri's gaze flickered toward it, his light eyes suddenly stormy and troubled—it was fear, Mattie realized. She had never seen Loharri afraid, and her mechanical heart beat faster, eager to see the creature that had such power over Mattie's creator.

The partition folded to one side, admitting a small, silver-haired woman with a face carved into narrow slices by myriad parallel wrinkles; her eyes, dark and bright, looked at Mattie with curiosity. "Ah," she said. "You made me my machine, and I thank you. Now, what can I do for you?"

Loharri stood, stooping. "I need your alchemy, but I would prefer to talk in private, most venerable Mistress Ogdela."

The woman raised her eyebrows, temporarily smoothing a few of the wrinkles. "Secrets from your own automaton!" she said. "How very quaint. Come along then, young man, and we will talk."

The two of them departed, leaving Mattie to watch the painted yellow and blue butterflies that flitted across the lacquered wood. She listened to the low buzzing of voices behind the partition, and rolled the word on her tongue: alchemy. A word powerful enough to make Loharri quiet and pensive. She did not know why it was so appealing to her; all she knew was that she wanted to learn Ogdela's trade.

When Loharri returned, a flask of clear liquid—paler than water!—clutched in his hands, Mattie had made up her mind.

"Most venerable Mistress Ogdela," she addressed the old woman. "With my master's permission, I would ask to be your apprentice." It was a shrewd choice, to ask in Loharri's presence—he would not deny her without a good reason while others were watching, and he would not betray his fear outwardly.

He shot Mattie a searing gaze. "I do not see why not," he said after a short pause. "As long is it doesn't interfere with your other duties."

"I've never taught an automaton," Ogdela said to Loharri. "Is she up to the task?"

Loharri sighed and handed Mattie the flask. "Sadly, yes," he said.

Mattie remained with Ogdela until the old woman decided that she was fit to go and open her own shop. Mattie had found a place just like Ogdela's—"To be more like her," she explained to Ilmarekh.

Ilmarekh listened to her story, his face drained of color, calm and placid like the surface of the Grackle Pond outside. The opium smoke had dissipated, and Mattie imagined that the consumed soul was done with flailing inside its flesh jail and had started to settle in its new place.

"So there it is," Mattie said. "I studied with Ogdela . . . I wanted to be an alchemist because of the power they hold over others. I hadn't realized then that not everyone is afraid of them, but I never regretted it, so it doesn't matter."

"The ghost . . . Beresta, she says she also studied with Ogdela. She will answer your questions." Ilmarekh stammered and stopped. Large drops of sweat swelled on his forehead, and he swallowed a few times.

Mattie guessed that the opium was getting the best of him; as the darkness descended outside, she remembered the family, still waiting by the porch, too fearful to enter their own house. "Perhaps I should take you home," she said. "You look like you need to rest."

Ilmarekh sat upright, the empty bowl at his elbow clanging with the sudden movement. "You'd do that?"

"Of course," Mattie said. "Why wouldn't I?" She regretted saying it as soon as the words touched the darkened air. Of course she knew why no one ever went to the Soul-Smoker's house, and Ilmarekh knew that she knew. To him, her feigned ignorance could only be interpreted as condescension, a feeble attempt to pretend that she did not know his disadvantage, the way people saw him. "I'd like to take you anyway," she said.

He nodded, slowly, and rose, leaning on his cane heavily. She hooked her arm under his, and he jolted at her touch—any touch, she guessed, would be a novelty to him. "Can you see in the dark?" he asked.

"Yes," she said.

He seemed relieved at not having to worry about finding his way and being able to use his cane for support only. His weight, small as it was, pressed on Mattie's arm, and she wondered at the birdlike thinness of his bones, at the feverish warm coating of flesh that knotted over them.

We watch from the secret places of the city—the rooftops and rain-gutters, the awnings of bakeries and the scaffoldings rising around new buildings—as the girl and the man walk through the dark streets. She doesn't bother finding the lit streets and cuts along pitch-black alleys and around dark ponds that reflect no stars; it is cloudy tonight. It is too dark to fear thugs or thieves, but we keep watch nonetheless.

We watch as she almost carries the frail man who seems

unsure on his feet all the way through the narrowing streets, through labyrinths of dirt paths of the shantytowns fringing the city, to the gate, to the wall. There, we do not follow, but we keep watch—we watch over her as the two of them exit the gate on the distal side and walk up the hill. The rain starts, slicking the path, and her mechanical parts creak louder as water gets trapped in her joints and delicate wheel-bearings. They are just a blur now, a double shape through the gray curtain of the rain and the night. The ground is still warm from the sun, and silvery mist rises and snakes along the path, clinging low over the wet grass.

There is a house on the top of the hill—no man's land, no-place, too steep for agriculture and too rocky for pasture, out-of-the-way and inconvenient for city dwellers and farmers both. This hill, the Ram's Skull, the bald forehead of the once-mountain worn to a nub by time (slipping, slipping, faster and faster) is nothing but bedrock and loose stones. The house on the top sits lopsided already, its northern corner sinking with the decay of the slope under its supports.

The mechanical girl and the Soul-Smoker enter the house—we hear the long squeal of a door as it opens and a slam as it closes behind them. We do not know what is happening inside, but we can guess—there is light in the fireplace and the gurgling of a kettle, and low, guilty voices. And we think of the souls and we count them—we had known every ghost in the city, and we can recall their names. We marvel at the cruelty of their fate without having the capacity to truly comprehend it—no more than to merely recognize it as grotesque. But, like the mechanical girl, we have no souls, and we are not afraid of the Soul-Smoker, we have no reason to worry that the souls inside him will somehow lure ours away and we will fall dead on the spot, abandoned by our animating essence. We think about the nature of souls and listen to the small domestic noises reaching us from the little house on top of the hill.

We sit all along the wall like giant gray pigeons, our hands clenched under our sharp chins, our wings folded primly, our eyes narrowed, and our ears pricked up. If someone were to wander by at this wet, ungodly hour, they would believe us turned into stone, inanimate like the wall we grip with our clawed toes. Or they would wonder what the gargoyles are doing out of their caves and hiding places, why are we out and about. But there is nobody here to pry or to wonder, and we watch and we listen and we wait, and we do not know what they are talking about.

Chapter 3

———

THE NEXT MORNING, MATTIE REMEMBERED THAT SHE STILL had to finish Iolanda's perfume. Fortunately, the night spent talking to the Soul-Smoker taught her more about regret than, she suspected, the entire city could. She found dried wormwood in her extensive apothecary, and prepared to sublimate its essential oil—she lit the burner and cleaned the aludel, and assembled it so that the smaller vessel sitting on top of the larger one was tilted at enough of an angle for the condensing vapor to slide down the concave walls into the waiting receptacle. As the wormwood heated, she crushed the brittle spiny leaves of rosemary, downy-gray, and mixed them with extractants and solvents to pry away its properties of memory.

One did not regret what one did not remember; Ilmarekh, who remembered every moment, every twinge of hundreds of former inhabitants of the city, told her that. The opium made him talkative last night, and the souls in his possession crowded and pressed, trying so desperately to look out of his blind eyes, struggling so valiantly to move his reluctant, cottony tongue. He spoke in a hundred voices; only one of them was Beresta, but Mattie felt that it would be impolite to ignore the rest of them, and she listened to their laments and reminiscences, to their complaints about children who grew up and never visited, about the sorrow of dark alleys and the cold, wet slither of a robber's knife.

Mattie listened, waiting for the small voice of the alchemist woman who could tell her about the gargoyles. But it was so crowded that she only had a chance to utter the name of her son—Sebastian, and the street he lived on. She didn't say anything else, but it was enough for now. Mattie thought that she would visit Ilmarekh again, perhaps visit him often. He knew so much, and yet no one dared to ask him questions for fear of losing their own souls. He was all Mattie's, and she was not a woman to miss her chances.

The warm smell of wormwood filled her laboratory, and she collected the few transparent, pale yellow drops that waited for her in the aludel. She blended them with rosemary and with the sage-and-myrrh concoction she had prepared last night. The musk of ambergris enveloped the rest of the ingredients in its sensual embrace, forcing them all together, the bark of the cypress and the sharp, bitter camphor softened by the gentle herbal scents.

Satisfied with her work, Mattie nodded to herself and let the mixture settle and blend. She was about to go out for a walk, and maybe pick up a few chemicals she had fancied for a while but had no means to buy until now, when a sharp rapping on the door announced a visitor.

She opened the door to see Loharri—dressed in a formal frock coat, he seemed especially thin and sharp-edged. "Busy?" he said.

"No." She stood in the doorway preventing him from entering. The smell of Iolanda's perfume saturated the air, and she could not risk him recognizing it later and guessing at Mattie's connection to Iolanda. "Going out?"

"Just an informal gathering," he said, although his clothes clearly begged to differ. "Lunch with some friends and colleagues. Would you like to come?"

"Of course," Mattie said. He rarely asked for favors nowadays, and she saw no reason to deny him. Besides, gatherings such as this always offered opportunities for eavesdropping. After her emancipation, she at first resented Loharri's friends who treated her as before—that is, as his automaton, a part of him that deserved neither recognition nor acknowledgment as an independent entity. Later, she saw the advantage of being invisible—she walked into a room where mechanics talked about their secret business and they never missed a beat, never remembering or caring enough to notice that she was an alchemist and therefore a political enemy. She just didn't know why Loharri kept giving her such opportunities.

"Hurry up then," he said. "You might even learn something about your new friends."

"Wait outside," Mattie said. "I need to change."

As she did—striped stockings, white and black, and a black dress with open neckline fringed with foamy white lace—Mattie puzzled over Loharri's words. Why were the Mechanics suddenly interested in gargoyles? They affected the politics of the city very little—figureheads, outwardly respected but inconsequential. They remained outside of the daily life of the city, subject more to lore and superstitions than laws and elections. Their patronage of the Duke's family and his court was symbolic—just like their predecessors who had undergone the inevitable transformation and now decorated the palace . . . they were even less important than the court, which persisted only, as Loharri often said, due to inertia and habit. Only the elected parties could pass laws, only they could command new construction and regulate commerce. But the Duke remained in his palace, useless and, as Mattie imagined, lonely.

Mattie descended the stairs and nodded at Loharri. He grimaced, pale and uncomfortable in his stern clothes. "Ready to go?"

She threaded her arm under his, and felt his tense sinews relax under the copper springs of her fingers. She hated admitting it to herself, but she stayed close to him because of the influence she had—she had the power to make him less concerned and more at ease, to make him smile even though it pained his broken face. She wondered at herself, at whether she would ever be able to forgive him for being her creator, for having such absolute control over her internal workings. For his love.

They headed uphill, toward the palace and the heavy gray architecture of the old buildings. Mattie suspected that the stone of which large rough blocks of the palace were hewn was the same as the stone gargoyles became, and wondered if there was a promising venue of investigation there; she made a mental note to take a mineral sample once they got to the old city.

"It's too hot to walk," Loharri said, even though the sun, still low over the rooftops, barely kissed the pavement and the air still retained the pleasant coolness of the night. His gaze cast about for a cab or a sedan.

"It's fine," Mattie said. "I enjoy walking, and you could use a constitutional. You spend too much time indoors."

Loharri scoffed. "I should've made you without a voice-box. Being lectured by my own automaton—why, that's an indignity no man should be forced to tolerate."

Mattie was used to his querulous tone, and simply changed the subject. "Did you know that Beresta had a son?"

"I heard," he replied, smiling. "I see you spoke to the Soul-Smoker."

Mattie inclined her head with a slow, ratcheted creaking of the neck joints. "I have. You should meet him."

"No thanks," Loharri said. "I prefer to keep a hold of my soul, thank you." He almost stumbled as a large puddle suddenly opened before them on the pavement, but circumvented it.

Mattie, whose legs were agile but not nearly as long as Loharri's, stepped into it, wetting the hem of her dress and soaking her slippers—she wore them for the occasion's sake, even though she had no need of footwear.

Loharri grabbed her elbow, pulling her out of the mess. "Look at that," he said. "I swear, the condition of these streets is just shameful."

"Why don't you do something about it?" Mattie shook out her skirt, spilling the murky drops onto the pavement. "You're in charge of the city—you and your friends, I mean."

"Priorities, dear." Loharri still held on to her elbow and dragged her along. The fresh air apparently energized him, since he was now moving in long, confident strides. "And besides, this is the Duke's territory, and he wants to keep it ancient and quaint. And it is only right to abide by his wishes—as long as they don't interfere with our plans."

Mattie was getting a distinct feeling that Loharri's willingness to discuss political and urban matters with her had a hidden purpose—perhaps he wanted her to talk . . . but to whom? Mattie was not a full member of the Alchemists' party, and as such she saw little interest in politics—why worry about something she would never have an impact on? She shook her head. Loharri was rubbing off on her, scheming and trying to guess people's motives and question everything—that was him, not her. Mattie only wanted to do her craft, and worry little about civic planning.

"What are the main priorities then?" she asked.

"Governance." He gave her a long look. "So, what did you hear about Beresta's son?"

"Nothing." Mattie shook her arm free and threaded it under his, as was proper. "Just that she had one. Why, is he famous?"

"Not in a way you'd want to be," Loharri said. "So, nothing about his current whereabouts?"

Mattie moved her head side to side, in a slow gesture of negation. "I just told you. I only learned that she had a son . . . she was not communicative."

"Hm," Loharri said. "I suppose you'll try and look for him then? To see if he knows of his mother's work?"

"Maybe," Mattie said. "Why?"

"Just curious. He's been missing for some time now. You'll tell me if you find him, won't you." Loharri did not wait for her answer—he turned under an arch of crumbling stone encrusted with pallid circles of lichenous growth, into a shaded courtyard. The wall of the building, gray like the rest of the district, was half-hidden under the living green carpet of toad flax, which already sent forth its tiny white flowers. Mattie recognized the building because of it—this seemed a side entrance into a little-used wing of the ossuary adjacent to the Parliament building. This wing contained no bones yet, and its echoey empty halls were occasionally used for parties and large-but-clandestine gatherings.

Loharri knocked on the small door half-hidden under the curtain of vegetation, and they were admitted inside. Lamps on the walls created warm semicircles of yellow light, and they overlapped, creating a scalloped edge on the walls and the floor made of large oblong slabs, destined to one day become the coffin lids of the notable citizens. The floor resounded hollow under the feet, always reminding of its ulti-mate purpose.

The mechanics were apparently throwing a party, but surreptitious business was the usual side effect of such events. These men, fastidious and solemn, did not seem to be able to remain in the same room with another human being without trying to figure out exactly how the fellow could be useful, harmful, or neither. They paid Mattie little mind, and no wonder—regular humans were mere clockworks to them, to be examined and figured out and, if necessary, taken apart; the automatons passed beneath notice.

Several serious fellows greeted Loharri with nods and reserved smiles—Mattie suspected that he was too lively for them, too moody, too unpredictable. His position of influence was assured by his proficiency and his many inventions—the most recent one already belched fire in every foundry, increasing their efficiency by some subtle but important percentage—but his demeanor and his disordered personal life earned him a few disapproving looks.

Loharri acted as if he didn't notice—he shook hands and chatted, and even came to say hello to several women sitting around the long tables, away from the men. They came as a decoration, and no one else seemed to pay much attention to them. Mattie wondered if she should join them and keep away from trouble, but her feet already led her after Loharri, the role of an obedient automaton as familiar to her as the sight of her own face.

She caught snatches of conversations—some talked about the Alchemists rallying for the next election; there were rumors that they were holding their most potent medicines in reserve, to be unveiled before the election, to wow and stun the populace. Imagine that, curing typhoid! Would there be anything but gratitude? Others mentioned that the Alchemists had been getting cozy with a few of the Duke's courtiers, seeking influence by the route of tradition rather than popularity.

And yet others talked about the gargoyles. Mattie stopped shadowing Loharri for a moment and listened, not moving, looking fixedly at her creator's back. The speaker—a small, rotund man of middle age whom she had met many times but whose name she could not remember, talked to Bergen—a man who looked as though pickled by many years that passed over his balding head. His dark clothes hung loosely on his desiccated body, and yet his mind was sharp; he was perhaps the only one in this gathering whom Loharri would call a friend.

"Think about it," said the rotund man, his face filling with alarming red color. "Without the gargoyles, what will the Duke be?"

"The Duke," Bergen replied. "Sure, the gargoyles and their sanctions might seem irrelevant, and perhaps they are. But without the third leg, this government will not be stable—we do need the court, you know. Otherwise, it'll be nothing but our squabbling with the alchemists."

"And that would be a bad thing?"

"Of course," Bergen said. "I for one do not think a civil war is such a good idea, and without the Duke we might have just that. Not that we don't have enough trouble already."

"But the gargoyles . . . "

"Are our history. This city is proud of its gargoyles, and there isn't much you can do about it," Bergen concluded and turned away from his interlocutor. "Spiritual guidance, be it superstition or tradition, is not always a bad thing. Some people need an external compass." His watery old eyes stopped on Mattie, and he smiled.

"Good afternoon, Messer Bergen," Mattie said in her flattest voice.

"Hello, Mattie," he said. "Your master around?"

She pointed wordlessly at Loharri, still leaning on the table by a cluster of brightly dressed women.

Bergen chuckled. "I don't understand what women see in him."

"He talks to them?" Mattie suggested.

"In any case, I need to talk to him," Bergen said, and walked up to Loharri, favoring his right foot. Goiter, Mattie remembered. The old man had goiter.

She moved behind Loharri, to stand still and listen. Loharri shot her a quick glance and a smile, and she momentarily felt grateful for that acknowledgement. Even though he had made her, with his own hands, put her together out of joints and slender metal bones, even though he knew more of her internal workings than anyone, he still managed to really see her as a whole.

Her attention was diverted by several automatons filing into the hall, their metal feet reverberating on the hollow floor of the sepulcher. They carried bottled wine and honeyed water, trays with fruit and bread and sweets, stacks of dishes and utensils. They moved in unison, their movements measured and devoid of any indication of free will. She had seen such servant automatons before, the mindless drudges that allowed for the leisure of the city's inhabitants. And every time she saw them she felt deep unease, a pervading sense of wrong—how could they make them like that? she thought. If they were to have a mind, they would've been miserable with their lives of servitude—Mattie remembered the dark sense of injustice when she was little but a maid—but at the same time they would have the choice of misery. Making them without minds removed a potential conflict, and Mattie thought of the slaughterhouses in the outskirts, the dank places that smelled of rust and iron and rot. She ventured there to buy offal that was used in some of her ointments, but sometimes she watched the animals. It was like that, she thought, remembering the panic in sheep's eyes; it was as if they managed to create a sheep that didn't mind being slaughtered after it was led into a dark steel barrel of a room where steaming blood stood knee-deep.

Loharri touched her hand. "What are you thinking about?" He traced the direction of her gaze and spoke softly, solicitously.

Mattie looked away. "Thank you for not making me like them." And added, before he had a chance to respond, "You should eat something. You look pale."

"I always look pale," he said but didn't smile as he normally would. "It really bothers you, doesn't it?"

She nodded. "They never had a chance. You removed the possibility of them even questioning if it was wrong."

He frowned a bit. "We'll talk about it later, if you don't mind."

She didn't; the mechanics continued to mingle, most of them carrying plates now, and to speak in their sedate voices. Mattie followed Loharri, listening for any mention of the gargoyles, but everyone seemed rather preoccupied with solving the transportation problem. Mattie listened just enough to conclude that the alleged problem was not a problem at all, but rather the way things had always been—the mechanics never tired of improving upon what was not broken. They felt that produce was slow to arrive from the farms, and that during the harvest the roads could barely sustain the crawling traffic of produce carts and the six-legged lizards that dragged them at a leisurely pace. It interfered with the deliveries from the mines, and during harvest the production of the factories often dropped. The mechanics, of course, thought that it called for automation of the lizards, the carts, or both. Mattie wondered if they would ever think of automation of the peasants.

"We would also need a bigger road," Bergen suggested.

"Or merely a better one," Loharri said.

Mattie grew bored of the conversation centering on roads and whether it was worthwhile designing a road that would move and carry stationary produce to the city, and wandered through the crowd, whirring and clicking, listening. She stopped by a small cluster of mechanics who spoke in low voices, often glancing over their hunched shoulders with a palpable air of secrecy. Mattie stopped a few steps away, far enough not to arouse suspicion but close enough to catch their whispers with her exceptional hearing.

"I know that they are up to something," said the rotund man that she recognized from earlier, and glanced around furtively. "Mark my words—exiles never go away peacefully; they always want to get back in. Always."

"Suppose you're right," said a young man, whose pimples and straight back testified that he was fresh out of the Lyceum. "What can we do about it?"

"Build fortifications," the rotund man said.

The rest of the group snickered.

"Isn't it a bit premature?" said one of them. "If you are concerned, perhaps some careful reconnaissance . . . "

"Enough of this nonsense," interrupted the man who appeared to be the oldest and crankiest in the group. "Wait for the problem to arise, then seek solutions."

Mattie thought that the mechanics were generally inclined to solve non-existent problems; she took a step away from the group when her leg shook and she felt faint. Her movements faltered, and she felt a fine tremor spreading through her arms and legs, while her head felt suddenly foreign and unwieldy. She stumbled and would have fallen, if the edge of the table had not presented itself to her dimming vision; Mattie grabbed onto it, her fine fingertips splintering under her weight.

She saw Loharri making his way toward her, worry on his face, and his fingers already unbuttoning the tall collar of his jacket. Before her eyes closed, Mattie saw him pulling out a thin chain and a blinding flash of light reflected from a polished metal surface. The flash grew larger and obscured the room and the dismayed faces of the mechanics, annoyed at such brazen automaton malfunctioning, and Mattie could only feel her creator's hands—loving, repellent—tugging the dress on her chest down, exposing her shame for all to see. And then she stopped feeling altogether.

MATTIE CAME TO—AT FIRST, SHE DIDN'T REALIZE THAT SHE was in the same room, lying on the same floor. Most of the lamps had been extinguished, and the people were gone. Only Loharri perched on the edge of the table, motionless and dark like a gargoyle in the gathering dusk.

She pushed herself up, and her hands clanged against the hollow floors, making them sing with resonance. Her fingers found the smooth window in her chest and traced its familiar oval shape. It was closed again now, secure and snug, but her heart whirred strongly behind it, all wound up and ready for another few months of labor. "I'm sorry," she said.

"It's not your fault." He didn't move, and she could not quite decide whether he looked tired or irritated. "Not the best timing, but these things do happen."

She stood, testing her limbs. He didn't seem mad at her for the embarrassment she caused him. She should be grateful for that, she thought, but instead she felt hurt. Violated. He exposed her heart for all to see, he wound her up with the key around his neck right in front of his friends. "I want to go home," she said.

He hopped off the table, and the floor echoed again. "As you wish. I'll walk you."

"No need," she said.

"I'd rather keep an eye on you," he said. "To make sure you're all right. I just wish you'd tell me when you need winding."

"I don't know when I do," Mattie said. "I just wish you had given me the key."

Loharri led her outside, into the uncertain, still-tremulous light of the streetlamps that were just starting to go on. "If I give you the key," he said, taking her hand into his, "you'll have no reason to spend time with me."

They had had this conversation often enough, and it always went in circles like that. Mattie reassured him that she would come and see him, but he shook his head and insisted until Mattie agreed that he was right. She wouldn't—oh, for a while she would feel dutiful and visit, and then the obligation would become a meaningless chore as the reasons behind it faded and resentment overcame loyalty. She looked away.

"Why do you hate me?" Loharri asked.

"I don't." Mattie faltered, unsure at the sudden change of tone and subject. She didn't, not really. He was just trying to confuse her, to take care of the uncertain, vulnerable state when her mechanisms settled after the recent disruption. "I honestly don't. I just . . . I just wish you'd given me the key."

He patted her arm. "All in good time," he said.

Chapter 4

Iolanda sniffed at the vial—Mattie had found the most expensive crystal, and the slanted sunrays lit the facets with red, yellow, and blue sparks—and smiled. "Not bad," she said. "A little bitter for my taste, but I suppose it suits. I'm pleased I have put my faith in you."

"Did I pass?" Mattie asked.

Iolanda's eyebrows plucked to perfect black crescents arched in pretended surprise. "Pass what?"

"It was a test, wasn't it?" Mattie said. "You wanted to see if I could follow your orders."

"I assumed you could do that," Iolanda said, and helped herself to a seat. "But yes, I wanted to make sure that you are good with deadlines and feelings—I know little of automatons, and I wondered if emotions are something you understand . . . "

"Why wouldn't I?" Mattie immediately worried that her words came out too defensive.

Iolanda shrugged, too languid to disguise her indifference. "You *are* made mostly of metal."

"I won't argue with the obvious," Mattie said. "But what does it have to do with feelings?"

"You have a smart mouth," Iolanda said, and smiled with faint approval. "I think I will work well with you. Now, I will depart, unless . . . "

Mattie waited politely for the rest of the sentence, but since it was not forthcoming, she saw it fit to ask, "Unless what?"

Iolanda rolled her eyes. "As I suspected, you do miss some subtleties. I was just trying to give you an opening to ask for favors."

"Thank you," Mattie said. She considered feverishly whether to ask about Sebastian—Loharri seemed so reluctant to speak of him and his disappearance that she felt she had no other recourse. Yet, she feared that she was becoming a part of something she didn't understand.

"Well?" Iolanda stood and tapped her foot on the leg of Mattie's laboratory bench. "I haven't all day."

"I wanted to find relatives of a . . . a friend. Not really a friend—a deceased colleague. Beresta."

"Never heard of her," Iolanda said. "What are her relatives' names?"

"There's only one I know of," Mattie said. "His name's Sebastian; he's a mechanic, I think . . . from the Eastern district."

Iolanda's smooth forehead acquired a thin horizontal wrinkle, which smoothed out as soon as she started to speak. "You ask for interesting favors, Mattie. Surely, you understand that associating with people like Sebastian is not good for you?"

Great, Mattie thought. A second undesirable in as many days. "No," she said. "I just need to talk to him about his mother's papers—I'm interested in her work, not him."

"I believe you," Iolanda said. "But that is of no consequence. Sebastian is not welcome in the city anymore—I imagine he lives outside the walls, perhaps on a farm somewhere."

"Or he could've moved on to another city."

"I doubt it. He still keeps in touch with some people here, and there's a rumor that he and his associates are not far away."

"What did he do?" Mattie asked. "And what does he want here?"

"He was a mechanic," Iolanda said. "The Mechanics cast him out. You better ask them."

Mattie bent her neck, indicating that she understood. "I will," she said. "Thank you for your help."

"Don't mention it." Iolanda straightened her skirt and smoothed the front of her blouse. "I've trusted you by hiring you—it is only right for me to be straight with you. Of course, I do expect the same back."

Mattie bowed, and waited for Iolanda, the crystal vial clutched in her smooth hands, to leave. Iolanda seemed so alien—Mattie had not considered it before, but Iolanda and her abundance of flesh made Mattie conscious of her own small, long-limbed body of metal and wood, jointed and angular. The only person she was close to before was Ogdela, old and dry like a matchstick. Then there was Loharri, but he was always there and hardly counted. But even he was long and thin, almost insectile—especially when he worked with his slow, deliberate movements that reminded Mattie of the praying mantises that populated the wild rose bushes that had been taking over the back yard of Loharri's house.

Mattie could not decide if she liked Iolanda—she liked her words and her apparent candor. But her fleshiness made her uneasy, and Mattie felt shallow because of that. And yet, the feeling persisted.

To take her mind off Iolanda, Mattie decided to go shopping. The money Iolanda gave her was certainly welcome, and Mattie decided to stop by a bookshop near the paper factory. It carried some books she had lusted after for as long as she had been on her own, after she had ended her apprenticeship with Ogdela—small, trim books with thick paper and ragged pages, books bound in cloth and leather, books with faded drawings painted with a thin brush dipped in ox blood.

Ogdela had given her a crude book printed on pounded birch bark and containing a number of simple recipes and a list of common ingredients. It was Mattie's treasure, even though she knew every word by heart—it was proof that she was a real alchemist; then there were others, acquired through varied means—some as payment, others bought with money she should've spent on other things. But she longed for the expensive books. She justified it to herself by her need to learn more arcane things—after all, to deal with the gargoyles she needed more complex potions and mixtures, new and exotic ingredients. But in her ticking heart, she knew that she just wanted the books as objects, as small solid leather-bound weights of palpable luxury.

She walked to the store; it was midday, and the streets swarmed with oxen, lizards, and mechanized buggies carrying people and goods to the afternoon markets; a few pedestrians weaved in and out of the traffic, but they grew rarer as she approached the paper factory—the sun had heated up the noxious fumes emanating from it, making the air yellow and thick.

Mattie tasted bleach and sulfur on her lips, until she passed beyond the factory, away from the river, and entered a labyrinth of narrow streets occupied by tenements and small shops selling wares both expensive and mysterious; a faint smell of polished wood and ancient fabrics hung over the area. She could see the palatial spires of the Duke's district far in the distance, piercing the low long clouds.

As she approached the bookshop, she felt a distant rumble underground, as if a thunderclap had struck deep within the earth under her feet. The air reverberated, and the windows of the shop—wide panes of glass—gave back a high-pitched, almost inaudible cry. Mattie paused, her hand on the handle. Its tremor, just on the edge of detection, transmitted to her fingers, making them itch. She opened the door.

"What was that?" she asked the shop owner, an old woman bent at the waist at precisely a ninety-degree angle.

She looked up at Mattie and smiled. "What was what, sweetness?"

"That . . . noise," she answered.

"I didn't hear anything," the woman said. "Want me to show you some books?"

"Do you have any books on gargoyles?"

The woman laughed. "Do I ever! Come with me, sweetness." She led Mattie to the back of the shop, where the shelves were covered with a thin layer of dust and books towered in haphazard piles, in almost unbearable opulence and bounty. The shop owner grabbed onto one of the shelves and miraculously straightened her back, as her hands moved up from one shelf to the next, ratcheting her to verticality. She pulled a few heavy books, thick and square, from the top shelf. "Here's something to start you with."

WE DO NOT LIVE IN THE BOOKS WRITTEN ABOUT US—WE CRAWL on the walls and we hide, but not within these pages. We do not even believe in these books.

Not that they are untrue, but these accounts lack the immediacy necessary for understanding, and we want to tell the girl to turn away, away—these books will lead her down twisty roads, long, confused byways, away from us. We want to tap on the window, but she is bent over the pages, lost in them. Already lost to us, and we consider weeping.

And then another explosion rocks the air, and we look away from the window, startled, and at first we don't see, we don't understand—but there is an empty space in the clouds, a space where the tall spire used to signal our home.

MATTIE STROKED THE PAGE OF THE BOOK IN DELIGHT, QUITE refusing to believe that the picture in front of her was a thing of artifice—it had the appearance and the texture of something completely natural, springing spontaneously from the paper thanks to some obscure magic. The gargoyle in the picture squatted, its wings folded, its fists supporting its sharp chin, its face serene. It was just like Mattie remembered the gargoyles from the night they visited her—so gray and alien and sleek in their winged beauty, their flesh hard and cold like stone.

She read the words below the picture and soon she was enthralled in the history of them—of how they sprang from the ground, uncounted eons ago, of how they talked to the stone and grew it—at first, shapeless cliffs shot through with caves and encrusted with swallows' nests; then, as their skill and numbers increased, they shaped the living stone whose destiny they shared—shaped it with their mere will!—into tall structures, decorated with serpentine spirals and breathtakingly sweeping walls, into delicate lattices and sturdy edifices.

The gargoyles needed no buildings, but when people came, the gargoyles built them—the Ducal palace was the first to rise from the wreckage of their former creations. They built for the joy of building while remaining elusive, hidden. And as people began to build their own houses and stores and factories, there were more places to hide. At night, the gargoyles went to the oldest of the buildings, to the palace, and they rested on its roofs and spires, haunch-to-haunch and shoulder-to-shoulder with their predecessors who had become one with the stone they had shaped. And they watched over the city as one would after a child.

Mattie closed the book and flipped through another—this one had no pictures and the words were crowded densely together, so that she had to extend her eyes a little to focus better. This book was full of dates and histories, and as far as Mattie could determine from her cursory skim, it was dedicated to proving that the gargoyles did not only grow stone but also had a power of controlling human souls, their thoughts and desires. The author argued in greatly heated and long sentences that the dynasty of the Dukes—the descendants of the first people to populate the gargoyles' creations—were complicit in the gargoyles' conspiracy, and that the source of their influence was not just social inertia but the hidden support of the gray creatures.

Mattie decided to get the second book as a gift to Loharri—even though he hadn't given her the key, he was kind to her. And, most importantly, it looked like something he would enjoy, and Mattie believed that everyone should get what they wanted, just for the sake of it.

She flipped the page to read more, and then she felt another concussion of the air and the faint trembling, tingling shudder of the windowpanes. This time it was stronger, and the floor under her feet groaned, and the boards buckled, as if trying to shake her off. The bookshelves tilted and creaked, and before she could step away they assaulted her with heavy tomes, their rustling pages fanned as if in anger, and their leather bindings scraping her face. She shielded it with her hands—she liked this face well enough to protect it, and the porcelain was fragile. A book hit her hand, and something cracked, shifted, and hung limp—Mattie had to look to confirm that two fingers on her right hand were nearly broken off, two slender metal coils that remained connected to her with just slivers of metal.

The shaking and rumbling stopped, and Mattie looked around at the toppled bookshelves and strewn books, and at the owner who had fallen back into her gallows shape and now stood open-mouthed, surveying the destruction.

"I'm sorry," Mattie said.

"What for?" said the owner. "You didn't do this . . . did you?"

"No, no." Mattie shook her head for emphasis. "How could I? I just wanted these books."

"Then take them and maybe come back some other time," the old woman said with a pained smile. "I'll have quite a bit of work to do here."

Mattie paid and headed outside but stopped in the doorway. "You have someone to help you clean up, correct?"

"Yes, yes." The woman waved her hand helplessly. "The neighborhood kids, they always come to help. Just go now, please."

Mattie left, her two books under her arm, her left hand cradling the injured right. There were people outside— everyone had rushed from their rumbling and shaking homes and shops, and talked excitedly. They all pointed in the same direction—west. Mattie looked too, but at first she could not discern what it was they were pointing at. She had to adjust her eyes again, and finally she discerned that blending with the low clouds a great puff of smoke and dust marred the sky, and that the spire of the palace had entirely gone from view.

"What happened?" she asked a young girl, a factory worker, to judge from her pale face and hair and chapped hands.

The girl squinted at the sky, her large, flat fingers tugging at the sleeve of her dark frock. "The palace's gone, I reckon," she said in a slow, thoughtful drawl. "Maybe an earthquake or maybe war."

"Don't be daft," a tall stern man said to the girl, never acknowledging Mattie with even a glance. He wore a thick leather apron, and Mattie guessed him to be a shopkeeper. "There's no war."

"The gargoyles are taking back what's theirs," said an

old woman, and wrung a wet shirt she held in her hands in apparent despair, or just out of habit—she must've been doing laundry when the quaking started. "Mark my word: they're pulling the stones back under the ground, where they all belong."

They stared into the sky, reluctant to move, as if any movement would upset the balance of their souls and bring the reality and its consequences crashing around them, like an avalanche of heavy books. Mattie was the first to break the spell.

She needed to learn what happened, and she had to talk to Loharri. A sickly tingling in her stomach, where all the sophisticated clockworks and mechanisms of her inner workings nestled, told her that her distress was greater than she had initially estimated. The gargoyles, she thought; the gargoyles. Had they been at the palace? Were any of them hurt?

She had almost reached home when with a wave of guilt she realized that she hadn't even considered the lives of people inside. The Duke and the courtiers had been away—it was the planting season, and they visited the farms to bless the fields. But the servants inside . . . Mattie was not sure if the palace employed any human servants except the housekeepers and the overseers; they would be dead, she thought. But her heart ached more when she thought of the mindless automatons buried in the rubble, their lifeless eyes and broken limbs now just so much refuse, just guts and metal left in the wake of human need for something . . . she did not know what. Like the sheep who never had the chance to feel any pain or to consider their imminent doom.

ON HER WAY, MATTIE PICKED UP SOME GOSSIP. SHE STOPPED by the public telegraph, a small structure painted yellow, where an ink pen on a long flexible handle endlessly recorded whatever news the operators fed it. She had no hope of reaching it to read herself—the telegraph booth thronged with people eager for the news, who shoved her aside like she was just an obstacle. Most ignored her questions, but from the snippets of their excited chatter to each other she learned the events, if not the precise details or reasons.

As she walked to Loharri's house, the information kept replaying in her mind. The ducal palace had collapsed; there was talk of an attack from the outside, but the structure imploded and crumbled inwards, and the consensus among the Mechanics was that explosives had been placed inside of the palace. The first explosion destroyed the outside walls and wings, and the second destroyed the palace itself.

Loharri was home. Like most mechanics, he had his own sources of information.

"What do you make of that?" Loharri said when Mattie, trembling with shock and unarticulated animal hurt, showed up on his doorstep.

"I don't know," she groaned. "I have to sit down."

Loharri wrapped his arm around her shoulders, and she was grateful for support and the gentle warmth of his breath. He almost dragged her to his living room that had grown even more cluttered since she last visited, and sat her on the chaise that wore a slight but unmistakable imprint of Loharri's angular form.

He examined her damaged hand, tisking to himself, and brought out the soldering iron. "I'll disconnect your sensors while I work," he said. "You'll lose all sensation in this arm—don't be alarmed."

"Thank you," she said. "I bought you a book."

He glanced at the proffered tome and smiled. "Thank you, Mattie. You didn't have to."

"I was at the book shop when the explosions happened," she said. "I don't understand who would do that. Unless . . . " She faltered and bit her tongue, but Loharri was too engrossed in his own thoughts and speculations.

"There's a pattern," he said. The iron in his hand hissed and exhaled thin streams of smoke that smelled of amber. "Today was the day when most of the court were visiting the countryside. Everyone knows that, so whoever staged it wanted no casualties."

"Or was looking for easy access without fear of being caught or interrogated."

Loharri nodded. "Good point, darling. That would indicate an outsider; I was thinking more of an inside job, but you just may be right. Also, note how the explosives were rigged."

"It collapsed on itself," Mattie said. "They didn't want to destroy other buildings."

"Yes, but those explosives . . . the whole city shook. I wonder who could make something like that."

Mattie did not have to answer—they both knew that the Alchemists were the ones with the capacity for making such things; Loharri was still sore since the time when the Mechanics had to go to the Alchemists with their heads uncovered and bowed to ask for their help in blasting a passageway through the mountains.

"Of course, the gargoyles can also command stone," Loharri said. He flipped through the book Mattie brought him. "Look, it says here that they rebuilt the palace after the earthquake five hundred years ago. They could collapse it if they wanted to."

He put the iron away and reconnected the sensors in Mattie's shoulder. She wiggled her fingers tentatively. There was some stiffness, but little pain. She hoped it would go away with some practice.

She cocked her head. "Why would the gargoyles do that? They've been aligned with the ducal family since times immemorial."

Loharri gave her a long look. "Have been brushing up on our history, have we? Be careful there, dear love—history leads to politics more often than you could imagine."

"I'm not interested in that," Mattie said. "Unless more buildings were to blow up."

Loharri paced the room, his long legs loping like a camel's. "I wonder if there will be. By the way, earlier . . . you said something, like you had some suspicions?"

"It's probably nothing," she said. "But at your gathering last night, I heard some mechanics talking about getting rid of the Duke."

"They always blab about that," Loharri scoffed. "It's just talk, understand."

"As far as you know." Mattie could not resist this barb.

Loharri bit. "Are you implying that my brethren might have secrets from me?"

Mattie shrugged. "Talk to Bergen if you're in doubt."

Loharri laughed—the same soft, almost soundless laugh she learned preceded his more extreme temper tantrums. "And yet you dare to fool yourself that politics is of no interest to you."

Mattie rose from her seat. "Your well-being is of interest to me. Talk to your friends. I'll talk to mine. Come by when you feel like you can talk without being angry."

Loharri seemed taken aback. "As you say, Mattie. Somehow, I missed the shift here—you talk to me like you are my master."

Mattie shrugged and craned her neck in pretend pensiveness. "Or perhaps you just think that someone who doesn't want to be your slave is aiming to be your master."

She didn't turn when she headed for the door, but all the way she felt Loharri's burning gaze on the back of her neck.

Chapter 5

———

THE SOCIETY OF THE ALCHEMISTS NEVER HELD REGULAR meetings. The news spread through the grapevine, and occasionally, when circumstances called for their special attention, they made use of the public telegraph. That afternoon Mattie decided to stop by the telegraph to see if a meeting was called—after all, the collapse of the ducal palace seemed reason enough to have one. Besides, Mattie thought, the other alchemists could not have missed the implications of large quantities of explosives that were apparently responsible for the disaster. It was only a matter of time before the Duke and his courtiers returned from their trip and started questioning the alchemists. There was also a concern about the gargoyles—always elusive, they never got involved in human disputes, but no one had ever destroyed their creations before; at least, according to Mattie's book.

In the carefully worded telegram marked "alchemists only" and protected by encoding, Bokker, the elected chairman of the Alchemists' Society, expressed his concern that the gargoyles might direct their displeasure at the Society's members, and invited the meeting in his shed—it was a rather spare construction, holding decades' worth of obsolete equipment, but large enough to fit all of the alchemists who would be concerned enough to attend the meeting. Mattie guessed that a hundred or so of them would show up—the same hundred that always stuck their noses into politics. This time, Mattie decided that she would attend as well.

After reading the missive, Mattie tucked her Alchemist Scrying Ring into her pocket, and her neck clicked pensively. She worried that the event would affect her relationship with the strange creatures she had grown quite fascinated with. She thought that she would not forgive her society if it indeed were their doing. Fuming and taken with dark thoughts, she headed for the meeting.

The Alchemists were not the majority party, and as such the society did not have the use of the palatial grounds. Mattie regretted it—she would've liked to see the devastation close up, but it was cordoned off by the courtiers and their enforcers.

She ventured as close to the palace as she could on her way, and was sternly stopped and turned around by a menacing, faceless figure in ornate armor, mounted on top of a mechanical buggy. Mattie could've sworn that with every day these ugly conveyances—clanking metal wheels wrapped in wooden frames, hissing and spitting steam engines perched on the bronze hulls, perilously close to their armored passengers—grew more numerous.

"Restricted area," the man in armor said. "Only mechanics and construction automatons are allowed through."

"Were there many casualties?" Mattie asked.

He shook his metal-encased head, and for a brief moment Mattie imagined him as another automaton, intelligent like her, and felt kinship.

"Be careful with that engine," Mattie said before turning around. "It looks hot . . . and dangerous."

"Mind your own business, clunker," the metal rider replied.

Mattie hurried away, her heart ticking louder and faster than her steps with suppressed fury. No one had ever dared to call her a clunker to her face, and the slur caught her off guard—like a sudden failure of her sensors, when everything tingled and then went numb. She almost fled the district, hurrying away from the glimpses of splintered stone and fine chalky dust over everything.

Mattie realized that she was running late. On her detour she wandered far away from the eastern district and the Grackle Pond, and she had to hurry through the streets, tracing a wide arc around the pond and emerging not too far away from the house on the embankment where she first met the Soul-Smoker. A concern flared, and a memory that really, she had to visit him and to see if Beresta would talk to her again. And Iolanda had said that Sebastian would likely be outside of the city . . . perhaps Ilmarekh would know something or had heard something from his house on top of the hill.

She passed the house of the recent death, where the funeral wreaths had already wilted and the liquid smoke had dissipated, and entered the wide streets favored by wealthy alchemists. Mattie eyed the houses, assessing the rent—this would be a nice place to live, she thought, both for the view and for the convenience. Loharri would be much closer, and the shops that sold especially exotic plants and animal parts would be nearby. And it would give her more time to work, which would certainly offset the expense; plus, with Iolanda's financial backing . . . she stopped herself from thinking in such a manner, since her alliance with Iolanda was a new affair, and was made all the more uncertain by recent events. If the court were to be forced to move out of the city, she realized, Iolanda and her revenue would be gone. She wasn't sure whether she should be proud of her far-sighted self-interest, or embarrassed at being so mercenary. Iolanda was right—she still had trouble knowing what the right emotion for a given circumstance was; she only hoped that people occasionally had the same problem, and Iolanda would thus be unable to catch her in a lie.

When she arrived at the appointed place, she found twice as many people as she had expected—the shed could not hold them all, and the meeting was moved to the hothouse, which took up most of the sizeable yard of Bokker's place. Bokker himself—a middle-aged man with white hair and no discernible neck—directed the late arrivals under the vast glass canopy. Mattie thought that it was a miracle that it still stood after the previous day's explosion.

Bokker nodded at Mattie curtly; even this small gesture turned his face crimson. "Haven't seen you in a while," he said.

"This seemed important," she said.

Bokker sighed. "You know, Mattie, everyone today said this. It makes me wonder, it truly does—is a disaster the only thing that can bring us together? Are we that selfish, that embroiled in our own lives? Is there a point to even having this society anymore?"

"Of course there is," Mattie said, and dared to touch his purple sleeve with her fingertips, as reassuringly as she could. "We don't have to see each other all the time to work together, do we?"

He sighed but looked somewhat consoled. "I suppose so, dear girl, I suppose so. We're lucky—two of our Parliament representatives came today. They'll tell us the latest rumors at the court and in the government."

Mattie headed inside. The hothouse was not exactly suited for gatherings—it was a huge indoor garden, with potted and hanging plants covering benches, walls, and ceiling. Most of the plants she couldn't even recognize—rare, exotic blooms nodded at her regally, iridescent blues and reds, and the air was thick with their cloying fragrance. She distinguished the smells of roses and orchid blossoms, of warm melting resin and sweet nectar.

The alchemists gathered between the benches, most of them sniffing and looking at the plants with appreciation. Bokker's collection was legendary among them, and it was the result and the perpetuator of his wealth. Bokker did not look down on selling his surplus, and the alchemists were always willing to buy the plants from him. Bokker had a reputation for not being petty: lenient with his bills and generous with his measuring scales.

Mattie followed the row of potted plants, all of them in jubilant bloom—reds and yellows, whites and blues—and the scents of musky lilies and earthy irises snaked into the sensors on her lips, filling them to saturation. Still, she discerned the smells of lush greenery and rotting peaches, the sweet decay of leaf mulch lining the flower pots, the dark, foreboding scent of rare orchids that twined their thick white roots around the branches of the small trees cultivated for the purpose of being the orchids' perch and sustenance.

She brushed her fingertips across a particularly lush, velvet petal, bright crimson streaked with gold, and it showered her fingers with bright yellow pollen. Her fingers smelled of saffron.

It struck her how large the hothouse pavilion was—two hundred alchemists milled about without jostling against each other or banging elbows, and some managed to carry on private conversations in soft blurred voices; despite her superior hearing, Mattie could not make out the words, but the overall tone seemed rather dark.

The gathering had filled an open area at the back of the rectangular pavilion, and stragglers had to strain to hear from the aisles between the benches. Bokker pushed past Mattie and took his place in the opening, among the garden hoses, buckets, and piles of peat moss. "Dear alchemists," he started from his inauspicious perch. "I need not explain why we are gathered here. I need not tell you that things that turn bad have a tendency to become worse. I do need to prepare you for the blame that will be thrown at us by the Mechanics, and I need you to restrain yourself from blaming them back."

"He has to be kidding," the woman standing behind Mattie whispered. Mattie had not met her before, but her Scrying Ring hung conspicuously around her neck on a thin leather thong. The woman spoke with a slight accent, and her dark skin betrayed her foreign origin; no other society in the city would have tolerated her. "He expects us just to sit back and take it?" Judging from the growing murmur around them, many alchemists shared her position.

Bokker turned almost purple and raised his hands, waiting for silence. "I do not ask for your acquiescence in the face of accusations," he said. "I ask for your tolerance and forgiveness. Do not lash back at those who accuse you, do not give them an excuse to rally the people and give power to the Mechanics. Realize that without ducal trust and support for our society, the Mechanics will rule the city."

"They already do," someone in the front shouted.

"Tides turn," Bokker answered mysteriously.

The woman behind Mattie tugged at her dress. "Excuse me," she said. "Why do the alchemists need ducal support? I'm new here, still learning . . . "

"The Dukes had always insisted that both alchemists and mechanics are represented in the government," Mattie said. "They represent two aspects of creation—command of the spiritual and the magical, and mastery of the physical. Together, we have the same aspects as the gargoyles who could shape the physical with their minds."

The woman nodded. "I'm Niobe," she said to Mattie. "And I thank you for your kind explanation. No one has been so nice to me here."

Mattie noticed the tension in the woman's shoulders, how she carried herself—as if not quite sure what to expect. "It's all right," Mattie said. "I'm a machine. No one explains anything to me either."

"We will remain calm and we will be vigilant," Bokker

said. "And I propose we start with finding out whether anyone had received any orders for explosives lately."

"Just from the goddamned Mechanics," said an elderly woman to Mattie's left. "You know that. You'd think they eat that stuff."

"That's a start," Bokker said. "Anyone else?"

A few more alchemists said that they had filled orders for the mechanics—their usual demolition, everyone assumed.

Niobe cleared her throat. "How do you know that the people who ask for explosives are really mechanics?" She raised her voice enough for everyone to hear.

"We have a system of identification," Bokker explained. "The Mechanics issue medallions to their members—unless one had graduated from the Lyceum and was initiated, they cannot get one of those."

"Could they be faked or stolen?" Niobe asked.

"I don't see why not," Mattie said loudly. "It is possible."

Niobe smiled gratefully, and Mattie's heart throbbed in sorrow. Niobe seemed so ready for anger and scorn, so surprised at any sign of kindness . . . Mattie had to remind herself that she really had quite enough problems of her own. Right now, she realized that the entire gathering was staring at her and Niobe.

Bokker clapped his hands. "Everyone who received an order, see me immediately. We will put together the list of names and verify with the Mechanics that these people are members in good standing and their requests were legitimate. We will also need to find out if any medallions had been lost or stolen."

"Like they will tell us if they lost anything," someone said—Mattie could not see who for all the greenery. "That'll put the blame on them."

"Any thoughts?" Bokker asked.

Mattie raised her hand tentatively. "I could find out," she said.

Bokker beamed at her. "Fabulous," he said. "Just don't do anything foolish . . . or suspicious."

"I won't."

The meeting was dismissed soon after, and Bokker and a few others stayed behind to work on the list. Niobe and Mattie left Bokker's house together.

"Where are you from?" Mattie asked. Niobe kept walking in step with her, and Mattie was starting to feel awkward about the silence.

Niobe gestured vaguely east, indicating the wide world outside of the city walls. "Big city," she said. "Beyond the sea."

"Oh," Mattie said. "You were not happy there?"

Niobe sighed. "Happy enough," she said. "Only . . . how can you sleep when the night is so dark it suffocates, how can you smell the incense in the air and wonder if there are different places, places your heart yearns to see? Didn't you ever wake up in the middle of the night and wonder if there are places where the alchemists use metals and not plants? Fire and not oil? How can you stay in one place and not want to leave?"

"I don't sleep," Mattie said. "And I don't wonder about other places."

Niobe rounded her eyes at Mattie in mock horror, and

laughed. "Maybe you didn't have to. You live in the City of Gargoyles, and maybe in the heart of wonder there is no more wonder left. But I . . . I so wanted to come here. I've been in this city a month now, and I've yet to see a single gargoyle." She pouted in disappointment.

They came to the Grackle Pond, and Mattie gestured to one of the wrought iron benches decorating the embankment. It was shaded by a slender cascade of willow branches, furry with pale young leaves, and Mattie judged that here they could sit in peace, enjoying the view and attracting little attention. "Let's rest a bit," she said, even though she was not tired, and drank in the thick smell of green stagnant water and silt. She trusted Niobe—she seemed so much like Mattie, and even though she was large and broad of shoulder, her flesh looked hard, as if carved of wood, so unlike Iolanda's.

Niobe plopped down on the bench and stretched her legs, sighing comfortably. "Come on," she said to Mattie. "Tell me about the gargoyles. You've seen them, haven't you?"

"Yes," Mattie said. She was unsure of how much she should divulge. "Only once. They hide during the day, and you can see them at night, if you want to, from a distance. Or you could at one time, anyway. They slept on the roof of the Duke's palace."

"Yes, I saw that," Niobe said. "But . . . none of them move, and you can't tell which ones are real."

"All of them are," Mattie said. "Most are stone, some few are still moving . . . but they all turn to stone eventually."

"We will all become one with what we were born from," Niobe said.

Mattie stared.

"Just a saying we have," said Niobe, and laughed and pointed at a flock of ducks and ducklings that paddled to the shore, their black, beady eyes somehow managing an expectant expression. "Oh, they are cute."

"Yes," Mattie said, without looking. "What did you mean, becoming one with what we were born from?"

Niobe shrugged. "People came from the earth and return to it once they die, and become dirt. The gargoyles are born from stone. So they become it." She laughed again. "Or something like that."

"What about the automatons?" Mattie asked.

Niobe stared at the ducks that shyly wobbled ever closer. "I don't know. We don't have anything . . . anyone like you back home."

Mattie nodded. She didn't have to ask, really—she came from Loharri's laboratory, born of metal and coils and spare parts and boredom; this is where she would find herself in the end, likely enough.

Mattie was fascinated with the change in Niobe—once they left the presence of the alchemists, Niobe seemed a whole new woman, laughing and moving freely. This is how Mattie felt away from judging eyes; the problem was, it only happened when she was alone, or with the gargoyles. Or Ilmarekh.

Her thoughts turned to the Soul-Smoker and the secrets of the souls that inhabited his weak, ravaged body. She felt selfish that she hadn't thought of him in so long. Him or Beresta. Or her work. She groaned a little.

"Don't be so glum," Niobe said, and immediately clamped

her hand over her mouth. "I'm sorry. I know the palace was important to you and your people."

Mattie nodded. "And the gargoyles. I wonder if they will raise the palace again or if there are too few of them left. Where will they go if they can't rebuild? Where will the Duke and his court go?"

"I'm sure it'll work out." Niobe patted Mattie's shoulder, and the clinking of her rings sounded muffled by the cloth covering Mattie's metal flesh. "I'm sorry to see you sad, and yet I'm happy that this misfortune allowed me to meet you. I haven't made a friend here yet."

"It can be difficult here," Mattie said. "Alchemists are not too bad—they won't be rude to you; at least, not to your face. But the mechanics . . . they're a conceited lot, and if you aren't one of them they'll spit on you. The man who made me isn't like that, but he too has his faults."

"I often wonder what it would be like to know your creator," Niobe said.

Mattie inclined her head. "It is aggravating," she said. "And humbling at times. Loharri . . . he can be difficult. Possessive."

Niobe laughed. "Of course he is. You're . . . " She paused, as if looking for the right word. "You're precious, Mattie. There's no one in the world like you. If I had made you, I wouldn't let you out of the house."

"I suppose I should be flattered," Mattie said and stood. "It is nice to meet, you, really, but I should be going."

"Oh no." Niobe grabbed Mattie's hand and peered into her blue porcelain face. "I've offended you."

"It doesn't matter," Mattie said. "It will pass."

Niobe stood too. "Listen. Come visit me the next holiday, all right? I live by the market, the one on the other side of Merchant Square. There's a jewelry shop downstairs."

"I know the place," she said. "It's owned by other . . . easterners? Like you?"

Niobe smiled. "That's right. Will you come?"

As much as Mattie resented being treated like a thing that could be kept indoors at one's whim, she thought that Niobe deserved another chance. After all, where else would she find someone as alone and mistrusted as herself? "Yes," she said. "I will visit you. Maybe you can tell me about the alchemy you practice."

Niobe's face brightened with a smile. "Yes! And promise you'll do the same for me. The alchemists here seem awfully protective of their secrets."

"They don't like outsiders."

Niobe raised her eyebrows. "Really? I haven't noticed."

Mattie shrugged. "They did let you in, like they let me in. Believe me, this is the best either of us will be treated."

"Unless we change that," Niobe said. "I'll see you the next holiday."

Mattie headed down the embankment, unsure whether to go home or to visit Ilmarekh. She decided on the latter; it wasn't just Beresta's secrets or her elusive son, but Mattie worried about Ilmarekh, of how he withstood the assault of the ghosts inside him. She headed west, for the city gates.

We mourn today as we will have mourned tomorrow, and we hide in the rain gutters and the attics, we smell dust and people's cooking. At night, we huddle on the roofs, the shingles rough under our feet, our folded wings chafing against the bricks of the chimneys. Sometimes, the wind blows and brings with it the sound of quiet laughter and the smell of lilacs, the humid breath of the water lilies in the Grackle Pond and the stench of bleach from the factory.

We are sad that we cannot smell cool stone, the dark moss pockmarking its surface, the rain and snow whipping its inert bulk and slowly, imperceptibly eroding it. And as we think of stone, we think of the things we haven't thought about in ages—of how stone heaved and buckled and split, releasing us into the world; of how it followed us, like the night ocean follows the moon, how it bounded toward our hands, like a loyal dog to the beckoning of its master. When we were many, we could breathe a barest whisper, and it heard and obeyed, it listened. And now our voices are few and weak, and we cannot rebuild what has been ruined.

Chapter 6

MATTIE FOUND ILMAREKH IN HIS HOUSE ON TOP OF RAM'S Head Hill, and immediately saw that he was unwell. She cursed herself for not thinking to bring a tonic or a strengthening elixir.

"What's wrong?" she asked Ilmarekh who sat, wrapped in a blanket, by the roaring fire despite a warm, balmy day outside.

He shivered in response. His teeth clattered so loudly that no words could come out.

Mattie moved closer, stepping carefully around dirty dishes on the floor and an occasional bowl of ash. She touched his forehead, and her sensitive fingers registered no fever, just a film of clammy sweat covering his brow.

It didn't take Mattie long to recognize the symptoms of opium withdrawal—the alternating sweats and chills, the body aches, nausea, uncontrollable sneezing and watering eyes—she catalogued them in her mind and hurried back to her shop.

There was little to be done about that but wait it out, but Mattie looked to diminishing the pain before cures. She thought of buying more opium but instead decided to use what few dried poppy flowers she had left—they would be enough to ease Ilmarekh's suffering and let him sleep.

She ran up the stairs, the light metal of her lower legs swinging over two steps at a time, and started her brewing. To opium, she added lemongrass against nausea, chamomile for a general calming, and vanilla to relax his knotted shoulders and let him sleep.

She flew through her shop, mixing and grinding, measuring and distilling, filtering and decanting. *A plain bottle would suffice*, she said to herself. *What does he care?* She rummaged through the jars and bottles and decanters crowding the shelf over the bench, and picked up an old apothecary vial shrouded with dust and cobwebs. She wiped the grime away and discovered on its side an image of a gargoyle in low relief on a flat medallion filigreed with gold.

When she was still living with Loharri, he sometimes took her eyes away as a punishment for disobedience, and she had to feel her way around for as much as a week. She still remembered her delight when her fingers stumbled upon a familiar shape and recognized it—a full, round surprise that made her heart bubble with joy. She remembered finding the vial with the gargoyle in it and secreting it in the folds of her dress, so she could trace the gargoyle wings in her room, in secret, and thus defy her blindness.

She cleaned the vial and poured her mixture into it. Surely the man who was blind for all his life was not immune to the joy of tactile recognition, she thought, and hurried back to the gates, the vial wrapped in the tight coils of her fingers. The elixir would make him better; she chased away the selfish thoughts of the questions she would ask him once he was coherent again. She needed to fix him, and did not dare to think beyond that.

Back in his shack, Ilmarekh had moved away from the fire; it still smoldered, ashes wet from a carelessly dumped bucket of water. He was now curled up on the bed, little more than a mere straw-filled mattress.

Mattie shook her head and poked at the wet ashes with the tip of her foot. "What are you going to do if you want fire later?"

He shrugged, sullen at the nagging note that crept into her voice.

"I brought you something," Mattie said, softer now. "Please drink it."

"Does it have opium in it?" Ilmarekh said.

"Very little—just to make you feel better. Why?"

He either shivered or shrugged, she wasn't sure. "When I don't smoke and my head is clear, the souls stop talking. I want them to stop talking."

"Just drink this," Mattie said, "and sleep—I promise they won't bother you."

"You won't . . . you won't do anything to hurt me, will you?"

From previous experience, Mattie knew that people didn't trust her just because she mentioned her good will or kind nature. Nowadays, she relied entirely on mercenary arguments. "Why would I do that? I still have questions to ask you."

Her words seemed to reassure him, and he propped himself up on one elbow, pulling a ragged woolen blanket around him. He grasped the bottle and drank, his long white fingers twitching on the glass, pulsating with every gulp as if they were the tentacles of an octopus testing the strength of its suckers. He was almost finished when his fingertips brushed across the glass medallion with the emblazoned gargoyle, and his blind white eyes widened in surprise.

Mattie was relieved to see a ghost of a smile touch his lips.

"Mattie," he said. "This is a truly lovely engraving. Thank you." He fell back on his mattress, still clasping the vial, and was asleep before he remembered to stop smiling.

Mattie guarded his sleep, which gave her plenty of time to look around. She knew the Soul-Smoker was poor, she just hadn't realized how much so. The house—the hut, if one wanted to be honest—lacked even the most basic necessities. There was no running water, and the fireplace seemed to be the only way to cook meals and heat water for a bath. There was just one room, one corner of it sagging perilously and threatening to bring down the entire house. The wooden floors, drafty and not covered by anything but sparse trickles of sawdust, were worn to a soft shine by the feet of many generations of Soul-Smokers; their daily paths were clearly visible—one led from the fireplace to the table, rickety on its thin, deformed legs; another shot from the table to the bed and the deep ceramic tub in the corner next to it; the third led from the bed to the fireplace. A simple triangle enclosing a life of privation.

Mattie did not have to ask to learn Ilmarekh's story—the Soul-Smokers were always the same, recruited from those who had no other choice. Usually orphans, usually crippled, those who had nowhere else to go and no one to turn for help to; those who had no chance surviving on their own, without the Stone Monks' dubious charity.

The orphanage run by the Stone Monks was the northernmost building in the city, its wall just a hair's breadth from the city wall by the northern gates. Mattie remembered coming there with Loharri—he seemed fond of coming there, with no other apparent purpose but to stand in front of the solid front wall, his hands in his pockets and his disfigured face twisted in an even more unpleasant grimace than usual. Mattie would stand next to him and occasionally ask questions to stave off boredom.

"Why did they put it all the way here?" she asked him once. "Their temple and the gargoyle feeders are all by the palace."

"Noise," Loharri said in a strained voice. "There'd be too much noise. They don't want anyone hearing."

Mattie cocked her head to listen then, but could not catch any sounds coming through the thick blind walls, just one door and no windows. The stone was too thick, too solid—the building looked like the ones in the ducal district, but the thin lines between blocks of masonry told her that it was man-made. "Why aren't there any windows?" she asked then.

Loharri turned around sharply and headed away. As she hurried to catch up, her skirts flapping in the rising wind, she caught the sharp sound of grinding teeth. "The windows give one hope, Mattie," he said. "This is not what this place is for."

Now, she tried to guess what sorts of horrors happened inside, and just could not think of anything that would push Ilmarckh and his predecessors to choose living in a tiny hut with hundreds of ghosts haunting his every moment, never leaving him alone; he only had time to be alone in his skin during opium withdrawal. She realized that her own experiences had been rather benign and limited in scope, yet it made her fear more. If they could do this to a man, what about a girl automaton whose position in the society was tenuous at best?

She rose from her seat on the floor with a jerking movement, eager to do anything so as not to think the awful thoughts that threatened to overwhelm her. She regretted spending the money on books; she needed to hoard it, to save it, because there could be a day when she would need to bribe people to save her life . . .

Mattie collected every dirty, crusted plate strewn on the floor and on the table, and dumped them all into the tub. Irritated, she ran outside into the nascent rain, and found a small, primitive well behind the house, halfway down the slope. She filled the bucket she found by the well with water and she brought it back, dumped it into the tub, and went back for more. She used to be a house automaton, after all, and she scrubbed the dishes and rinsed them in cold water, she swept the floors with a fury of a tornado, she whirled like a broken mechanized dancer. The familiarity of the movement comforted her momentarily, but soon was supplanted by other memories.

She remembered Loharri's house, as a house servant sees it—straight planes of the desks and benches and shelves that gathered dust, her habitual irritation at the piled up parts and flywheels and counterweight mechanisms that cluttered everywhere, and Loharri's insistence that she mustn't touch them and yet keep the place clean; the desolate expanses of wooden floors that needed to be waxed. Like him or not, but he did let her go—partially, at least.

She fetched another bucket of water and scrubbed the floors with unnecessary force and vigor, her metal bones creaking with the effort. The more she tried to understand what moved those around her, the more she failed—especially with Loharri. She remembered the women who came and went like the seasons; she remembered his long spells of ennui and seclusion, and then visits to the temple and the orphanage, the night stalking of the sleeping gargoyles, immobile and light like birds. And how he always brought her with him.

She soothed him; oh, how she soothed him. She remembered the cool lips on her porcelain cheek, the slight trembling of hands as they touched the metal and the whalebone inlays of her chest, the breath fogging the window behind which her heart whirred and ticked. The almost hungry caress of the fingertips as they traced the outline of the keyhole on her chest, and made her heart tick faster. The taste of human skin on her lip sensors, salty and precipitous, and the feeling in her abdomen that some great misfortune was about to befall her mixed with light-headed giddiness. The smell of leather and tobacco trapped in her hair afterwards.

And then he recovered and worked in his shop, and she cleaned, and the procession of dark-lidded women with heavy thick hair and small, secretive smiles resumed. Women like Iolanda who asked Mattie worrying questions. Mattie was a woman because of the corset stays and whalebone, because of the heave of her metal chest, because of the bone hoops fastened to her hips that held her skirts wide—but also because

Loharri told her she was one. She thought then that he loved her; and yet, as soon as she was emancipated she forbade him to touch her.

She dried the dishes and stacked them neatly in the rack by the fireplace. She scrubbed the fireplace free of wet ash and brought in a fresh armload of logs, stacked outside under a sailcloth canopy protecting them from the rain.

Ilmarekh stirred in his sleep and sighed. Mattie settled on the floor by the fireplace and waited for him to wake up. She tried to keep her thoughts on a single track, from Sebastian to gargoyles, from the Alchemists to the Mechanics. The machinery in her head made small insect clicks, a familiar and comforting sound, and if she listened closely, she could hear the whisper of the undulating membrane, which, as Loharri had told her, imprinted her thoughts in her memory.

Ilmarekh sat up and smelled the air, his narrow nostrils flaring. "Who's here?" he asked in a hoarse voice.

"It's Mattie. I didn't want to leave you alone."

He wrapped himself in the blanket but did not shiver. "Thank you," he said. "You did not have to do that. And thank you for your medicine—it is wonderful."

"Are the souls bothering you now?" she asked.

He cocked his head, listening. "I hear naught but whispers," he said. "Thank you. I can rarely afford such a break."

"Why not?"

He grimaced. "It is painful. Besides, the souls need a link to the world. If I sever this link and refuse to open my mind to them with opium, they will go insane. And insane souls are not a pretty sight."

Mattie thought a bit. "How long do they stay with you?"

"Until I die," he said. "Every blessed one of them. When I die, my original soul leads them to their rest, and we all are free." He smiled a little. "My predecessor died old, very old, but the one before him was quite young. They say, he went mad from being unable to contain the multitudes. They killed him then; I only hope that I manage longer than he."

"I'm sorry." Mattie couldn't think of anything else to say.

He reached out and she moved closer, to let his spatulate fingers touch hers. "Don't be. You've been kind to me. Kinder than anyone else. I'd like to help you."

"Just ask Beresta of the whereabouts of her son," she said. "I mean, when they . . . the souls are talking to you again."

"I know where he is," Ilmarekh said. "I'm sorry I didn't tell you earlier, but I didn't think it was my place."

Mattie squeezed his hand. "Where is he?"

"Where you wouldn't look for an exile," he answered with a smile. "In the heart of the city. I saw him at the temple—Beresta recognized him. She didn't tell me but I felt it."

Mattie shook her head. "The Temple? But . . . why didn't anyone recognize him?"

"Because people don't pay attention to those who are covered with mud and carry buckets with gravel for the gargoyles' feeders," Ilmarekh said, and sneezed forcefully.

"Thank you," Mattie said and stood. "I have cleaned the house, and now you can just rest. If you wish, I can bring you food from the market tomorrow morning."

He shook his head. "No, dear girl. Leave me be—food does not agree with me in this state. But rest assured, I welcome your visits."

"There has to be something else I could do," Mattie said.

He shook his head, mournful. "There's nothing to be done. Just go, leave me to my silence."

Mattie walked out of the door, feeling no joy that the object of her search was so near. She tried to imagine what it was like for the Soul-Smoker, to be finally free of the torments of the multitude of whispering residual lives and yet to be too ill to enjoy the silence. If his one true happiness was just to lie on a ratty, straw-filled mattress, his eyes open, drinking in the silence like a desert wanderer drinks in water, what was it to her?

And yet, she couldn't shake her anger as she walked downhill. Not at Ilmarekh but at those who chose that life for him —just like the anger she felt when the soldier on the metal mount called her a clunker. There were these people—she wasn't sure exactly who they were—who kept telling them what they could and could not be. And Mattie was quite certain that she did not request her emancipation just so she could obey others besides Loharri. She prayed for Iolanda's protection and help, yet she hoped that there would never be a day she would need either.

IN THE NIGHT, MATTIE'S HEELS CLACKED EVER SO LOUDLY ON the gray stone by the ducal palace. The enforcers were gone for the night, and only chains stretched between the black and glistening lampposts; their light was weak that night, as if its energy was sapped by the recent disaster. And not even the gargoyles stirred in the darkness. She was alone, as alone as Ilmarekh currently was in his skull. She shrugged off fear the best she could.

She crossed a wide swath of cobbled pavement—it used to surround the palace, but now that it was gone, it looked like empty no man's land, strewn with rubble, seeded with a thick smell of sulfur and charcoal. She circumvented the rubble heap—so much stone!—as quickly as she could, afraid to look closer out of the superstitious fear that there was someone watching, and he would see and catch her the moment she locked eyes with him.

The building of the temple loomed behind the former palace; it was a dark place, rarely visited by anyone but the Stone Monks. And, apparently, the gargoyles—they studded the cupped roof of the temple, immobile and asleep; Mattie wondered if they mourned their stone friends who perished in the explosion, if the gargoyles ever mourned anyone. Mattie stopped and watched for any sign of movement on the roof, but the gargoyles appeared soundly asleep. No monks ventured outside in this dead hour, and she was now far enough from the palace to smell freshness in the air, the wet dust and stone—a reminder of the recent rain.

She passed the temple and approached the low wall that stood there as a reminder rather than a true obstacle—one could clear it in a single long leap if one were so inclined, and Mattie was. She picked up her skirts with one hand, placed the other on the mossy furry top of the wall, and vaulted over it, the springs of her muscles coiling and propelling her with ease. She now stood in a small courtyard that contained nothing but large stone urns half-filled with gravel, and a single tree, long dead but still reaching for the moon with the broken black fingers of its branches.

Mattie found the urn in which the level was the lowest, and crouched low next to it. The feeders were refilled at night and she waited, waited for the footsteps and clanging of the bucket filled with shattered stone, the gargoyles' favorite food.

She did not have to wait long. Before the dawn arrived, the low gate connecting the courtyard to the temple swung open, and a tall figure appeared, a bucket in each hand. Mattie felt disappointed—it had to be an automaton, to carry such a weight, and she was about to leave her hiding place and depart, when the figure started to whistle. The mindless automatons did not whistle, and Mattie's heart ticked faster.

The man with the buckets walked toward her hiding place, and as he got closer Mattie realized that his skin was the same color as Niobe's, and she remembered that Loharri referred to Beresta, his mother, as an easterner. She wondered how he managed to remain hidden.

The man rested one bucket on the cobbles of the courtyard with a dull thump, and picked up the other with both hands. Mattie was close enough to see the ropy muscles on his arms tense under the ragged, unbleached linen of the shirt as he dumped the contents of the bucket into the feeder. The gravel rattled against the stone wall of the urn, and Mattie pressed her cheek to the rough surface, listening to the stone tumbling inside.

The man heaved up the other bucket and emptied it into

the urn. He picked up both buckets and made a move as if to leave, but then he spun back around and looked straight at Mattie. "Are you gonna stay in there all night, or are you gonna say hello?"

She stood, trembling and feeling stupid. She just assumed that as a human he couldn't see in the dark. "How did you know I was here?"

"You're ticking, girl," he said and cocked his head to his shoulder. "You might want to have that checked out."

"No I don't," Mattie said. "It's my heart, and there's nothing wrong with that."

"I was joking." His teeth glinted briefly in the dark. "You're an automaton, aren't you? Haven't seen one that clever before."

"Not clever enough to remember that my heartbeat makes a sound," she said, and extended her hand. "I'm Mattie. And you're Sebastian."

He touched her hand carefully. "My name is Zeneis. I don't know who Sebastian is."

"I looked for you on bequest of your dead mother," she said, looking him straight in the eyes, so lost and dilated by darkness. "I spoke to the Soul-Smoker, and Beresta told me to seek you out."

He hesitated just enough to convince Mattie that he was indeed Beresta's son. "I don't—"

"Hush," she interrupted, in her best imitation of Loharri's imperious tone. "Don't lie when there's no need. I have no interest in anything but your mother's work. I'm an alchemist, and I want to know what she was doing for gargoyles. Of course, if you decide to not help me . . ."

He sighed. "Dear Mattie, don't threaten those who are stronger than you. I'll wring your little metal neck faster than you can say 'Aqua Regis'. You were stupid to come here all by yourself, weren't you?"

She backed away from him. He did look strong, but Mattie suspected that she was just as powerful. The trouble was, she did not know how to fight.

He stepped closer, and the empty buckets clattered to the ground. "I'm sorry. I hate to hurt you, even though you're just a mechanical thing. But I don't trust those who threaten my safety and know my whereabouts."

"I wasn't threatening," Mattie said and took another step back. "I was trying to help you."

Sebastian smirked. "Help, eh? I've heard that one before. But every time someone in this city offers me help, I get worried. And remember, you came to ask me for help, not the other way around." He sprang forward, his arms reaching out with the speed and strength of pistons, and grabbed Mattie's arm.

She wrenched it free, and heard the thin bones of her forearm grind together. Shooting pain came a moment later. She swung a fist, aiming at his jaw, but he ducked, and she just caught the edge of his ear.

He hissed in pain. "You're really going to get it now," he said.

Mattie raised her hands to protect her face, and waited for the blow.

WE SHOULDN'T INTERVENE, EVEN IF THERE IS A GIRL WITH THE *dead boy's hair, and she is cringing in anticipation of a blow;*

we cannot bear the thought of her face shattered, the underlying gears exposed for all to see. We cannot bear having to ask another for help. And the man, we know him, as he is now and how he used to be—and we remember that he knows about us. Still, we shouldn't intervene.

We flap our wings, and they both freeze as they are; she is covering her face, one blue eye looking between thin fingers hopefully in our direction, and he—imposing—with his shoulder thrown back, his elbow ready to release the tension of wound muscles, the fist heavy and bony and dead, as we feel his resolve draining away.

And then we arrive—we glide like leaves, like gray ugly stone leaves, we descend in a graceful arc, we float. We surround them, insinuate ourselves between them, gently pull them away from each other. We smooth her hair and chase the fear from every facet of her eyes, we tenderly take his hand—like a lover would, perhaps—and unclench his fingers, rest his arm by his side. We erase the frown from his high forehead, we smooth her dress. We position them with caring hands, with solicitous wings, to face one another.

"Now talk," we say, and we wait for one of them to utter the first word.

Chapter 7

———

EVERYONE HAD A STORY; MATTIE HAD LEARNED THAT A LONG time ago when Loharri explained such intricacies to her. She remembered it well—a sunny afternoon when wide slats of sunlight painted the dark wooden floors and striped the furniture, giving it a semblance of trembling and very quiet life.

"Sit down," Loharri said.

She obeyed, sinking into the pillowed couch of his living room. There would be a lesson, she thought. She wasn't yet sure how she felt about them.

"Do you know where you came from, Mattie?" He did not sit down but paced across the living room floor, his stockinged feet making no sound. It irritated her, his silence of movement—hers were not like that.

"Yes," she answered. She was already learning to mimic some body language, and folded her hands over her breast and inclined her head, like a child reciting poetry by rote. "You made me just last week."

"Two weeks," he corrected. "A week has passed; time does not stand still."

"So next week it will have been three weeks?" she asked.

He nodded. "As time goes by, things happen to you. You learn new things. You make yourself a story—your story. Everybody has one."

"Do I have one?" Mattie asked. She was not sure why but she wanted so desperately to have it.

He sighed and raked his fingers through his dark hair that was long enough to touch his collar. "Not yet, Mattie. But you will."

"Next week?"

He breathed a laugh. "We'll see. It takes a bit of time, usually."

"What is your story?" she asked him then.

"It's not important," he said, and paced again. "Let's concentrate on making you one."

Mattie's story started in the mechanic's workshop and continued among the shining pots in the kitchen, among the floor wax and wide windows that gathered soot like it was precious, and culminated in a small alchemical laboratory of her own.

And as it turned out, this is where Sebastian's story started. He looked around Mattie's alchemical bench and smiled at the sheep's eyes and bunches of dried salamanders like they were old friends. "It's just like my mom's place," he said. "She lived not too far from here."

"Eastern district," Mattie said. She still worried a bit about his presence among so many breakable and valuable chemicals and glassware—he seemed so awkwardly large in the narrow, cramped space that every time he moved his arms, she reached out involuntarily, ready to catch alembics and aludels he was sure to knock down.

He nodded and finally stepped away from the bench to sit down in the kitchen. "I grew up watching her work . . . I probably still remember some of the salves she used to make for ailing neighbors."

She hurried after him, secretly relieved and already regretting letting him into her home—it was not safe, with Iolanda and Loharri liable to drop by. Why did he agree to come?

"So, you wanted to know about my mother's work," he said.

"Yes," she answered. "Did she find out how to stop the gargoyles from turning into stone?"

"They still do, don't they? No, she didn't find the cure. She kept saying that it's the stone that held them hostage, that they were one flesh. And only if she could break the bond with the stone . . . " He cut off abruptly and gave her a sly smile. "This all sounds like nonsense to you, doesn't it?"

"No," Mattie said. "Not at all. It makes perfect sense."

"This is why I became a mechanic," Sebastian said, and stopped smiling. "The alchemists . . . you just babble nonsense and pretend that it means something."

"It does," Mattie said. "How did they let you into the Lyceum? You . . . you're not like them."

"My mother pulled some favors," he answered, frowning. When he got angry, he seemed to get bigger, and the stool under him looked ready to give up and crumble, abandoning its duty. "But of course, once they let me in, they watched me like a thief in a jewelry store. I could do no right. No matter what I proposed, they refused it, and then acted like one of them came up with that idea. And it's just relentless." He slapped his knee. "Every day, every day!" His impassioned speech brought color to his cheeks, and despite her preoccupation, Mattie noticed how attractive he looked.

"You are very beautiful," she said.

He looked at her—she couldn't quite comprehend his expression, but it reminded her of the time she first asked Loharri for her key. "Not an hour ago, I almost hit you," he said, quietly and slowly. "If it hadn't been for the gargoyles, I would've killed you; you'd be just a pile of springs and gears. Why do you talk like that?"

Mattie realized that she had said something wrong. "You didn't kill me, though," she said. "You're not my enemy."

He shook his head. "How did you come to be an alchemist, anyway? And how come the gargoyles chose you?"

"That's what I wanted to be," Mattie said. "You became a mechanic because you were raised by an alchemist; I became an alchemist because a mechanic made me."

He smiled at that, showing small, uneven teeth. "Fair enough. What about the gargoyles? They seem protective of you."

Mattie nodded. "Yes. But I don't know why they chose me after your mother. Because we are both women? Because we are resented for what we are?"

"You got that right," he muttered. "She told me that the alchemists were better with the foreigners than the mechanics, but not by much. They just take the trouble to hide it a little."

"That's something, isn't it? I feel grateful to even be emancipated, let alone accepted into the society."

Sebastian studied her for a while, as if considering how she fit into his view of the world. "Emancipated, eh? And how did you manage that?"

"I just asked my master to be an alchemist," she said.

"As I got better, he decided that making me clean his house was a waste, and he made me new hands and built another automaton for housework."

"It must be nice to have someone do for you the work you loathe," he said. There was a hint of disapproval in his voice.

"It was a mindless automaton," Mattie said. "Whatever the case may be, when I asked to be emancipated, my master agreed and signed the papers. I only see him when I want to."

"Congratulations," Sebastian said. "Who is your master?"

"Loharri," she said. "Do you know him?"

"A little," Sebastian said. "He's not quite as awful as the rest of them."

"He can be pretty awful," Mattie said. "He was the one who told me that you were exiled . . . but he didn't tell me why, and neither did you."

Sebastian laughed. "I only just met you," he said. "Suffice it to say, I've done nothing wrong."

Mattie did not think it sufficed at all, but just nodded her agreement. "Why are you still in the city then?"

He stood. "I still have business here," he said. "Do me a favor, don't tell anyone you saw me."

Mattie shook her head. "I won't. Before you go, promise you'll tell me if you remember anything else about the gargoyles and your mother's work."

"Will do." He stepped to the door but paused on the threshold. "Come and think of it, I remember something else. The gargoyles have no souls."

"Everyone knows that," Mattie said, disappointed.

"That's what she said," Sebastian answered with a careless shrug of his large shoulders, and left. His heavy footsteps rattled down the stairs.

Mattie started on her daily work, potions and salves the apothecary downstairs bought from her as often as she offered them, her movements smooth and habitual, honed by long repetitious hours in the same cramped space. A small window over the workbench offered a small but welcome glimpse of the early morning sky, pinking around the edges, the clouds gilded by the still-invisible sun. Mattie worried if Sebastian would make his way to the temple undetected and scolded herself—of course he would; he survived here just fine, without her knowing or worrying about him.

There was a cadence to the movements of her hands, a rhythm to the small shuffling steps she took as she moved back and forth along the bench, mixing herbs and powders, cutting the sheep's eyes open and squeezing the clouded jelly smelling of mutton into the bowl. Mattie tasted the air—still good, but she would need to stop by the butcher's soon. She let her thoughts drift, and they tumbled in her head lazily, in beat with the whirring of her insides. Memories wafted in and out of her mind, and she watched them like a detached observer.

When she was first made, she did not feel pain. She fell and broke her face, and Loharri made sure that she knew hurt. "It's for your own protection," he said. "Pain is good—it warns you that you are about to hurt yourself."

A week later, she passed out on the floor. He took out her key and wound her, and she flinched away. Then, he made her feel pleasure. Being wound had been the only pleasure she knew.

Until now, she thought, until she became an alchemist. Her hands flew, and her mind drifted, and her heart beat in a steady happy rhythm.

MATTIE LEFT THE HOUSE AND HEADED DOWN THE STREET toward the river; she meant to go to the butcher's eventually, but for now she decided to take a walk along the embankment, away from the paper factory toward the western district, where the trees smelled sweet and cast cool shadows, where large, soft leaves absorbed the noise of the traffic.

She walked through the shaded alleys, enjoying the peace and the silence that did not belong to her. She stared at the whitewashed fronts of the houses, at the groomed trees in front of them. That was the only thing she missed about living with Loharri—the quiet and self-satisfied demeanor of this neighborhood. She felt exiled for no reason.

As she entered the streets that led to the market, the noise grew—there was a clip-clopping of oxen hooves, scraping of lizard claws, soft hissing of the buggies, and a clang of metal from some indeterminate source.

"Out of the way!" She heard a voice from behind, and bolted to the curb. She turned, to see a mechanized contraption she hadn't seen before—it belched fire and twin streams of steam as it crawled down the street. The contraption had several pairs of stubby piston legs that gripped the cobbles of the street; its jointed back bearing several chairs (empty for now) moved in a sinusoid curve as the thing slithered down the street. A lone mechanic presided over the front end of the contraption; he sat on a small shelf jutting out of the monster's flat metal face, and moved two long jointed levers.

"What is it?" Mattie shouted over the roar and hiss of the mechanical beast as it passed her.

"It's a caterpillar," the mechanic shouted back. "It can carry ten people at once."

"What if they are going to different places?" Mattie asked.

The mechanic did not grace her with an answer—the mechanics often ignored stupid questions, especially if they came from automatons and easterners—and steered the metal caterpillar down the street. Mattie had a feeling that soon enough more of them would crawl through the narrow streets, displacing pedestrians and buggies and spooking the lizards.

She realized that her feet, of their own volition, were taking her to Loharri's house. It was only natural, she supposed—she passed this market so many times, up the slight incline of the ancient hill eroded almost to nothing, to the white house almost hidden by overgrown rose bushes. Loharri paid little mind to the plants now that Mattie, who had planted them, wasn't there to take care of the succulent green growth that seemed to become more audacious with every passing year. Ten years since she first planted the roses, and now they were taking over, erecting themselves into a formidable hedge. The first pale and red blooms studded the thorny branches, a decoy of beauty hiding their murderous intentions. Mattie imagined that one day the plants would take over the house and bury Loharri within . . . she could almost live with this thought, if it weren't for the key he wore around his neck.

Mattie circled the house to check on the plants in the back yard, and she had to fight her way through the roses that crowded the path leading to the back door and grabbed at her skirts with their thorns. She tried the back door—unlocked as usual, and she pushed it open.

Despite the brilliant light outside, the kitchen remained subsumed by velvety dusk. This home had a special quality of light and air about it; it softened and gilded everything inside, and it was kind. Mattie's eyes needed a second to adjust to it, and the familiar objects came into focus—the generous hearth, the glinting of kettles and pans suspended over the table in the middle, the reassuring solidity and slight woody smell of the cutting boards, the automaton in the corner . . .

The presumed automaton turned to face Mattie and she belatedly realized that it was a woman—scandalously under-dressed at that, lacking her corset and bustle and even a skirt, wearing only a white shift flimsy enough to reveal the curvy, fleshy body underneath.

Mattie looked away quickly. "I'm sorry," she said.

"Don't be," said the familiar voice. "I was just getting a drink of water. How've you been?"

Mattie dared to look up into the woman's face. "Iolanda."

Iolanda shrugged and the thin strap of her shift slid off, revealing a round and freckled shoulder. "You seem surprised."

"I didn't think . . . you liked him," Mattie said.

Iolanda moved closer, silent on her bare feet. "I don't," she whispered. "And yet, here I am. And here you are."

Mattie reached for the door. "I'll come back later."

"It's all right," Iolanda said, and grabbed Mattie's wrist. "Don't be so uptight." She dragged Mattie along, yelling, "Loharri! Look what I found!"

He was in his workshop, thankfully dressed. "You don't have to scream your head off," he said. "Don't they teach you any manners at the palace?"

"There is no palace," Iolanda said cheerfully. "The Duke is moving."

"Where?" Loharri and Mattie said in one voice.

"To his summer mansion, by the sea." She gestured vaguely east, and laughed.

Mattie thought that she had never yet seen Iolanda like that—so energetic, so giddy, crackling with some hidden excitement. And the fact that she was here and undressed . . . she decided to ponder the implications later, when she wasn't so distracted.

Loharri apparently thought the same. "What are you so happy about?" he murmured, and pretended to study a copper spring with greater attention than it warranted. "Eager to bathe in the sea?"

Iolanda giggled with a girlishness Mattie had not suspected in her. "I'm not going," she said. "I'm staying here. A whole bunch of us are."

"By 'us' you of course mean 'courtiers'," Loharri said, dropping the spring on the workbench and picking up a half-assembled clockwork heart—another automaton, Mattie guessed.

"Yes!" Iolanda clapped her hands. "You should hear the marvelous rumors . . . "

"I hear them all day long, and there's nothing marvelous about them," Loharri said. "If they call one more emergency session, I'm going to leave this wretched city and go to the sea with the Duke."

"You won't," Iolanda said. "You love this place as much as I do, and you are dying to find out what's going on."

Loharri shook his head. "Children," he said. "You are all dumb, spoiled children who don't recognize danger because you have no concept of what it is. People died in that palace, you know."

Iolanda pouted. "Don't be a spoilsport. There weren't that many—maids and cooks, and that's it."

"And of course they don't matter," Loharri said, frowning.

"I never said that. It's just that there weren't many people hurt. Just automatons." She huffed and spun around, and danced out of the workshop.

Loharri smiled at Mattie. "Speaking of automatons. What can I do for you?"

You can give me my key, she wanted to say. Instead she asked, "Have you seen those mechanical caterpillars?"

"Oh yes," he said. "Adorable, aren't they? And with their legs they don't damage the streets as much as buggies, or even lizard's claws. And they can run faster than either of those. It'll cost a bit to build a few more and establish regular routes, but in the long run they'll pay for themselves in repair costs."

"I don't like them," Mattie said.

Loharri shrugged. "It's just too bad then. You came all the way to voice your grievance with the mechanics' way of running the city? Did your society send you?"

"No," Mattie said. "But we are doing our own investigation. Can you help me?" She folded her hands pleadingly.

Loharri sighed. "Why do you always have to ask for things?"

"Because I cannot get them myself," she said with a coquettish tilt of her head. "Will you help me?"

"Depends on what you need," he said.

Mattie thought a bit. She did not want to tell him too much, yet she saw no other way of obtaining the information she wanted but direct request. Breaking into the office where the mechanics kept their records seemed risky, and Bokker told her not to do anything dangerous. "Can I trust you with a secret?" she asked, although she knew the answer.

He seemed startled. "Yes," he said. "Of course. Have I ever betrayed your confidence?"

"No."

"What do you need then?"

"Just some of the mechanics' records. Nothing big, just if you issued any replacement medallions at any point—we think that someone could've ordered explosives by pretending to be a mechanic."

"I can do that," Loharri said. "This is not a bad idea, actually."

"You wish you had thought of that?" Mattie said.

"We have an even better idea," he said. "I can't wait until the alchemists learn of it—they'll pitch a fit. I would bet money that they'll try to block us from getting to the city funds, but the Duke's not here to lend them his support, so I believe there is nothing they can do." He laughed softly.

Mattie knew him well enough to realize that only an invention he had an immediate interest in would please him so. "What is it?" she asked.

"A machine," he said. "An automaton, but without a body, just pure mind, like yours—only bigger. It's like a hundred of your brains stuck together, made for analysis. We tell it what happened, and it figures out who had the most to gain and therefore who is responsible, and what we should do next. Amazing, no?"

"Wouldn't its answer change depending on what you told it?" Mattie asked.

Loharri stopped smiling and squinted at her in suspicion. "Of course it would. So we'll just tell it everything."

"You don't know everything," Mattie said. "No one does."

Loharri frowned now. "Seriously, Mattie. We certainly know enough about this city and what's happening here to give it enough information to figure things out. And imagine, a rational machine that can figure out the future! We won't need the Stone Monks' cryptic advice anymore . . . not that I ever thought it was useful, but maybe with this machine others will realize how ridiculous they are."

"Maybe," Mattie said. "I just doubt it would be much more reliable."

"I doubt you know what you're talking about," Loharri said. His scar paled, and the skin around it turned a shade short of purple, indicating an alarming redistribution of blood. "Come by the Parliament building tomorrow morning, I'll have the list of missing medallions for you. But now, I'm busy."

"Thank you," Mattie said.

Iolanda waited for her in the kitchen, by the door. "I'll come by later," she whispered, her lips urgent and warm by Mattie's ear. "I'll have a big order for you."

Mattie walked all the way to the slaughterhouse on the southern edge of the city. Troubled thoughts churned in her mind, like they had been doing lately. She considered Iolanda's semi-naked presence in Loharri's house and her giddy excitement about the demolition; she thought of Sebastian and his words about the gargoyles, but even more so she tried to find a benign reason for him, a mechanic who had more than a passing familiarity with alchemy, to be in such close proximity to the palace. No matter how she turned it in her head, she failed, and she could not help but feel suspicious.

She passed a factory belching fire and steam, obscuring the sky. It was a bad area, surrounded by the slums where small workshops threw together crude automatons destined for the mines and factories. She had heard rumors that people worked in the mines too—they were more flexible, and could reach the more distant passages. Their fingers were also quick and precise, and if there was an avalanche or a collapsed mine, they were cheaper to replace than the automatons.

There were several caterpillars running at full speed toward and away from the factory, carrying metal from the mines just south of the wall, in the hills. The dull glint of copper and iron grew brighter in the light cast by the factory flames, and Mattie smelled sulfur and hot metal on the wind. She hurried past—she did not like the factory, and after it the sight of the slaughterhouse seemed a relief.

The butchers knew her by sight, as they did most alchemists—they waved her past the killing floor to the large wooden barrels filled with offal. She nodded to a few colleagues who were already picking through the barrels, their noses pinched shut with wooden clips. Mattie did not find the smell unpleasant, and moved leisurely. She grabbed a sheet of wax paper from the stack by the barrels, and walked along the row of barrels, looking for eyes.

She noticed a tall woman bent over a barrel, her skin a familiar dark hue. "Niobe," she called.

The woman looked up and smiled. "Mattie," she said. "I didn't know you people used animal parts."

"I didn't know you did."

Niobe held up a glass jar, half filled with sloshing of dark and thick blood. "We don't. But I've learned some blood alchemy in my travels." She handed the jar to Mattie.

"What does it do?" Mattie asked.

Niobe smiled still. "Come on. Get your eyeballs, and I'll show you."

Chapter 8

———

THE STREETS IN THE CITY RUN LIKE VEINS IN A LEAF, LIKE *paths in our very own labyrinth. We keep our hand on the wall at all times as we follow, unseen, gray on gray stone. We flatten ourselves against the stones, and we crawl in small and swift movements, like monstrous geckos. We follow the two women—one mechanical, the other alien to us, foreign—a child of shifting sand dunes and red earth, not of stone. Both smell of blood and hidden excitement, both carry jars filled with dark and viscous redness; it sloshes as they walk, laps at the walls of the jar with quiet hissing, and it reminds us of the ocean we've never seen but often imagined.*

We think it amusing that lately we cannot love our children—children of stone, children that came from those who first settled in our creation; they do not seem to love us either. They have destroyed what we have built, and they think of us no longer. Our feeders are not refilled today, and we go hungry. It seems fitting somehow.

We remember another woman born of red earth on the other side of the sea. We remember her thin arms, fingers like bird claws. Her face covered in a cobweb of wrinkles, her dark-hooded fatigued eyes. Her soft, accented voice, always warmed by the elusive promise of salvation.

"Why did you turn to me?" she asked us, at a time when

her hands were too tired to move and her heart was ready to give out. Why me, *a plaintive cry of every lone soul in this city, alone as the day they were born.*

We cannot explain this feeling, this stirring, wistful like the smell of linden blooms in the blue moonlit night. We only feel, we feel the absence of love from the stone, from the city, we feel uprooted from our soil. And we seek salvation from all the unloved children of the world.

ON THE WAY, NIOBE RELENTED UNDER MATTIE'S PITIFUL stare (she extended her eyestalks for that very purpose), and confided that blood alchemy had many uses—love spells and divinations, as well as darker purposes. She told Mattie that in her homeland the blood homunculi were used to temporarily trap restless spirits, forcing them to divulge their secrets and use their incorporeal nature to peek into the time yet unwashed over the world but accessible to spirits, unmoored as they were from their physical confines.

"How far into the future can they see?" Mattie asked, fascinated.

Niobe smiled. "It's unpredictable. Sometimes they confuse future and past, or even present—it is all the same to them. Know where we could catch a few spirits?"

"Yes," Mattie said. "The Soul-Smoker has them all. But I doubt he'd give any of them up."

"Soul-Smoker?" Niobe asked, frowning. "What's that?"

Mattie explained what Soul-Smokers did for a living, and told Niobe about Ilmarekh and his sad state.

"Isn't anyone happy in this place?" Niobe said.

Mattie considered her answer. "Some are. All are, at one time or another. I'll bet even Ilmarekh is happy occasionally."

"That's not what I meant," Niobe said but did not elaborate further. Instead, she quickened her step and sang a tune Mattie was not familiar with, swinging the blood-filled jar in rhythm with her song.

Mattie hurried after, intensely curious about the blood alchemy now. "I wonder if Ilmarekh would agree to let us trap a soul or two before he gets to them. Or maybe he'd think it's cruel."

Niobe laughed. "Patience, Mattie. Let me show you some simple stuff today. Besides, if I go to see the Soul-Smoker with you, won't he steal my soul too?"

"He doesn't steal them." Mattie felt protective of Ilmarekh. "It's just your soul might decide to join the rest; believe me, he doesn't need another voice whispering to him."

"He must be crazier than a fighting fish," Niobe said. "You have strange friends."

"Only strange people want to be friends with a machine," Mattie said.

Niobe laughed. "I suppose so."

Mattie caught up to Niobe, and looked around. They were in the part of the district she rarely visited, and she realized that there were many dark faces among the passersby. It made sense to her, she supposed, that foreigners settled close to each other—people seemed to like company of their own kind.

Niobe seemed to know many people—she constantly smiled and waved, and people smiled and waved back. The smells that wafted from the doors and windows, open on account of warm weather, set Mattie's sensors afire with their strangeness—she recognized sandalwood and incense of some sort, fermenting bread, fresh berries, and unfamiliar cooking.

"There seem to be a lot more of your people here since I last visited," Mattie said.

Niobe shrugged. "People move, they bring their families. They help each other too—when I first came, I had nothing with me but my bag and an address. And these people were strangers to me back home, but here they treated me like family, took me in, helped me find a place. Without them, I would never have figured out how to join the society and apply for an alchemist's license. We have to stick together—I bet you stick together with your own kind too."

Mattie shook her head. The vision of the automata at the mechanics' gathering moving along the walls in a blind, shambling procession, deaf and dumb and as unaware of the world as the tables around them, flashed in her mind. She wanted nothing to do with them.

"Why not?" Niobe persisted, simultaneously making a pretend scary face at a gaggle of small barelegged children that ran through the streets with an air of great joyful purpose.

"I'm not like them," Mattie said, "Well, most of them. There are a few intelligent automatons around; a few of them are even emancipated. But you know, nobody likes making them. And they . . . we don't even like ourselves."

"I'm surprised to hear that." Niobe turned into a street too narrow for proper traffic, animated by just a few pedestrians. There was a low buzz in the air, a suppressed droning of a multitude of voices at a distance, and Mattie guessed that they were getting closer to the market. "I would think that intelligent automatons would be valuable."

"They are expensive," Mattie said, "but not valuable at all. We make poor servants—one advantage automatons have is that they don't talk back or complain. Very few tasks need an actively engaged mind."

"And the mechanics and the alchemists have it covered," Niobe said. "I understand."

The market had become larger too, and Mattie regretted not visiting it more often. There were quite a few booths that sold herbs and minerals and bits of rare wildlife. She couldn't help but stop every few steps, craning her neck at a lovely display of boars' hooves or bottles with golden oil of uncertain origin.

Niobe followed her, asking occasional questions about the use of plants. She seemed curiously ignorant of their properties, and Mattie quite enjoyed explaining that two piles of small dried blue flowers were, in fact, quite different—one was lavender, the other veronica, and each had its own properties.

Niobe sniffed at the flowers and laughed, and told Mattie that where she came from, all plants were subdivided into blood plants and water plants, plants with yellow sap, and plants that cured nausea. She scoffed at dried salamanders and insisted that only live ones were suitable for harnessing elemental powers, she lingered over large shapeless chunks of rock, her long fingers tracing the silvery veins of precious metals and her soft voice reciting their affinities to sulfur or volcanic fire. Mattie could not remember the last time she had been able to lose herself in conversation so completely.

She lost track of time as well, and the sun was starting to tilt west when they finally emerged from the battleground of the markets, both loaded with precious ingredients and professing mutual surprise at how little they managed to spend in the face of overwhelming temptation.

They entered one of the side streets, and Mattie recognized the jewelry store—the only one in the city that carried lapis lazuli, mother-of-pearl, and large chunks of amber. Mattie used to come there with Loharri—he picked through the precious stones for his projects, while she browsed through the piles of amber, looking for pieces with entrapped insects or bubbles of air from long ago.

As if answering her thoughts, Loharri emerged from the doorway of the jewelry shop. His sharp eyes slid over Mattie to her companion and lingered a bit, before meeting Mattie's gaze. "Slumming?" he said. "Don't worry, I am too. Who's your friend?"

"I'm Niobe," Niobe said. "Forgive me for not shaking your hand." She shrugged apologetically at her many parcels.

"Forgiven," Loharri said. "What's in the jar?"

"Sheep's blood," Niobe said. "What's your name?"

Loharri frowned a bit. "Loharri's my name. I am a member of the order of Mechanics. Surely you've heard of us?"

Niobe nodded. If she felt out of place or intimidated, she didn't show it, and Mattie marveled at the difference in her demeanor compared to the latest alchemists' meeting. "I've heard of you. You're the ones who build all those factories that make it impossible to take a stroll by the river."

Mattie cringed—Loharri didn't like being challenged, or addressed in such a familiar manner.

Loharri produced the coldest smile in his repertoire. "Everything has its price. Yet, we managed to do some good—I'm the maker of your friend," he said, pointing at Mattie. "I'm sure she mentioned me."

"In passing," Mattie said. She found it easier being rude to him while Niobe was nearby. "Niobe's an alchemist, too."

"I noticed." Loharri gave a cursory nod of his head. "You will excuse me, but I have a business meeting to attend. I'll see you tomorrow, Mattie."

Niobe turned and watched him disappear behind the corner. She then smiled at Mattie. "Quite a character."

"Yes," Mattie said, undecided on whether she should feel proud of Loharri or embarrassed by him.

"What happened to his face?"

"I don't know," Mattie said. "He rarely tells me anything about himself."

Niobe sighed and started up the stairs. "They never do," she remarked in a low voice, apparently addressing herself more than Mattie.

Niobe's craft proved to be as difficult as it was fascinating. In her cramped laboratory, smaller than Mattie's and twice as cluttered, Mattie learned to burn blood and refine it through a long, sinuous alembic; Niobe showed her how to mix the blood essence—black powder that smelled of burned horn and rust, and crumbled in Mattie's fingers—with the viscous resin of rare trees, how to shape the resulting sticky mass into tiny figure and imbue the lifeless homunculus with powers curative or destructive—it didn't seem to matter to the homunculus, who absorbed poison or antidote with equal ease.

Niobe spoke at length about the properties of blood—its affinity with metals and earth, its ability to transform any element to its most basic and potent character. Its love of human flesh, the command it held over human mind, the raw power of both healing and ruin.

"Would your potions work on automatons?" Mattie asked.

Niobe shrugged. "I never tried it, but I think so. You are made of metal . . ."

"And bone," Mattie interjected. "Whalebone."

"And human hair," Niobe said, looking over Mattie's short dark locks that barely reached her shoulders. "That's unusual."

"Yes," Mattie agreed. "I don't know of any other automatons who are made this way—I don't even know why Loharri made me like this."

"Do you know where he got the hair?"

Mattie shook her head.

Niobe smiled, stretched, and stepped away from the bench. She had to light the lamp as the darkness gathered outside, and the high, tense voices of the children fell silent and were soon displaced by those of adults, coming from the people carrying leisurely conversations, sitting on their porches or standing by their windows, chatting with the neighbors across the street—a street so narrow that people on opposite sides could almost touch hands if they wished to do so.

Mattie stood by the window, listening to the night voices—

more resonant, it seemed, than during the day, and kinder, more sedate, lulled by the evening meal and impending sleep. Many spoke in a language Mattie did not understand, but the sound soothed her all the same.

The house across the street from Niobe's workshop had its windows open, and the second floor apartment had a window box, brimming with blooming lavender and small irises, blue like the night, bright white arrows on their lower lips shining in the darkness. Mattie smelled the sweet and bitter aroma of the flowers.

Niobe stood by her side. "This is my favorite time of day," she said. "I feel that I will grow to love this city."

"I like it too," Mattie said. "I feel . . . invisible and yet a part of it."

"Invisible is good," Niobe said.

"Loharri doesn't understand that," Mattie said. "He always wanted to show me off, even when I thought I'd rather die than go out."

"Of course he doesn't understand." Now that they were alone Niobe did not bother to hide her contempt. "Even that scar of his . . . How do you expect him to know shame if he never had to hide in his life?"

Mattie shrugged, the metal bones in her shoulders grating together with a long dry whisper. "Maybe he has. I know so little about him. He has many lovers, and other mechanics hate him—that's it, really."

Niobe laughed. "Who would've thought?"

"But it's true," Mattie said. "Why, just today . . . " She broke off, suddenly remembering Iolanda's whispered promise.

"What?" Niobe prompted.

Mattie shook her head. "Nothing. I just remembered something. I have to go."

"It's getting late anyway." Niobe yawned. "Stop by soon, all right? I like working with you."

"I will," Mattie promised. "Thank you for teaching me—I'll teach you next time."

She clattered down the stairs and into the sweet-smelling night streets. The eastern district was vast, and she had a long way home before her. She decided to run.

She picked up her skirts, her bag of offal and the jar of blood tucked under her arm, and she ran like the wind. Loharri discouraged her from running—her joints were delicate, and he did not want them to wear out too soon. Mattie decided that one time would not hurt her; besides, she enjoyed running.

Her feet struck the cobbles with an alarmingly loud noise, but Mattie did not care. The cool breeze washed over her porcelain face, and thick locks of her hair streamed behind her, like the wings of a night bird. Her skirts, awkward and bulky, hitched by her knees, rustled as she ran. She needed no air, and she felt no fatigue, but the rhythmic motion helped her think.

She felt closer to Niobe than anyone else. She loved Ogdela, but the old woman had never forgotten about the gulf between her and Mattie. Niobe was less polite than Ogdela, and occasionally her comments made Mattie self-conscious; yet, there was less of a chasm between them. Mattie resolved to teach Niobe her favorite formulae, even the ones she discovered herself and guarded as jealously as any other alchemist would.

She slowed only once she saw her house and the apothecary sign in its downstairs windows. She straightened her skirts and walked up with calm steps, expecting to find an angry note from Iolanda or a bored messenger.

Instead, she discovered Iolanda her own self. The joviality of the morning had disappeared, and she frowned at Mattie and rose from the steps where she sat like a commoner. "Where have you been?"

Mattie held up her parcel and the jar of blood.

Iolanda's nose wrinkled. "That's disgusting. And it smells like a dead sheep."

"Would you like to come in?" Mattie asked, and led the way up the stairs.

Once inside, Iolanda marched straight to the kitchen. "Can I trouble you for some liquor?" she asked, a shade more politely than before.

Mattie poured her a glass of currant brandy she kept for especially distraught visitors.

Iolanda tossed it back with one swift motion and grimaced. "Thank you," she said. "I've been getting quite a chill."

"My apologies," Mattie said mildly. "You didn't give me an exact time, and I had errands to run."

"I understand," Iolanda said. "In any case, I have a request for you. Just give me a second to collect my thoughts."

Mattie poured her another glass and waited, patient, as the fireflies outside lit up, one by one, yellow in the blue and thick darkness. Mattie wondered where they came from.

MATTIE'S MEMORIES HAD SHAPES—SOME WERE OBLONG AND soft, like the end of a thick blanket tucked under a sleeping man's cheek; others had sharp edges, and one had to think about them carefully in order not to get hurt. Still others took on the shapes of cones and cubes, of metal joints and peacock feathers, and her mind felt cluttered and grew more so by the day, as she accumulated more awkward shapes, just like Loharri collecting more and more garbage in his workshop.

To remember things, she had to let them come to her, as the sounds and the sights around prompted and jostled some of the shapes loose; otherwise, she had to pick among the clutter, despairing of ever finding the pertinent piece of her past in the chaos.

Seeing Iolanda sitting in her kitchen, absentmindedly rolling the empty glass—back and forth, back and forth— between her soft palms reminded Mattie of another night in this kitchen, a year or two ago.

Loharri had showed up unexpectedly then; it was raining, and his black wool suit was soaked through, and the overcoat hung in heavy folds impregnated with water, like the broken wings of a gargoyle. Water pooled in the brim of his hat as in a rain gutter. "Do you have anything to drink?" he asked.

Mattie always kept a bottle for her clients—most of them needed it before they could speak freely of their troubles and ailments, of their need to make the garden grow or to fix the crooked spine of a spiteful child, of their misery. Back then, business was better than today—people would still rather buy a potion to make a servant sleep less and work harder in preference to buying an automaton, they still trusted alchemists more than mechanics. She had many clients, and bought a bottle of fruit brandy a week.

Loharri sat down heavily, not bothering to remove his rain-soaked overcoat; she had to free his listless arms from the sleeves and carefully lift the hat off his head, trying not to spill more water than was unavoidable. She hung the overcoat on the back of a chair by the burning stove and poured him a glass.

Loharri drank and then he talked. Mattie had not seen him like this before, even though she was familiar with his mood swings and proclivity to ennui. The words poured out of his mouth in a constant stream, and Mattie understood little of it. He spoke of people she had never met, of places she had never visited.

"Why are they afraid of us?" he said, plaintively. "We are just trying to help; we're making things better. Without us, they wouldn't even have running water, and yet . . . "

His voice trailed off, and Mattie considered if it would be impolite to ask who 'they' were; she guessed that 'we' referred to the Mechanics.

"You are my only hope, Mattie," he muttered, alcohol blurring his voice. "You are the only worthwhile thing I've ever done."

"I'm not a thing," Mattie said.

"It's not the point," he answered. "The point is that I have nothing besides you."

She comforted him the only way she knew how—she let him stroke her hair with his trembling fingers, the bone-white cuff of his shirt brushing against her cheek. She tolerated his searching, restless hands, let them entangle in her locks; she let him pull her close and touch her face with his lips.

He let her go. "I'm so sorry," he whispered, and poured himself another drink.

Then he talked again, about the oppressive walls and the dark skies that thundered and spewed lightning, of the stone closing in, of the strange malaise of the mind that made one reluctant to think, to break away from the tyranny of the gargoyles' city. No matter how the Mechanics modified and rebuilt it, the ancient unease remained, threatening to wake up at any moment and to engulf them all, pull them back into the stone the city was born from; then he talked about the new road the Mechanics were blasting through the hills, the road that would reach the sea and bring in prosperity and reason.

"Shh," Mattie said and stroked his shoulder. "Have another drink."

He obeyed, then fell silent and brooded awhile, and Mattie kept stroking his shoulder, unsure whether she was still responsible for giving him comfort, or if she were free enough to tell him harshly to go home.

She could never quite bring herself to hate him—she teetered on the brink often, never crossing over. She had learned resentment and annoyance while being with him, and cold gloating joy; but there was also contentment and sympathy, and pity and gratitude.

"This city watches you, always," he murmured. He pulled Mattie closer, his arms wrapping about her waist and his face buried in her skirts. Mattie thought then that it was rather sad that he sought comfort by embracing a machine—the construct that was not built to give it. But she tried, and the trying threatened to rend her heart in half.

T HIS MEMORY WAS SO VIVID THAT SHE COULD NOT HELP BUT clasp her hands together.

Iolanda looked up from her glass, and smiled sheepishly. "I'm sorry," she said. "I was lost in thought there."

"Me too," Mattie said.

"What were you thinking about?" Iolanda asked.

"Loharri," Mattie answered. "He seems so vulnerable sometimes."

Iolanda raised her eyebrows and took another sip from her glass. "Really? I did not see it in him."

"Maybe not." Mattie sat on the stool by the kitchen table—she was not tired, but she knew people appreciated being on the same eye level as their interlocutors. "What were you thinking about?"

"My order for you," she said. "It's not easy for me to ask it . . . but can you make something that would compel a person to listen to me?"

"To listen or to obey?" Mattie asked.

Iolanda shrugged. "Either would be fine. I need someone's attention to persuade them, but if you can help that persuasion I will not say no."

Mattie watched the fireflies flickering outside. She knew about compulsion; she understood coercion—like only an automaton with the key in somebody else's hands could understand. True enough, Loharri was good—he never threatened her with the key, but the very fact that he could if his heart turned that way was enough.

And yet, if she was coerced, was it wrong of her to do it to others? "Who is it for?" Mattie asked.

"Your master," Iolanda answered, not looking away. "I promise I won't harm him."

"No," Mattie said slowly. "It's all right. I don't really mind if you do."

Iolanda arched an eyebrow. "Is that so?"

Fireflies crowded by the window; the lone lamp in her kitchen must've looked like one of their brethren to them, trapped inside an incomprehensible, impenetrable barrier, alone like an air bubble trapped in amber. The poor sods strained to get through, not realizing that any semblance of kinship or recognition was just an illusion, and there was nothing hidden from sight; there was nothing but the surface, and the surface lied.

"Yes," Mattie said. "Do as you will. You want him to love you? To tell you secrets?" She tapped her metal fingers on the jar lid, sending waves through the red sticky liquid inside. "I'm learning some new tricks, and I will bind him to you by blood, I will twist him to your liking."

"Something tells me you would want more than money for this service," Iolanda said. Her high cheekbones flushed with color, alcohol or excitement, joy or fear, and who could tell them apart anyway. "What do you want?"

"My key," Mattie answered. "All I ever wanted was my key and he has it. You can't steal it, it is bound to him. But he can give it to you, and he won't give it to me."

Iolanda touched Mattie's hand. "You poor thing," she whispered. "I had no idea."

"Do you understand then?"

Iolanda nodded. "Show me a woman who wouldn't. I promise I'll try to get you your key back."

"Don't promise," Mattie said. "Just try. As for the rest, it is not my concern."

Iolanda rose from her seat. "Bind him well," she said. "And I will see you soon."

Chapter 9

———

Mattie went to the eastern gates to see the Duke and his court depart from the city. Despite the public telegraphs reassuring the populace that the measure was temporary, an uneasy air hung over the mostly silent crowd, occasionally punctuated by the crying of infants, which did little to lighten the mood.

"I can't believe this is happening," said a woman in a dress grown murky-gray from too many washes.

The man standing next to her nodded, but his eyes kept glancing away from her at Mattie. "Oh, it's happening all right." He spat on the ground, undeterred by the dense crowd. "His father must be trying to crawl out of his grave by now. The Stone Monks should be denouncing his treason from every roof, and it's about time they did something useful. Disgrace, that's what it is."

The first buggies carrying the courtiers and the servants, flanked by shambling columns of automatons, passed the crowd. There were a few boos and a few restrained curses, but most of the people remained silent. Apparently, Mattie was not the only one who took the Duke's leave at its symbolic value.

She looked over the crowd, moving her eyes separately to focus on different parts of the gathering; she saw a few familiar alchemists, but did not feel compelled to greet any of them. She looked for Iolanda or Niobe, and hoped not to see Loharri. Whatever happened between them, she did not feel eager to face the man she had betrayed. She did not go to the mechanics' lodge the day before; she did not retrieve the information about the missing medallions. *I'll do it tomorrow,* she thought, *or the day after, or perhaps the day after that.* Whenever she could bear the look of his slanted heavy hazel eyes that always seemed to see right to her heart and always forgiving her—even when she had done nothing that needed to be forgiven. Now at least he would have a reason.

The crowd shifted, breathing, sniffling, like a large animal. A small girl held high above the crowd on her mother's shoulder sang in a small shy voice, and people whispered. Mattie's sensitive ears picked up bits of conversation nearby and farther away. The Duke's leave did not sit well with anyone.

"The gargoyles didn't leave," a male voice behind Mattie said. "The Stone Monks are still with us. Why is he so special that his hide needs to be saved before the city?"

"What's he gonna do?" someone else asked.

"Nothing, like he done nothing for years. The Parliament will decide, and the Parliament will run things like they always have. Nothing's gonna change."

"He was only here to sit pretty in the palace," the man who spoke first said. "If he ain't gonna do that, why does he think he can tax us?"

The murmur hushed when the sound of screeching metal and heavy pounding reached down the street. Mattie stretched her eyes as far as they would go, and she glimpsed the rest of the procession, up the hill—the giant lizards resplendent in their brown and gold scales, their claws tipped with mercury and silver, dragged open carriages behind them. As they pulled closer, Mattie saw a number of well-dressed people swathed in yards of silk and brocade stiff with gems and rich thread as they smiled and waved at the crowd from the carriage. The Duke himself, a middle-aged clean-shaven man with kind and tired eyes, held hands with his wife; their daughters, all pretty and haughty in their youth, looked straight ahead of them, pointedly ignoring the rabble catcalling to them. A few more men and women crowded together; normally, the Duke's favor conferred certain advantages to them, but now they looked fearful, realizing that the favor of a powerful man often had a downside.

The enforcers in full armor drove in small buggies, surrounding the carriages with a protective shield; but those who had foresightedly brought vegetables in regrettable condition were not deterred from throwing them. The enforcers made a move toward the crowd, and the vegetables ceased.

Mattie looked up the street, at the approaching caravan of mechanical caterpillars that hissed with steam and carried the courtiers, dressed somewhat less extravagantly than the ducal family and their favorites. They were less protected by the enforcers, and whatever produce remained in the hands of the displeased populace was thrown at them with guilty alacrity and a few constrained verbal outbursts.

Mattie was ready to turn away as the first carriages of the procession approached the eastern gates, leaving the city with a leaden finality, telegraph's reassurances notwithstanding.

It was almost as though a part of the city was detaching itself, leaving the place incomplete somehow, although not necessarily worse. There was a sense of freedom in having a piece missing, in having a void that could be filled with something new.

A man jostled past her; he was garbed in the habit of the Stone Monks, but did not move with the usual humility of the clergy—he strode through the crowd, parting it with his heavy shoulder. Mattie stepped aside, giving way, and so did a few of her neighbors.

The man walked past, and only then Mattie noticed that his right hand was deep in the pocket of his robe. Just as she thought that he was about to hurl a spoiled apple or a turnip at the courtiers and judged such behavior inappropriate for a monk, the man pushed into the street, steps away from the ducal carriage.

The object he extracted from his robe was neither a fruit nor a vegetable, but a large clear bottle filled with thick transparent fluid.

The enforcers turned the buggies toward him, screaming warnings. Some of them drew muskets and leveled them at the man, still imploring him to step back.

The man swung and threw the bottle at the carriage and ducked into the crowd just as the first shots rang out. And then all was chaos—Mattie was pushed and almost knocked off her feet as the people around her screamed and ran, as several people from the first row of the crowd fell under the musket shots. Mattic could not look away.

The bottle burst loudly with a flare of hungry fire that

engulfed the side of the ducal carriage. The lizards thrashed, trying to escape the inferno, and got tangled in their tack. Their tails whipped madly, knocking over the carriage. The lizards of the carriages that followed reared up and turned away, some dragging the carriages into the crowd, others upsetting theirs.

The fire spread, engulfing two other carriages. Their passengers wrestled from under the wreckage, even as their clothes and their hair caught fire.

The crowd pushed Mattie away from the sight of the explosion, and she only saw snatches of the raging fire, of a bleeding woman, her face smashed on the cobbles into a smoldering ruin. A giant lizard, its scales glistening red, lay on its side, its broken leg a mess of red twitching meat and fragments of sharp, pink bone. It shrieked in a strange voice, like a child crying. Mattie had never heard the lizards utter anything but an occasional hiss before.

Mattie strained to see over the jostling bobbing heads of the fleeing crowd. She saw the slow mindless automatons snap to action—they did as they were told, and they started to clean up. They moved among the wreckage, picking up the bloody fragments of the bodies torn by the initial explosion. There was nowhere to put them, so they stacked them all in the middle of the street—bloodied limbs, charred corpses, lizard bones, the shattered wood of the carriages and torn pieces of tack. No one paid any mind to them—the street cleared, and before Mattie was swept along with the panicked crowd, she saw the gruesome pile built by the automatons growing higher, as they labored, slow and creaky and not at all perturbed. As far as Mattie was concerned, they were the most horrible thing she had ever seen.

MATTIE WAS SHAKEN ENOUGH BY THE DAY'S EVENTS TO GO see Loharri. On her way, she stopped by the telegraph, which was thronged as she expected. There were fewer casualties reported than she expected; two of the Duke's daughters were dead. The Duke himself, along with his wife and the surviving daughter, were badly burned. The Stone Monks were caring for them, with their vast pharmacopoeia and the favor of the gargoyles. People whispered that this momentous event had even brought the gargoyles out of hiding, and that they watched over the injured, perched on the temple's roof.

Loharri was not home, and she headed for the ducal district, expecting to find him in the Mechanics' chambers of the Parliament. She realized the folly of her intentions as soon as she approached the Parliament, abuzz in movement, swarming with automatons and people, alchemists and mechanics both. A mechanical caterpillar stripped of its seats stood in the street, chuffing idle steam. Eight lizards harnessed double-file waited patiently in front of a low sled. Mattie guessed that the mechanics were evacuating valuables from the Parliament, afraid of another attack, and that Loharri would likely find no time for her.

She passed the open doors of the ossuary, and couldn't resist peeking inside. The sealed sepulchers embedded in the floor offered no sight of interest, but the piles of bones stacked along the walls, the skulls in neat piles in the corners, never failed to fascinate Mattie. Loharri had told her that the bones were those of previous dukes and their wives, their courtiers and favorites, their children and servants. The skulls shone softly when the sunrays from the open doors, filled with dense clouds of motes, struck their suture-seamed yellow surfaces, the domes of the foreheads high and round, the eye sockets mysteriously dark, dripping with untold sadness and wisdom.

"In much wisdom there's much sorrow," Loharri used to say. Mattie thought that she agreed as she watched the skulls, their sockets seemingly following her every move from their corners. They smelled of old parchment and dry earth crumbling into dust.

Listen. A faint whisper caught her attention, and at first she thought that it was just the wind trapped inside, rattling the old bones.

Listen, again.

She stepped inside, looking through the dusk filled with remains. There were just bones, but then she caught a glimpse of movement out of the corner of an eye. And then—like in an optical trick the traveling performers entertained their customers with, where one was supposed to look at the jumble of leaves to spot a deer, a lizard, and a giant bird, and once one saw them they would not go away—she saw the folded wings and the gray skin blending with stone, she saw the heavy horned heads and slit eyes, the folded hands, the bent knees. And the mouths opening like fissures in the age-old stone to whisper to her urgent words.

Listen, they spoke in one voice, the voice of the stone the city was carved from. *We will tell you a story.*

THERE IS A NOTION OF TIME AS AN ENEMY, BUT WE COULDN'T tell you how fast it was passing until we heard the human heartbeats, counting the seconds as they fell into the eternity. So many million heartbeats ago, when you were not yet here and the eastern woman, the stranger, the daughter of red earth was young, there were two boys.

Three boys, maybe. We can't remember, and we sometimes confuse death and sleep, sleep and oblivion. But in any case, there they were—feral children living off scraps and rotten fruit left in the market square after the market was over. They had forgotten how to speak and only snarled at pigeons and stray dogs if they went after the scraps the boys had their eyes on, and they spat and hissed at the passing of the Stone Monks, who were the greatest fear of all children, parented or not.

We weep often, for the Monks carry our name and everything that they do is attributed to us. But what can we do? We are weak and dying, and they fill our feeders, so we keep our thoughts to ourselves; we shove the gravel into our mouths hastily, rent with guilt, and we do not speak.

But the boys, the boys . . . one is raven-haired, narrow-eyed, and so beautiful, dirt and grime and lice notwithstanding; another is white-haired like an old man, and he moves on all fours, feeling his way like a crab. Yet another is quiet and small, and he cries often. He has no words, and his anguish wails and sobs through the night alleys, and we watch over them, like we watch over everyone who is marked for

*destruction by the grindstones of the world. There is nothing
we can do but watch over them.*

MATTIE STARTLED AT THE SLAMMING OF THE DOOR BEHIND
her, and the gargoyles fell silent, blending back into the
surrounding walls.

"Anyone in here?"

"Just me," Mattie answered. "Sorry, Master Bergen."

The old mechanic shuffled closer, his limp more prominent
now, accompanied by the tapping of a cane. "Mattie? What
are you doing here?"

"The door was open," she said. "I was looking for
Loharri."

"Of course you were." His voice was paternal, soothing,
and the look of his rheumy eyes kind. "We're a tad busy here,
but he's around. I'll help you look if you want."

Mattie followed him to the exit. "What's happening?"

"You've heard about the Duke, of course."

"Of course," Mattie echoed. She decided not to tell him
that she was there—she was indisposed to answer questions,
to relive the fear and the disgust she felt watching other
automatons, purposefully excluded from the context, gathering limbs. "Terrible, isn't it?"

"Yes," Bergen said without much conviction. "Terrible.
Only now, who's next?"

"You're not leaving the city, are you?"

"Dear girl, no, pox on your tongue." He gave a feeble laugh.
"What, leave and let the alchemical vultures pick apart everything we've built here?"

"They're not vultures," Mattie said, narrowly avoiding using 'we'.

Bergen shook his head. "Perhaps I'm being too cautious in my old age. But we are just moving the archives and machinery, in case they decide to bomb the Parliament. One must be careful—dark times, dark times."

They walked to the Parliament building, Mattie tactfully restraining her step so as not to overtake Bergen. He kept talking about the intrigues and the damn alchemists, of how things weren't what they used to be—Mattie saw no virtue in arguing with the latter point.

Inside the Parliament building, the chaos was even more overwhelming than outside. Mattie bumped into people who ran without heed, and narrowly avoided an automaton that shuffled by with a stack of papers high enough to completely conceal its torso and face. She looked around but saw no alchemists. She cursed her cowardice—if she got the list of the missing medallions in time, maybe her society would not need to be afraid to set foot in Parliament.

"He'd be in the archives," Bergen said. "I must be getting on now, but you should find him—check all the way up the stairs, on the fourth floor."

Mattie squeezed through the crowd, going against the stream of people and automatons. The stone steps under her feet were worn concave, and her feet nestled securely in the depressions made by many generations of human feet, giving her comfort and a fleeting sense of belonging to the great tradition. Even though she could neither vote nor be elected, she felt a part of it.

The crowd thinned after she passed the second floor where the offices and the chambers were, and almost disappeared by the fourth. When she set foot into the echoing silent crypt of the archives, it felt like she was the only person there—no, the only person left on earth, so desolate it was.

She found Loharri at the small desk tucked away in the back, where he sorted through stacks of hand-written and printed documents and scrolls. "Loharri," she called.

He jerked his head up, as if coming from deep sleep. "What's the matter, love?"

"I know it's a bad time," she said. "But the medallions."

He nodded. "Here you are. I copied it for you last night and set it aside. Glad you came."

She took the proffered scroll with only a dozen or so names on it. "Thank you," she whispered, guilt washing over her anew. "I can't believe you remembered."

He smiled lopsidedly. "Have I ever forgotten you? Have I ever broken a promise?"

"No," she said. "But with everything that's happening . . . I thought you'd have better things to do."

"But you still came," he said with a shrug and pushed away the stack of papers in front of him. "See? Great events might shake our foundations, but we still remember our little inconsequential promises. And I bet you money that everyone still carries on as normal—people eat, children wail, couples fight and fuck. These things are the true edifice of the city, not dukes or buildings, not even the gargoyles. How's your work going, by the way? Found Sebastian yet?"

"It's difficult," Mattie answered. "I'm in a new territory—our formulae are all for people's needs, not the gargoyles'. Imagine if you had to design a musket for creatures with eight arms and no legs."

He laughed. "They wouldn't run, and could reload much faster. But I get your point, dear girl. Stone isn't flesh."

"Or metal," Mattie said. "I don't even know how to begin thinking about it; I mean, I do, but I have no idea what makes sense and what doesn't."

He nodded. "I'll let you know if anything occurs to me. Anything else you need?"

She thought of the gargoyles' story and mentally cursed Bergen for interrupting. "Just a question," she said. "Do you know the Soul-Smoker?"

His smile remained but changed, as if his mirth had drained away and only its ghost remained behind. "No," he said. "Can't say that I know the gentleman. I've seen him, of course."

"Have you ever known him? When you were children?"

He shrugged. "Maybe. This city is not that big, and you know how children are, always running in packs. Why? Did he say anything?"

"No. Just wondering," Mattie said. "He seems very lonely and very sick."

"Comes with the job." Loharri cleared his throat. "Now if you don't mind . . . "

"Of course. You have work to do. I will see you soon," Mattie said.

As she turned to leave the archives, she heard a weak voice

calling Loharri's name from downstairs. She cocked her head, listening. "Can you hear that? Someone's calling you."

"They can come here," he answered. His former good spirits were gone, replaced by bile. "What am I, an errand boy?"

"I think it's Bergen," Mattie replied. "It's hard for him walk up the stairs."

Loharri heaved a sigh and cursed under his breath, but stood and followed Mattie down the stairs. They met Bergen halfway between the second and the third floors.

"Loharri," the old man wheezed. "Come quick. The enforcers arrested the man who threw the bomb at the Duke."

MATTIE THANKED HER STARS AND HER LUCKY STONES THAT Bergen was too perturbed to pay attention as she followed him and Loharri to the jail adjacent to the Parliament building. The old man worked his cane as if it were a hoe, reaching with it in front of him until the metal-clad tip caught between the cobbles and pulling himself along, his limp pronounced but apparently disregarded. Even Loharri's long loping strides were barely enough to keep up with the old man, and Mattie trotted behind, hitching up her skirts slightly higher than was proper, but forgivable under the circumstances.

The enforcers crowded the courtyard of the jail, their buggies clanging against each other and chuffing, the hiss of steam sounding almost identical to Bergen's wheezing breath—a pleasing symmetry, Mattie thought, since Bergen was the inventor of these buggies, and it seemed only right that they replicated their creator's habits in such harmony.

The enforcers, armored and menacing, looked at Bergen and Loharri with suspicious eyes through the narrow slits of their bronze helms, but let them through; Loharri grabbed Mattie's elbow and dragged her along, without giving the guards a chance to ask her any questions or consider her admittance.

"Thank you," Mattie whispered, his kindness a stab.

"If anyone ever hassles you," he whispered back, "just tell them you're mine. Damn your pride and just say it, all right?"

"All right."

"Promise?"

"Promise." Her heart felt ready to give, to pop the rivets that held it together and explode in an unseemly shower of metal and springs and wheels toothed like dogs.

They entered the low arch, decorated like everything around this building with carvings of gargoyles—a show of gratitude from the city, from back in the day when the gargoyles were strong enough to grow a jail at the city's request.

They had grown it large and sturdy, with a monolithic door that required twenty men to move it aside. There were no windows or water pipes or air ducts, and the jail, one with the stone that birthed it, was cold in winter and hot in summer, and not many lasted long enough to experience both extremes—one or the other killed them before that. But that was for the prisoners condemned for serious crimes; those who were found guilty of lesser offenses were transferred to the southern copper mines, or to the northern fields, where they died slower and side-by-side with people who had done nothing wrong apart from being born to an unpleasant lot in life.

They found the prisoner just inside the jail. He was dressed in the habit of a Stone Monk, torn at the shoulder, exposing a large gash crusted over with blood. The skin of his shoulder, smooth and brown, was stained with blood and bruised, and his thick lips opened and closed in quick, gulping breaths.

Mattie noticed his hands shackled together by an elaborate brass device consisting of several metal semicircles nestled inside one another, latching onto the wrists of the man in an overlapping lattice. She also saw the depression in his side, where the robe flapped, seemingly not touching the body.

"His ribs are broken," she whispered to Loharri.

He nodded and narrowed his eyes at her, as if to warn her to stay silent.

Two mechanics and an alchemist surrounded the man; they were inflicting no violence on him, but their taut faces told Mattie that they wanted to.

Bergen caught his breath, and addressed the prisoner. "Were you working alone or did you have accomplices?"

The man just stared, his eyes startled and wide, his mouth still straining after each shallow breath.

"The bastard can't even speak properly," one of the mechanics said.

"Or he doesn't speak our language." Bergen cleared his throat and moved closer to the prisoner. He spoke slowly and loudly, as one did with children or feeble-minded. "Alone? Were you alone?"

The prisoner gasped. "I did nothing," he whispered.

Mattie tugged Loharri's sleeve. He frowned and shook her hand off. "What?" he whispered with a fierce expression on his twisted face.

"That's not the right man," Mattie whispered. She hadn't realized how silent the room was, until her whisper resonated, and made everyone turn toward her. "It's not the right man," Mattie said, louder, addressing Bergen and everyone else. "I was there, I saw. The one who attacked the procession was much bigger. And he wasn't an easterner, he was local. I saw his hand—it was pink, like yours." She pointed at Bergen's hand gripping the pommel of his cane.

Tense silence filled the room, palpable, broken only by the ticking of Mattie's heart and the ragged breath of the prisoner who watched Mattie with almost religious hope on his face, mixed with open-mouthed wonder.

"Nonsense," Bergen said, and turned away.

The rest of the mechanics coughed into their hands and shuffled their feet, covering up their visible relief.

"Loharri," one of the mechanics said. "Perhaps you should take your automaton outside—she seems prone to hysterics. I guess all women are like that, mechanical or flesh."

Loharri did not say a word and gave Mattie a gentle shove. "Run along, now," he said softly. "I will see you soon."

Mattie turned to the door, the gaze of the prisoner imploring her not to leave him. She gave a small shake of her head and walked out, the panicked eyes of the man, their whites prominent and blinding like those of the sheep in the slaughterhouse, burned into her memory.

Chapter 10

―――

We follow the girl as she walks through noisy streets, *crawling with the vile mechanical contrivances that did not come from the stone. The girl walks as if blind, stumbling over the cobbles, and we hear her heart whir and whine deep inside her, creaking with tears she will never weep. We are glad that she is gone from the place of sorrow, where so many of our children have perished and so many others have behaved badly.*

Content that she is on her way home, we turn and leap from roof to roof, our toes grasping shingles like steps; our wings balance us, keep us steady. We follow the inverse labyrinth of the buildings, the negative reflection of the streets between them, to a different location.

We see a small, white-haired man who used to move like a crab when he was little, but who has now learned to walk upright, with dignity and grace. He has words now, and we are proud of him, as proud as we are of any we like to follow. He moves toward the place the girl has just left, the pulsing streets converging on the ugly stone heart of the city, and we almost wish we hadn't built it.

Everyone flees at his approach; the soulless creatures like ourselves are the only ones who are immune to his repulsive charms. We remember the time he swallowed his first soul, as we remember all the countless others, gone up in smoke and inhaled by his wide loving mouth. He is nothing but loving.

The courtyard of the jail is filled with people, but they too flee as he gets closer; they go into the jail building and wait inside. The only man left in the courtyard is the stranger—red earth, salty sea, hands bound, feet shackled, and nowhere to run.

The white-haired man, the smoker of souls, stands before him, quietly, mildly. "Are you ready?" he asks, his eyes of milk staring over the stranger's head into the infinity of the jail walls.

The stranger shakes his head side to side, the frantic motion of a terrified child.

"Shh," the blind man says, "shhh." He takes the face of the prisoner into his hands, and the stranger goes limp and docile.

The blind man's hands are soft and gentle, and he touches his lips to the stranger's.

The stranger tries to keep his mouth closed, but it is of no use. His soul, sensing the companionship of many others, presses on his lips from the inside, and he finally gives with a loud exhalation. His lips brush against the blind man's and open, and the two men stand for a while, eye-to-eye, mouth-to-mouth, and we listen to the hissing of the escaping soul, we watch the stranger's eyes go white and empty like the clouds, and we hear the clink of his shackles as he collapses on the pavement, formless and soft like water.

A mindless automaton enters the courtyard and approaches the blind man who is motionless, his narrow chest expanded as if by an impossibly big breath.

"You have done your duty," the automaton says in a grating

141

voice, uncolored by either emotion or understanding. "Write your report by tomorrow morning; someone will be by to pick it up."

We regret that he has to do it, we regret that among the souls that could not find rest there are others, to whom rest was denied in favor of extracting confessions. We know that our children are mendicant—they speak of never killing anyone, but they let buildings and the smoker of souls take the lives of those they cannot be bothered to kill themselves.

We did not want it to be like this, but what can we do? We are naught but a shadow of a distant memory, whispering in the rain gutters, clambering along the rooftops; we are nothing but decorations on the building, amusing in our grotesque bodies and webbed wings. We have heard of other cities where the buildings are decorated with statues of angels with golden wings, but we doubt that these angels were ever alive or even real. Most beautiful things are not.

We regret not having finished the story we started to tell to the girl—our understanding of time is vague, but we have a nagging feeling that it would've been useful to her. We resolve to tell her soon, and try harder this time, perhaps hold onto her skirts and plead with our eyes. Listen, we should say, listen.

We turn our attention back to the man and the automaton in the jail courtyard. The automaton gives its orders once again. The white-haired man nods and heads back home, the memories and the terror of the newly inhaled soul sloshing inside him heavily, like water in a bucket.

———

AS THE DAYS WORE ON, MATTIE NOTICED THE TROUBLING changes in the air—even though she rarely left the workshop these days, preoccupied with her work. She tried to get to the meaning of Sebastian's words, of understanding the very soul of stone. For that purpose, the burners belched blue flames, and the alembics filled with ground stone were heated to a red glow.

She studied the transformation of stone. It turned the flames yellow and blue and sometimes green, it could be dissolved in Aqua Regis, and with enough heat, parts of it sublimated, leaving behind a hard and latticed carcass.

The stone was complex, as Mattie realized, consisting of many minerals so blended together that one could have no hope of separating them for individual study, and had to deduce the composition of it from its behavior during many transformations she subjected it to.

Mattie also taught Niobe—not about the blood alchemy but of the elements and their manifestations. She described the salamanders that lived in and commanded fire as golden lizards, and Undinae—as small girl automatons fashioned with webbed fins instead of arms and legs. Niobe laughed at her claims that she was able to see the salamanders, and Mattie did not really mind. She offered small sacrifices to the salamanders by burning some fragrant herbs along with stone, asking them to help her solve the riddle of the gargoyles.

But the stone alchemy was not the only thing that occupied her days and nights—having no need for sleep, Mattie felt superior sometimes at being able to accomplish twice as much in a day as any other alchemist. She worked on the stone during the day, when the light was bright enough to see the spectral colors and emanations; during the night, she practiced blood alchemy.

A deal was a deal, and she learned the new craft with dark satisfaction. She made a small homunculus from rendered sheep blood, with the heart woven from Iolanda's and Loharri's hair. The homunculus was still, waiting to be awakened in order to ensnare Loharri's soul. The process took her longer than she wanted, but her learning was hindered by her inability to ask Niobe pertinent questions—she was ashamed to ask about compulsion and denial of will, and she feared that if Niobe found out about such practices, she would think poorly of Mattie. So Mattie saved the darkness for the night; night was for wounding.

During the day she helped Niobe decipher the recipes from her little birch bark book, and explained to her the properties of herbs and metals and sheep's eyes. She showed her how to mix salves that reduced fever and unclouded the troubled mind. Day was for healing.

As the days passed, Mattie noticed a growing unease in Niobe. Mattie's guilty conscience bounded to her mind's surface, sending jolts to her heart and making it creak and moan faster and faster, its ticking loud and quick like the song of some demented cricket.

"What's wrong?" Mattie asked her finally, as the two of them stood at Mattie's laboratory bench, grinding herbs and extracting essential oils, each lost in her own private musings. "Are you mad at me?"

Niobe looked up from her fragrant aludel. "What? Of course not, Mattie. You're the only friend I have—why would I be mad at you?"

Mattie shrugged, her pestle grinding against the porcelain interior of the mortar. "You seem upset lately."

"It's because I am, but it has nothing to do with you." Niobe sighed and stirred the ground herbs, encouraging the oils to express. "You stay home, and you don't see. But if you came by my neighborhood, you'd know."

"What's happening there?" Mattie tried not to feel too guilty about not visiting—among her crimes, this one seemed the most trivial.

"The enforcers swarm like black flies." Niobe crossed her arms over her chest as if she grew suddenly cold, and paced alongside the bench. "They think that it is us, the foreigners who blew up your palace and your Duke."

"Why do they think that?" Mattie interrupted. "I saw the man they arrested, and it was the wrong man . . . I tried to tell them but they wouldn't listen."

"Of course they wouldn't," Niobe said. "They decided to blame those they don't like. They took the jewelers, and they took the bookbinders. They question everyone, men and women, and they threaten to call the Soul-Smoker every time something speaks against them. Half of the easterners left the city to go back home."

"The Soul-Smoker is a nice man," Mattie said.

Niobe laughed. "I suppose he is, right up to the moment

when he sucks your soul out of you."

"He has no choice," Mattie whispered. "And I have no soul."

Niobe shrugged. "We all have our burdens."

"You can stay with me," Mattie said. "Unless you want to go back home?"

Niobe shook her head. "I thought about it, but I won't go back—at least, not now. I won't give them the satisfaction."

"Then stay here," Mattie said. "It's safe here, and I can protect you from the mechanics."

Niobe smiled a little. "You? Protect me? They won't listen to you."

"But they'll listen to Loharri," Mattie said. "And I have money for bribes, lots of money."

Niobe nodded slowly. "I suppose you don't have to spend it on food."

"No." Mattie folded her hands, pleading. "Stay with me, I promise I'll buy you food."

Niobe laughed and hugged Mattie, her soft breasts giving under Mattie's hard metal chest, pressing against the keyhole of Mattie's heart. Mattie hugged back, guilty and grateful. "Thank you, Mattie," Niobe said. "I would love to stay for a bit—it's always safer for two than one."

Mattie thought that she could tell Niobe anything—well, almost anything. She was reluctant to confess her misuse of blood alchemy, and instead decided to confide her next most bothersome secret. "Niobe," she whispered even though there was no one there to overhear her. "I know a man with a skin like yours . . . he is in hiding, but I worry that now they will pay closer attention to him and find him out. What do you think I should do?"

"It depends," Niobe said. "What did he do to have to go into hiding?"

"He told me that it wasn't his fault. I do know that sometimes what people tell you is not the truth; I just don't know whether to believe it to begin with."

Niobe shook her head. "Mattie, bless your clockwork heart. You don't decide to believe—you either do or you don't."

"I wouldn't presume as much as not to believe someone just because people lie sometimes."

"In this case, you should probably let him know that he is in danger. Only can you do that without endangering yourself? If someone sees you talking to a suspect—and believe me, he is a suspect—your master's influence won't save your little metal parts."

Mattie thought a little. "Yes," she finally said. "I think I can; we just need to wait until darkness."

"Great." Niobe smiled. "Where do you want me to sleep?"

MATTIE KNEW HOW TO MAKE BEDS, BUT SHE WASN'T in possession of one. She decided to create a nice soft bed for Niobe in the warmest place, by the kitchen hearth—the nights were still occasionally nippy. Besides, it would be as far away from the bench as the apartment allowed, and Mattie did not want Niobe disturbed by Mattie's nocturnal work.

She found a couple of quilts given to her by grateful but poor customers, and collected most of her dresses into a heap.

Once she covered them with the quilts, the bed acquired quite satisfactory appearance—not of poverty but of whimsy. Mattie liked that, and so did Niobe.

The sun was still high enough in the sky, and they walked to the market to buy some provisions for Niobe. As they browsed, Mattie noticed a few suspicious stares in Niobe's direction, and a few merchants refused to trade with them outright.

Niobe just shrugged, even though Mattie guessed that the deepening of the color on Niobe's cheeks meant that she was more perturbed than she showed.

Nonetheless, Mattie led her to the booth that sold a good variety of herbs, and tried to distract Niobe by explaining how one decided on the plant's usefulness. "You see," she pointed at the dried plant with purple flowers, "its leaves are heart-shaped, which means it is suited for heart trouble."

"Are you referring to the actual heart, or love problems?"

"The latter," Mattie said. "See? Its shape is not of a real heart but of its symbol."

"Symbol of a symbol," Niobe muttered. "I see. What about this one?"

She pointed at the glass jar filled with fresh flowers, plump and red, their three petals dripping with nectar. "That's for the liver," Mattie said. "See the three lobes?"

"And this one?" Niobe picked up a dried stem clustered with strange fruit—brown and transversed with fissures. "Brain problems?"

Mattie nodded. "That is its signature, yes. Every plant has one. The plants with red sap are used to purify blood, the ones with yellow sap—clear out urinary infections, and so on. See, it's easy. It's getting to the potent chemicals inside them that is hard."

"I see," Niobe agreed. "Every plant has medicine, as long as you can figure out how to get to it."

"That's the tricky part," Mattie agreed. "This is why it is essential to keep a journal and record every transformation, so if you find something you can recreate it and share it with the rest of the society."

"If I want to."

"If you want to."

"Are you going to buy anything?" the woman who owned the booth asked. There was no open hostility in her voice, and her face expressed carefully cultivated indifference.

"Just a bunch of maiden's hair and two of bladderwort," Mattie said. She paid for her purchases. "Thank you, Marta."

Marta muttered an acknowledgment under her breath, and Mattie and Niobe traded looks.

"Let's go home," Niobe said as soon as she picked up a loaf of bread and some olives. "I'm getting tired of all the hostility."

Mattie nodded that she agreed. She hadn't realized how rigidly she had held her back, how taut the springs of her muscles were. Just being outside was tiring to her; she could not imagine how Niobe was able to hold up, with her weak flesh body. And she had been enduring it far longer than Mattie.

Mattie took Niobe's hand in a gesture of support.

"Don't," Niobe whispered. "You don't want to associate with me like this. It's dangerous." But she didn't take her hand away.

"I don't care," Mattie whispered and twined her fingers with Niobe's, metal against flesh, springs against bone.

THE NIGHT FALLS, AND WE HEAR THE GIRL CALLING US, AND we leap over the chasms that open below our feet at the precipitous drop-offs of the roofs. We hurry, and we rehearse our story in our minds, and yet there's hope swelling up in our hearts, subterranean. A secret hope that the girl will throw the window open, her blue porcelain face as expressionless as ours, and tell us that we don't have to fear time any more. We suppress the hope, and we mutter out loud, no no, it's not going to happen. She just wants to hear our story, and we will tell it to her. Listen.

We run up the fire escapes and slither across the walls, we leap, we run, we crawl and finally we reach the high window, warm yellow light spilling from it swarming with fluttering of white moths; fireflies flicker on and off above the roof. A nightingale is starting his song in the trees nearby, and we pause for just a moment to listen to the sweet trilling.

Listen, we whisper to the girl framed in the window. Her skirt floats wide, her waist cinched by the belt glistening with bronze rivets. It's so small, we could circle it with one hand, and we wonder if there's anything in her middle besides a metal joint that holds her lower and upper body together. She seems so fragile.

There's another shadow in the room, and we smell ripe grapes and generous red earth. The second woman gasps at the sight of us but remains quiet otherwise.

"Listen," the girl says before we can utter a word. "The man who fills your feeders is in danger."

"He is gone," we whisper back. *"He left the day you met him, and the monks are neglecting our feeders."* We feel pathetic, complaining like this, and we bite off the rest of our words.

"Where did he go?" the girl asks, panicked.

"He is hiding," we say. *"He's hiding in the rafters of warehouses, in the roofs and in the gutters. The city is his cradle."*

"The next time you see him, tell him to be careful. Tell him to come and see me when it is dark."

We eye the other woman, and we don't want to talk in the presence of strangers—we feel shy and recede away from the window.

"What about the story you started to tell me?" she asks.

We take a deep breath and move closer again. *"There were three boys."*

The three boys who did not expect their lives to change, until the monks took them. We could not see them in the orphanage, for it has no windows, and only if we pressed our ears against the cold stone—dead now, cut up by human hands, dismembered and dumb—could we hear the ghosts of their voices.

We saw them when the monks took them out for walks in the courtyard, at night, when there was no one around to see their gaunt faces and their fingers raw from hard work, the skin of their hands stripped away, oozing a clear liquid we have no name for.

We saw the alchemists and the mechanics coming to the night courtyard, illuminated only by the blue and distant moon, and pick among the children, selecting the agile and the clever. The rest, the ones who stayed behind, were trained for other jobs. All cursed us, because we only watched—but what else could we do?

We saw some of the smaller children—the boy who cried often among them—stuffed into small cages that would restrict their growth, keeping their bodies small and squat, bowing their legs; their arms seemed simian and long in contrast, thin enough to fit between the bars of their cages and grow free. Those children were destined for the mine-shafts, for picking out precious stones from rubble with their thin, flexible fingers.

Of course, not all could bear such treatment, and many died. The boy who cried often wilted in his cage, and every night as they wheeled him out he seemed smaller and paler, shrinking away from the bars, not growing into them. He curled up on the floor and cried, and called for help in his animal tongue. The blind boy sat next to him, whispering unarticulated comfort.

The beautiful boy with long hazel eyes was quick to learn the language, and both the alchemists and the mechanics who came to trade eyed him with interest. The monks asked a high price, and they came back to haggle. Once, a mechanic remarked that the boy was too beautiful to be smart; the next night he came out to the yard with his face bandaged.

The small boy who cried often died the day before they took the no-longer-beautiful boy away. The blind boy held his hand as the small boy drew his last breath; the blind boy sensed the presence of the disembodied soul, watery and shapeless, and he

*cradled it to his heart until the dead boy's soul nestled into his,
like a child's face into a pillow, like stone into our hands.*

*The monks let the no-longer-beautiful boy cut off the dead
boy's hair, and when he left, his hand held firmly by a stern
mechanic with a slight limp, long tangled locks slithered under
his threadbare shirt.*

THE GARGOYLES' STORY STUCK WITH MATTIE, AND SHE KEPT
turning it over in her mind, over and over. The fact that
Ilmarekh was an orphan did not particularly surprise her, but
the fact that he had chosen this profession, that for him it was
an act of kindness and not desperation, touched her in a way
she couldn't fully explain even to Niobe.

She was also puzzled by the role Loharri played in it; especially the part about the dead boy's hair—she did not think of
him as a sentimental man. Even on his frequent visits to the
orphanage he seemed angry and bitter rather than pensive or
distraught. She resolved to ask him at the first opportunity,
but for now, there were plenty of other things to worry about,
and they won over other concerns due to their urgency.

She went to the public telegraph to check on the news
and to see if Bokker had replied to her missive sent a week
ago, containing the list of the missing mechanic medallions.
To her shock, she found only warnings to stay at home, and
reports of unrest.

It seemed that the Mechanics increased the pace of building
and introduction of caterpillars; their request for additional
buggies for the enforcers and their work on the machine
that Loharri had been so enthused about taxed the coal and

metal mines to capacity. The Parliament, led by Bergen and his mechanics, drafted many peasants for mine work—it was fraught with danger and required more thinking capacity and mobility than most automatons could provide. Instead, the automatons were sent to the fields to replace the peasants whose labor was repetitive and simple, and where they were not likely to need to be replaced.

Mattie shared the news with Niobe over breakfast—that is, Niobe was eating breakfast, and Mattie was sitting at the table in solidarity.

Niobe shook her head. "They will rebel, especially with the Duke so gravely ill."

"How do you know?" Mattie asked.

Niobe shrugged. "There's only so far you can shove a person until they shove back. I've seen it happen before."

"What will happen?" Mattie whispered.

"Riots, probably. If the mechanics are smart, they'll send enforcers right away to quell them before they even start. Give people money, double the miners' wages. If not . . . if the miners rebel and quit, the city will grind to a halt without coal."

Mattie was about to answer when someone knocked on the door. Only Loharri knocked with such arrogant insistence, and Mattie went to open. To her surprise, it was Sebastian.

"The gargoyles told me you were looking for me," he said.

Chapter 11

Mattie clicked along with a greater sense of determination than ever. Iolanda's request receded on her mental landscape, its bothersome shape pushed deep and wedged between other concerns she did not want to think about just yet; it fit right next to her uneasy curiosity about Loharri and the dead boy's hair, two thoughts caught together like the teeth of two interlocking spur gears.

Instead, she worried about the gargoyles and Sebastian, who had become, unofficially, her ward along with Niobe. There was no reason for Mattie to protect Sebastian and to tell him that the mechanics were interested in his whereabouts and that the enforcers were eager to arrest any easterner and hand him over to the Soul-Smoker. But still she felt compelled—for the vague but persistent feeling of kinship she felt for his mother. When Beresta had broken through the chorus of voices shouting through Ilmarekh's mouth, it was only to say, "Find my son. He lives in the eastern district." At the time, Mattie assumed that Beresta's tortured whisper was for Mattie's benefit, to help her sort out the gargoyles' business; now she was not so sure. She felt as if Beresta had entrusted her son to Mattie's care from beyond the grave, and she couldn't very well ignore the request.

But her place was getting crowded. Between Niobe and her

bed by the fireplace and Sebastian's large frame curled up in the corner of the laboratory, by the waste drain, there was barely enough place for Mattie to stay upright, let alone pace, and she spent her days working at the bench, pulverizing and sublimating stone, and running outside to buy food for her visitors. Something had to change soon; and she needed advice.

She avoided Iolanda for now, and Loharri was the last person she wanted to alert to the nature of her hesitation and Sebastian's presence. When she closed her eyes—rather, retracted them into her head to give them a rest from constant stimulation—the visions of hair plagued her. She saw the dead boy's hair, curled up like a sleeping snake against the naked smooth skin of Loharri's stomach, and Loharri's and Iolanda's strands, twined together in a deadly betrayal masquerading as love. Mattie shivered.

She put her shoes on and headed for the door.

Sebastian woke up. "Where are you going?" he said in a voice rough with sleep.

"Out," Mattie said.

Sebastian sat up, his face gathered in a suspicious frown. Mattie had learned most of his expressions, and this one was as familiar as his smile. The blueprints of his face wedged deep into her memory, like the alchemical recipes she never forgot because she mustn't. "Out where?"

"To talk to your mother," Mattie said, softly. "Keep quiet—you'll wake up Niobe."

"Can I come too?"

"You know you can't. But I will give her your regards. Any questions I should ask her?"

Sebastian shook his head, his face relaxing, pensive. "That wouldn't be right. The dead are dead. Aren't they?"

"Not until the Soul-Smoker is dead." Mattie headed for the door.

The night city embraced and buoyed her, the air sweet and blue and dense like water sloshing in the Grackle Pond, mysterious and forbidden. The streets seemed different, the buildings twisting and leaning dangerously into the streets, their shuttered windows distorted in an inaudible moan. A few times Mattie worried that she had lost her way somehow—even the familiar landmarks acquired a menacing air. It was a while before Mattie noticed that the streetlamps had remained unlit—no doubt, the mechanics had braced for the shortage of coal.

It was windy outside the gates—the open blasted earth afforded no cover for the lashings of the gale, and Mattie had to wrap her skirts around her legs as tightly as she could, afraid that they would catch the wind like sails and carry her away, into the dark sky salted with the rough crystals of the stars. Loharri had told her that there was no air between the stars and this is why people couldn't live there, but Mattie did not need to breathe, and she imagined herself floating in the black void, only her puzzled memories for company.

She hurried up the hill, toward the shining beacon of the lit window and the sweet smell of opium smoke the wind brought to her.

Ilmarekh was not surprised at her visit—as soon as she knocked on the door, he called out, "Come in, Mattie."

She entered. "How did you know it was me?"

"Who else would visit me in the middle of the night?" he answered.

"The enforcers."

He pointed to the previously vacant corner of the room, where a small portable telegraph gleamed with its brass knobs and copper rods. "They need me so often, they installed the machine. I hear it go off, I just head for the jail." He heaved a sigh. "I don't like this, Mattie—every time I tell them the soul was hiding no secrets, they just laugh and tell me that they'll keep looking."

"I'm so sorry," Mattie said. She meant the souls of the innocents and Ilmarekh himself. "Can't you refuse?"

"They will kill them anyway," he answered. "Or the jail will. This way, they're safe with me. And they never lack for company. I listen to the stories they tell, Mattie—what stories! I didn't know how different the world was, and how beautiful—they show me cities of white stone and golden roofs, they show me gardens so fragrant, my head swims. And the sea, Mattie, the sea! Have you ever seen it?"

"No," she answered. "I want to."

"You should. You'd think it's just like the Grackle Pond but bigger, but it's nothing like that at all. It has waves—so big!—they rise like solid walls of green glass, heavy with threat and exhilaration. It changes color—from blue to green to black—in seconds, and it is the most beautiful thing one can imagine, especially when the waves are breaking on the shore, topped with white foam." Ilmarekh clasped his bird-like hands to his chest, overcome with feeling.

Mattie looked away. "I'm glad you're getting something out of it."

Ilmarekh's smile faded. "I'm not the only one."

Mattie felt immediately sorry—she thought that for a soul sentenced to death even a temporary home shared with hundreds of other inhabitants, even a small delay was of benefit. "I'm sorry," she said. "I didn't mean it like that."

Ilmarekh shrugged, and sat down on his mattress. "Of course you did. I don't suppose I blame you."

There was no point in blaming him for carrying out the decisions others had made, and Mattie sat next to him. "Can I talk to Beresta?"

"She hasn't been talking at all lately," Ilmarekh said. "It happens sometimes—the souls who have heard too much cocoon themselves off, build a wall around themselves, and I cannot reach them."

"Can she hear us?"

"I think so," Ilmarekh said.

"Beresta," Mattie called. "Your son is safe. He sends his regards."

They both waited for her answer, and finally Ilmarekh's cheeks and eyes bulged as if he were about to vomit. Instead, a quiet whisper came. "Tell him that I miss him," Beresta said. "Did you find the cure for the gargoyles?"

"Not yet," Mattie said. "Sebastian told me to break the bond with stone, and I've been trying to—"

"Does he eat well?" Beresta interrupted, a bit louder this time. "Does he look well?"

"Yes, very much so," Mattie replied, suppressing a wistful

sigh. "He is a strong man now." She decided not to mention the details of Sebastian's exile and the hiding.

"It makes me so happy," Beresta whispered. "Now, about the bond . . . you cannot break a thing free of its foundation—it withers like an uprooted plant or floats away, like a boat off its moorings. Before you break them away from stone, find something you can bind them to, something that is alive."

"Thank you," Mattie said.

Beresta fell silent, and Ilmarekh sighed. "I guess she's still around then. Did you come to talk to her, or do you have other souls you wanted to talk to?"

The dead boy, Mattie wanted to answer but bit her lip. Not yet, she told herself. She had more pressing concerns than to decipher Loharri's hidden history. "I have some people— easterners—hiding from the enforcers," she said. "In my apartment."

"What have they done?" Ilmarekh asked.

"Nothing, just like the ones you have engulfed."

Ilmarekh's pale cheeks pinkened, with shame or anger Mattie was not sure. "I see your point. What do you want from me?"

"I can't risk them being discovered. Can you tell me where they can hide without being found?"

"Here," Ilmarekh said. "Although being in my vicinity would rather defeat your purpose." His face distorted, and his lips quivered, as if holding back a moan. And then the spirits talked.

"Take them to the farms," one advised. "There's nothing

but automatons there since they herded us all into the mines, haunted, cursed."

"Take them to the eastern district, where they can blend in," another shouted.

"No, what are you, stupid? The enforcers practically live there, dragging out every soul and exiling all they can."

"Leave the cursed city, go back home," yet another voice shouted. Ilmarekh's lips contorted as hundreds of spirits fought over control, and his small body shook in great spasms. "Underground!" "No, the farms!"

Just as the assault of the opinionated spirits started to subside, another voice, smooth as silk, persuasive, spoke. "There're other people like them," it said. "Like you. There's a resistance, a rebellion growing. It started off with just a few, but now . . . "

"How do you know it?" Mattie asked, suspicious. "And if you know it, wouldn't the enforcers know it too?"

"No," Ilmarekh said in his normal voice. "I don't tell them what I know. I'm an executioner, not a snitch . . . unless it is a confession of a real crime."

"So you know about the resistance?" Mattie asked, still skeptical.

Ilmarekh nodded. "Do you have friends in high places?"

MATTIE RETURNED HOME IN THE MORNING, WHEN THE gargoyles on the temple roof were outlined against the pink sky with streaks of golden clouds. On the way, she considered whether she trusted Iolanda enough to ask such questions, and every time she thought about it she recalled her obvious joy at the Duke's leaving, and her desire to stay behind to see what marvelous changes would take place.

Then again, her joy was too obvious. If she were indeed involved with anything illegal, wouldn't she hide it better? Mattie felt the beveled gears in her head speed up and heat with friction as they manufactured one febrile thought after the next. Loharri, she thought. Maybe she should talk to him.

She chased the thought away, and momentarily worried that he had built it into her, this need to run to him for help or advice every time she needed it. Would he be this calculating? *Sadly*, she thought, *he could be.* This is exactly the sort of thing he would've done—but did it invalidate his willingness to help?

She reached her building fevered and distraught. Mattie stumbled up the stairs, her head on fire. There was a smell of burning hair, and as she touched her face she discovered that below the cool surface of the porcelain, the metal sizzled, and that the roots of her hair smoldered.

Sebastian was up. He took one look at Mattie and forcibly sat her by the bench. He grabbed a piece of cloth she used to dry her glassware with, wet it in the sink, and wrapped Mattie's head in it. Steam rose from her brow, and she felt her eyes retract deep into her head against her will. Her thoughts bubbled to the surface, the steam escaped with a slow hiss through her eye sockets, and her heart fluttered in an irregular beat.

It's the spirits, she thought. *It's Loharri and Iolanda and Sebastian and the gargoyles and too many things to care about, and too many dangers to avoid.* That's what broke her.

Blind now, she heard Niobe's worried voice. "What's wrong with her?"

"I don't know," Sebastian answered. "She's overheating."

"Can you fix her?"

Mattie felt Sebastian's rough fingers search under her jaw line and on the sides. "Don't," she wanted to say, but her voice box must've gone out too. Sebastian popped off her face, exposing her, helpless and naked, to the world.

"Oh," Niobe whispered. "She is . . . so intricate."

Sebastian sighed. "Yes, she is. The man who built her . . . I don't even know what to call this. I've never seen anything like it before."

"So you can't fix her," Niobe said.

Sebastian's fingers probed something sensitive inside. "I could try . . . I don't know what else to do."

"Call Loharri," Niobe said. "There's nothing else you can do."

Mattie wanted to call out that no, it wasn't a good idea. Through a great effort, she managed to loll her head to her shoulder, and more steam escaped through some malfunctioning gasket.

"I'm calling Loharri," Niobe said. "You better find a place to hide."

"You can't go out," Sebastian answered. "It's not safe."

"I'll find someone to take the message."

Mattie's ears rang with persistent piping, but even through the ruckus she could hear the window being opened, and Niobe's strong voice calling over the rooftops and the city below, "Hey, gargoyles! Your friend is in danger."

Then the ringing grew louder and ceased suddenly, and all sensation left Mattie's limp frame.

WE HEAR THE CALL, AND WE RUN, ALL THE WHILE WONDERING whether we should be more dignified than to run errands. But the girl is ill—we saw her, her face torn off and the rest of her so broken we would've wept if we could. So we do the next best thing, and we rush. People in the streets crane their necks to see us bounding across the rooftops, in the clear light of the day, with no time to hide, and they point and shout. We think dimly that they must think that it was the recent events at the palace and the eastern gates that disturbed us so greatly.

The house where the girl was made, where she used to live is almost invisible for the solid wall of weeds and rose bushes— there's a narrow path leading through the vegetation to the door. The house stands apart from the rest, and we have no choice but to descend and run across the ground, like fast gray dogs, running on all fours through the fragrant hedge. It lashes out at us, and the branches whip and slide off our hard gray skin, and we wonder if it is growing harder, if small fissures are starting to appear, and if last night another one of us has gone, to leave us fewer and weaker. We knock on the door politely.

A woman answers the door, a woman in loose gown sliding off her round shoulders, a woman with tangled hair and sleepy eyes, which she rubs with her fist like a child. She rubs them again, as if expecting us to disappear back into her dreams, but we remain, stubborn.

"Can I help you?" she says cautiously, after we start wondering if we should speak first.

"We need to speak to the mechanic who lives here."

"What is that about?" Her eyes are awake now, curious.

We hesitate. "It's about his mechanical girl," we say.

She gasps. "Mattie? Is she all right?"

"She's broken," we say. "We need to talk to the master of the house."

She moves aside and beckons us in, but we remain outside, where we would not be easily trapped.

She disappears inside the house, and we wait, hidden among the bushes from the curious eyes of any passersby.

And then he comes out with a small bag of tools, and we recognize him, even though he has grown tall and thin and hunched, his eyes still long and narrow, his face no longer beautiful. He is pulling his jacket on as he walks out on the porch where we are waiting. "Where is she?" he asks.

"In her apartment, high above the streets, her face is off and she is broken."

"What happened?" he says, but already we bound away, our message delivered.

MATTIE WOKE UP TO THE FAMILIAR TOUCH. SHE EXTENDED her eyes carefully, fearful that she still wouldn't be able to see. Loharri's stern face swam into her field of vision. She looked past him to Niobe standing by the window, her forehead lined with worry, her arms crossed over her chest.

"What did you do?" Loharri asked.

Mattie sat up from the floor and touched her face to make sure it was back in place. Sebastian had seen her naked, she remembered. She did not find the thought altogether repellent; she liked the way his calloused fingers fit under her jaw, how swift and unapologetic he was . . .

"Mattie!"

She startled at Loharri's insistent voice. "Nothing," she said. "I've done nothing wrong."

Loharri shook his head. "Mattie. You don't even know why you got ill, do you?"

She shook her head. "I was working too hard."

His face remained composed, but she recognized the slight slow movement of his jaw, as if he were trying not to grit his teeth. "You were ill," he said, "because you went against your desire to see me. I told you that you always must do so. Didn't I?"

She nodded. "I didn't know."

"Wait a moment," Niobe said and stepped forward. "You booby-trapped the poor girl's head and didn't even tell her? Just to make sure she didn't get away from you?"

"Don't talk to me like that," Loharri said without even looking in Niobe's direction. "You're forgetting your place— what, the alchemists let you join and you think you are their equal?"

Niobe shrank away as if from a slap, but her eyes blazed.

"Don't be like this," Mattie pleaded and folded her still trembling hands over her heart. She remembered Loharri's temper—he often spoke harshly, but it passed.

"I'm sorry," Loharri said to Niobe. "I do appreciate your calling me and being here for Mattie—but please do not meddle in things that don't concern you."

Niobe didn't answer, and Loharri turned his attention back to Mattie. "Now, what did you want to talk to me about?"

"About the bombing," Mattie answered. "I told you last time that you got the wrong man, and yet you killed him."

"How do you know that?"

"The gargoyles. And you keep taking people and banishing them from the city, and—"

"Enough," Loharri interrupted and rubbed his face. "I don't like it either, Mattie, but that's politics for you. People are restless, and they need someone to blame."

"This is it?" Niobe said. "That's your entire excuse?"

"It's not an excuse," Loharri said. "Things started to change when you people showed up."

"Your people show up in our cities," Niobe parried. "We don't make a fuss about it."

"You would if your own people were losing jobs to the foreigners."

"Your people are losing jobs to your machines," Niobe said. "You put mechanizing everything and making it efficient above your people's happiness, and you wonder why they aren't happy?"

Loharri stood and turned to Niobe. "Don't try to come between me and my automaton," he said. "Seriously. I have no interest in finding scapegoats, and I'm not going to tell anyone about your presence here; you don't need to worry about that. But if I have to remove Mattie from your company, I will. She does not need your influence." He grabbed his bag of tools and was out of the door before Mattie had a chance to say thank you or goodbye.

Niobe waited for his steps to fall silent in the stairwell, stretched and laughed. "What an unpleasant man," she said.

"He really isn't," Mattie said. "He has his problems, but he's better than most. You just need to get to know him a little."

"I have no desire to." Niobe gave Mattie a quick hug and a pat on the shoulder. "Don't worry, we all have friends everyone else hates. Just don't let him hurt you."

"I have other plans." Mattie reached for the shelf over her bench, and picked up a jar sealed with a glass stopper, the figure of the blood homunculus visible inside.

NIOBE'S HELP PROVED TO BE INVALUABLE—SHE WAS BETTER versed in the darker uses of blood alchemy than Mattie expected, and she managed to get the homunculus moving about and chanting strange words. It wobbled and bubbled along the bench, back and forth, unable or unwilling to get down, and hissed and sputtered. Its heart, woven from two-colored strands, pulsed with grim life.

"How is it supposed to work?" Mattie asked.

"This creature, while alive, holds two wills together as one. Whichever one of them feeds it can command it, and the other person obeys."

"What does it eat?" Mattie asked.

"Blood. Isn't it obvious?"

"I'll tell Iolanda to get sheep's blood then."

Niobe shook her head. "If she wants to command the other, she'll have to feed it her own blood. Don't worry, it doesn't eat much—just a pin prick will sate it for a week. The longer you feed it, the stronger it gets, but it only commands for a short time."

Mattie watched the creature, fearful of it and yet fascinated. Just like Mattie, it was made, not born; and yet Mattie felt no kinship to it, the slimy, organic thing, not with her pristine metal and bone and shiny, hard surfaces. Not vulnerable to the creature, yet unable to command it, for she had no blood to feed it.

It occurred to her that her only kinship was with gargoyles and their affinity for stone and hard skin, with their tormented not-quite life. She felt sad when she realized that freeing them from fate would mean breaking the bond she felt with them, yet, to refuse it would be unkind.

"What are you thinking about?" Niobe asked.

"Sebastian. You think he's safe?"

"I think so. He said he'll return tonight to check on you, to make sure you're all right."

Mattie flustered. "Do you think he really cares about me?"

"Of course he does. He . . . " Niobe paused and grabbed Mattie's arm, and spun her around to face the light from the window so that Niobe could take a better look at her eyes.

Mattie could not avert them, so she retracted them instead. "What?"

"Oh, dear whales in the sea," Niobe whispered. "You are in love with him, aren't you?"

"I don't know," Mattie said. "Should I be?"

"I haven't realized that you could . . . Oh, dear me. What am

I saying? Of course you can. You are. This is why this bastard booby-trapped you, this is why he was so cross. He knows you love someone else, Mattie. What will happen to you?"

Mattie weighed her words. "I don't know. I haven't accumulated enough history to know things like that. I will ask Iolanda to protect me." She pointed at the homunculus. "I'll ask her to make sure that he gives me my key back."

Chapter 12

Iolanda did not take long to show up. She burst through the doors in a whirlwind of wild hair and flared skirts. "Mattie! Are you all right?"

Mattie nodded. "I'm fine."

"What happened?"

"Loharri," Mattie said. She explained the device planted in her head, and her desperate need to get her key back. She needed Loharri out of her head and her heart, she said.

Iolanda smiled at that. "Indeed," she said. "I know exactly what you mean." She pushed past Mattie to the laboratory, and took a step back once she saw Niobe. "Who is she?"

"Niobe," Mattie said. "My friend. She was helping me with your request."

"Ah." Iolanda walked through the laboratory to her habitual seat in the kitchen, and laughed at the sight of the pile of Mattie's dresses covered with a blanket. "How cozy! You're sleeping here?"

"Yes," Niobe said, showing neither embarrassment nor anger. "Mattie has no need for beds, so I have to make do."

"A fellow alchemist then," Iolanda said. "Thank you for helping with Mattie—I'll pay you too."

"There's no need—"

"Of course there is." Iolanda sat and played with a

long strand of her curly hair. "There's always a need for money."

"Iolanda only employs women," Mattie said to Niobe.

"How do they let you get away with it?" Niobe asked, visibly warming up to Iolanda.

"They don't notice," Iolanda answered, and both of them laughed.

Mattie did not quite understand what was so funny about hiding oneself, about being allowed to do what one pleased while no one was looking. They, the women, were like the gargoyles, Mattie thought. Respected in words, but hidden from view of those who ran the city and managing to live in the darkness, in the secret interstices of life.

"All right then," Iolanda said and helped herself to the decanter with pear liquor. "Let's see what you've cooked up for me."

Mattie took the blood homunculus out of its jar.

"Ew," Iolanda said. "What is it?"

The homunculus seemed to recognize Iolanda with the hair coiled in its chest, and it toddled up to her and grabbed at her skirts with its stumpy fingerless hands, leaving dirty traces on the fine silk.

"We better put it in the jar." Niobe scooped the weakly resisting creature into its glass jail and stopped the jar before it could crawl out. She handed the jar to Iolanda. "There."

Iolanda studied the creature through the glass, her full lips twisting in disgust.

Niobe explained how to feed the homunculus, and Iolanda looked even more doubtful.

She turned the jar this way and that, but no matter how she tried to turn the blind embryonic visage away from her, the homunculus always managed to turn to face her. "I don't even know if it's worth it," Iolanda said. "Don't get me wrong, I appreciate your fine work. It's just—"

"That's fine," Niobe said cheerfully. "I'm sure Loharri would pay double for it—his hair is in too, so he can command it as well as you."

Iolanda frowned, then unexpectedly laughed. "All right," she said. "You made your sale, clever girl. Say, would you like a nicer bed than what you have right now?"

"And what would that entail?" Niobe asked, still smiling.

"Come stay with me. No one would hassle you there."

"What will I do?"

Iolanda shrugged. "Minor remedies. And keeping me company. Most of my servants are automatons, not nearly as clever as Mattie, and they are dreadful conversationalists. In fact, they do not speak at all, they only listen and do as they are told."

"That may be," Niobe said. "But what do you really need?"

Iolanda shook her head in mock exasperation. "I want you to keep an eye on this thing you just so cruelly entrusted me with. I don't want to see it or hear it. It looks like it might bite."

"It has no teeth," Mattie offered.

Iolanda continued as if she didn't even hear Mattie's interjection. "I won't treat you as a servant. I know how stuck-up you alchemists are. Just take care of it for me, all right? And I promise I'll protect you from the enforcers."

"You're too kind," Niobe said.

"All right then! Get your things." Iolanda thrust the jar with the homunculus in Niobe's hands, all too eager to get rid of it. "Come on, come on!"

As Niobe hurried to pack up her clothes and her alchemical ingredients, Mattie stood by her bench, unable to quite articulate her hurt. She did not fault Niobe for choosing a better arrangement and greater protection than Mattie could offer. She didn't even mind that it meant that she chose Iolanda over Mattie. But she was injured to the core that these two had such an easy time liking each other and trusting each other, despite the gulf that was supposed to exist between them. That the flesh women had some secret bond that Mattie did not share, that by implication she was excluded from their thoughts like she was excluded from their conversation. She was just a machine, a clunker one only acknowledged when convenient. For a moment, she regretted betraying Loharri to them—at least, he never made her feel like she did not belong.

With Niobe gone, Mattie distracted herself with her work on stone. She had mixed blood residue with stone dust and given the homunculus a small shaving off her finger for a heart. The animating essence of the blood stirred the slow, lumbering stone, and the homunculus awakened. Mattie had just started to make an emulsion of various minerals and gemstones to feed the homunculus and prod it to talking and divulging its secrets, betraying the bondage it had over the gargoyles. She felt so close now. Then came a knock on the door.

As Mattie walked to open it—just three steps—many thoughts darted through her mind like startled pigeons. It was Niobe, she thought, who had come back to apologize and stay with Mattie despite the inconvenience, because they were friends; it was Iolanda, holding the slender shaft of Mattie's key in her soft, manicured hands; or it was Loharri who came to take her home forever, because she could not be trusted out of his sight, not even with the traitorous gears ticking in her head, monitoring her heart for any sign of doubt in him.

She opened the door. It was Sebastian—the only possibility she had not considered because she was afraid, Niobe's insinuations still buzzing subsonically deep in her mind. *You're in love, you're in love,* Niobe's voice teased, *and he does not love you back because you are beneath noticing, you're nothing but a mindless automaton that can be shoved aside as soon as it starts getting in the way of what a person wants. You are nothing.*

Sebastian grabbed her hands and smiled. "Mattie? You're all right!"

She nodded and took her hands away, demurring. "Loharri fixed me."

His face grew somber. "I'm sorry I couldn't."

"It's all right," Mattie said. "No one expected you to."

"No." He frowned and sat by the table, in the chair recently vacated by Iolanda. "It's my fault. I haven't been practicing my work in years—do you know how much you forget this way? Can you imagine not practicing at all? I couldn't rejoin the society now if they asked me."

Mattie looked at him askance. He seemed so alien—always

coming and going at odd hours, seemingly untouchable by either the enforcers or mechanics. He was like a gargoyle, hidden, having the gift of making himself invisible—a natural gift, Mattie thought. "Your name was on the list," she said.

"What list?" He seemed momentarily disoriented by the change of topic but smiled. "What are you talking about, Mattie?"

"Your mechanic medallion was reported missing," Mattie said. "I saw the list."

"So? I'm sure there were plenty of others."

"Yes." Mattie paused. "Don't you want to know why we had the list?"

He forced a smile. "Why, Mattie?"

"Because only the mechanics can legally order explosives from the alchemists," she said. "We suspect that maybe there was a stolen medallion involved."

Sebastian shrugged. "I wouldn't know anything about it, Mattie. Ask the gargoyles—they saw me every day; they know I wasn't involved in anything, no matter who the mechanics want to blame."

"The gargoyles complain that their feeders are empty."

"I'm sure the monks will find someone," Sebastian said, his face coloring with a dark blush. "If they haven't already."

"Maybe." Mattie studied him—she did not suspect him, not really. But there were questions that gnawed at the edges of her thoughts, leaving a latticed pattern of doubt and confusion. And she could not forget that he was a mechanic who knew something of alchemy—and who could say how much he picked up from his mother? Maybe the mechanics kept perfecting their art, making more and more complex things every day, but explosives had been made the same way for centuries. The alchemists enjoyed tradition and camaraderie more than efficiency; Niobe was right about that.

"So what, you gonna start suspecting me now?" Sebastian said. His years spent at playing simpleton with a bucketful of gravel had left their mark in his speech—she noticed it more when he got defensive, retreating into a pretense of simple-mindedness when questioned or confronted.

Mattie shook her head. "I would never suspect you, Sebastian."

He smiled, still uncertainly. "And why is that?"

She saw no point in pretending—her mask was a part of her, her real face, her clean boyish features. "Niobe thinks I love you," she said.

Sebastian stopped smiling and looked away. She made him awkward, Mattie realized—everyone felt awkward when they had to say no to someone who'd been kind to them. And occasionally, just out of gratitude, they said yes. "I'm flattered," he said. "But even people could be mistaken about such things—why, you barely know me."

"Barely."

He coughed and got off the chair with an air of determination. There was nowhere to go so he just paced the length of the kitchen—three steps to the door, three back. "Have you seen the new contraption the mechanics are building?" he asked after a bit of frantic pacing.

"No," Mattie said.

"They're building it by the pond, not too far from the park.

You really should see it—it is fascinating. They call it the Calculator."

"Oh," Mattie said. "Loharri mentioned it before—it's the machine that is supposed to figure out the answers and find those responsible for the bombings, and help us figure out how to run and defend this city."

"Yes," Sebastian said. "My, you know a lot of things before they become public knowledge, don't you?"

Mattie nodded. "Loharri doesn't keep secrets from me. And the mechanics always talk freely when I'm about—I don't think they take me seriously at all."

"It's their loss," Sebastian said. "Trust me on this. Will you go see it?"

"Why do you want me to?"

"I thought you would like to meet another very smart machine," he said.

Mattie shook her head. "It is not smart. It just analyzes—anyone could do that."

"Why don't they?"

"Because they don't know all of the parameters," Mattie said. "And the same is true for this machine—it doesn't know everything, and it is unable to decide what's important."

She went to see the Calculator anyway. She saw it from afar—its smokestack rose over the trees of the park, gray and white, occasionally colored with the yellows of sulfurous fumes. The machine itself disappointed her—Mattie never dared to think it in such words but she expected an intelligent automaton that looked like her. Instead, it was a gigantic contraption, clanging with metal pistons and spewing steam from multiple pipes and openings covered with grating. It was like an angry house that was hissing and spitting at Mattie, and she did not know why it was so upset.

There were several engineers tinkering with one of the many square modules at the Calculator's side. Loharri was among them, and Mattie's instinct was to turn away and run home before he noticed her. She turned and hurried toward the safety of the street, where she would be hidden from his eyes by the buildings and the brightly colored but still-subdued crowd. The absence of dark faces was noticeable to Mattie, and she moved uneasily through the crowd, so homogeneous that Mattie stood out like a red roof in the gargoyles' district.

"Mattie!"

She turned with ready moan of exasperation, to see Loharri running after her.

"Wait!" He slowed to a somewhat more dignified walk and weaved through the crowd, long and sinuous like an eel. "You don't have to run every time you see me and make me chase you through the streets. It doesn't look proper."

Mattie shrugged. "I wasn't running. I just didn't like your Calculator."

He grinned, briefly flashing his very white teeth. "Please don't tell me you're jealous."

"Of course I'm not." Mattie shifted on her feet, uncomfortable, all the while studying his face for any subtle change induced by Niobe's alchemy. "I just think it is loud and dirty."

He laughed, and bowed with an exaggerated flourish. "You, of course, are much prettier."

Mattie huffed. "Has it occurred to you that being pretty might not be the height of my ambition?"

"Yes." He smiled still. "It worries me quite a bit, actually. You were made to be pleasing to the eye and interesting to converse with, not to run off and take up a trade which frankly isn't that different from the nonsense the Stone Monks ply."

"Why do you hate them so much?"

He shrugged. "They are not rational, my dear girl." That was his standard explanation for any dislike of others he had ever exhibited. "So all right, the gargoyles grew the city. It was awfully nice of them, but I don't see why we're supposed to worship them."

"Not worship," Mattie said. "Feed them and help them when they need it. And maybe listen to what they have to say."

"Sure. This is why we have the monks in the first place, for feeding and helping. And now, apparently, you've joined the ranks of the helpers and listeners. Why would they need the rest of us?"

Neither of them mentioned the trade in children, the horrible deformed creatures, colloquially known as spiders for their short, round bodies and long, thin limbs, the pitiful terrors that emerged from the mine shafts every night. Honestly, Mattie was glad she did not have to see them—the stories were enough.

Mattie watched the traffic, now mostly caterpillars and just a few lizards, flow by with its usual hissing and groaning and metal clanking against stone. This is what this city is about, she thought. The metal against stone, the constant struggle, and the mechanics against the alchemists. Only now there was no doubt as to who had won—the mechanics had the upper hand; it was their city now.

"What are you thinking about?" Loharri asked.

"Nothing," Mattie said. "Everything. The Soul-Smoker, for once—did you know that he had been in the orphanage?"

"Yes." Loharri scowled. "I have to go back—the Calculator is malfunctioning."

"What's the problem?" Mattie asked.

Loharri shrugged. "We ask it how to increase the coal supply, and it tells us to send everyone in the city to dig for it."

Mattie laughed. "It's not just ugly, it's also dumb."

"You may be right. But we know what the problem is, we can fix it now." Loharri turned away.

Mattie waved after his long, narrow back, clad in black wool despite the warmth and the sun. "That's what you always say," she whispered when she was certain that he could not hear her.

With Mattie, it was like this—her first weeks of life were spent on the bench in mostly- or half-assembled state. She retained snatches of those memories, even though they scared her with the sight of her own disembodied legs standing on the floor all by themselves, and several porcelain faces staring at her with empty sockets while she cried out, naked and alone. Loharri called it 'growing pains', and she agreed at least with the second part. He kept finding new problems and new solutions that in turn caused more problems, until Mattie was quite sure that she would never walk, would never be made whole. And then, as if by a miracle, she worked, complete and functional. In his weaker moments, Loharri called it a celestial intervention. Whatever the cause was, here she was now, Loharri's voice still ringing in her ears. *I now know what the problem is; I can fix it.*

SHE RETURNED HOME TO FIND SEBASTIAN PREOCCUPIED with one of her books—the one about gargoyle history. She watched his profile for a while, his crinkled forehead, his lowered thoughtful eyes. Perhaps Iolanda was correct—perhaps Mattie was in love. Or perhaps it was just desperation to break free of Loharri's hold.

Sebastian looked up over his shoulder and smiled. "Mattie," he said. "I've been thinking about what I said earlier. I didn't mean to dismiss you; I didn't mean to imply that . . . " His large palm stroked his short hair absent-mindedly. "How do I put this?"

"You can't love a machine," she said. "I understand."

He shook his head. "That's not what I meant. I just don't know . . . how."

His skin, soft and smooth, beckoned her hand, and she touched his cheek, and felt the pulsing of blood under her fingers and saw the blooming of a dark blush a moment later.

"What are you doing?" Sebastian asked, but did not move away.

She remembered the words, even though she had never uttered them before. "Making love," she whispered.

Sebastian remained seated, his black eye looking at her askance, as if unsure what to do.

Mattie was rather at a loss for ideas herself, and she bent down and wrapped her arms around him; her fingers touched on his chest, her cheek pressed against the back of his neck.

He grabbed her arm and pulled her in front of him. "Let's take a look at you," he murmured. "You know, I have no idea what you look like under this dress."

Her fingers picked up the fabric of her skirt, lifting it demurely just above her ankles.

He studied the double bones, shining and slender, meeting at the metal joint that held the front and the back parts of her foot together—metal toes and wooden heel. He reached under her skirt, his warm fingers stroking past the roundness of her knee joint, brushing against the polished inner surface of her thigh, long and curved, and came to rest against the smooth metal plate between her legs.

"Not like this," Mattie whispered, and touched his hand to her chest, pressing his palm against the tiny glass window.

He finally understood and pulled her into his lap. He yanked at the fabric concealing her breast, and his mouth found the keyhole as if by instinct. She froze—a troubling mix of fear and lightheaded pleasure—as his tongue circled the circumference of the keyhole. He forced the tip in, once, twice, and she felt the vibrant life flood her. He wasn't winding her, but her whole body responded, rocking in rhythm with her heartbeat, she squirmed in his lap and his kisses and caressing fingers grew hungrier, more urgent. He pulled her dress off her shoulders, touched her inlays like piano keys, tangled his fingers in her hair. His mouth pressed against her lips and then her breasts, and then her lips again.

———

MATTIE FLED TO THE SOUL-SMOKER—IT SEEMED LIKE HE and his many ghosts were the only ones she could still talk to. Confusion overwhelmed Mattie as she ran through the streets, so alive and yet so different from what she remembered. In search of any distraction to prevent her mind from latching onto the single thought—*I have let him touch me. I made him touch me*—she stopped by the public telegraph. The small foyer that hosted the apparatus and the long yards of tape it spewed incessantly, recording the news, passing messages, mounded in front of it, like some grotesque tapeworm tangled beyond any hope. The clerks let it be, sitting in their little niche, protected from the ravages of the public by thick bars.

"Anything for the alchemists?" Mattie asked.

The clerk, a young redheaded man named Janus, yawned. "Not since three days ago."

Mattie felt a guilty pang from not having checked in so long. "May I see it?"

The clerk dug through the large metal case divided into hundreds of private enclosures, where the important messages went to sit for a week before being disposed off.

"It's very quiet today. You were mobbed last week."

The clerk, his shoulders and bony elbows moving energetically as if he were kneading dough, laughed. "Yeah, and two days ago everyone just decided, screw this. There's so much bad news you can absorb before wanting to close your eyes and curl up in a corner, yes?"

"What happened two days ago?" Mattie asked the young man's back.

"The Duke died," he said. "His wife and daughter recovered enough to join the rest of the court."

"Thank you." Mattie's mind tried to figure out what it meant for the city, and as chaotic as her thoughts were, she felt that the changes she considered were already in motion, the great blocks of stone that tumbled slowly into place, locking things in like the slab of the jail door slamming into its doorway, sealing off all sunlight and hope.

"Here's your message," the red-haired clerk said. "It's encoded."

Mattie took the ring out of her pocket and quickly read the message. She had to read it several times, since her eyes slid off the words, refusing to absorb their meaning.

The message was from Bokker, who had looked through the alchemical records. One of the names in the missing mechanics' medallions showed up—Sebastian's. The medallion was presented by a man who had ordered some quantity of explosives. Moreover, Bokker advised that the man who had used the medallion was tall but wore a hood obscuring his face; but by the color of his hands the alchemist thought that the man was an easterner—Bokker was especially insistent on mentioning this detail, as well as the fact that there were very few easterners admitted to the Lyceum, let alone to the society itself.

Mattie left the telegraph building, feeling a freezing cold starting at her heart and spreading outwards, freezing every emotion out of her. She tried to think of it logically—

perhaps Sebastian's medallion was listed because it was lost or stolen from him, perhaps someone else was using it. And yet, she knew that the medallion was on the list because he failed to return it after he was banished. Maybe he lost it afterwards, maybe he didn't have anything to do with it. And yet, it fitted with his disappearances and his closeness to the palace, it fitted the overall pattern and his insistence that he could not leave the city. No matter how Mattie tried, there was no way of fitting it any other way without invoking a complex conspiracy—and as she knew, those were almost never true.

She hoped that Ilmarekh would offer her some advice, but she knew that she was beyond advice, beyond being able to cheer up at mere words. She needed to do something.

Having made a decision, she turned around and marched away from the gates. She passed by the factories, under the low-hanging clouds of smoke and soot, through the incessant banging and clashing of the machinery; she walked past the hovels and the hollow-eyed old people who passed the last of their days looking for sun in the endless haze, and hacking up gray pieces of their lungs.

"Friends in high places," Ilmarekh had told her the last time. Iolanda. Mattie was willing to overlook the friend-theft at the moment, and instead decided to ask Iolanda for one of her many promised favors. She needed to know what was the right thing to do, and how the two of them fitted inside the machine of the city, more metal than stone now.

Chapter 13

———

MATTIE HEADED NORTH, FOR THE WEALTHY DISTRICT surrounding the former palace, where the houses were few and spacious, enveloped by delicately maintained gardens and tall hedges that tastefully contributed to the landscape yet managed to keep the owners' private affairs in and the interlopers out. Her footfalls resonated in the wide, quiet streets lined with old shade trees that softened all other noises into a rich, velvety background that made her aware of her own noisy workings.

The wealthy district lay a good way away from the gates, nestled in the very heart of the stone city, embraced by the semicircle of the palace district in the south and the park on the north. There were a few ponds here the names of which Mattie did not know, but even they seemed different from the Grackle Pond—the water here was pure like crystal, with the barest hints of blue shadows playing within; the schools of red and orange fish—some solid, some patterned—played in the emerald green tangles of the lake grass, their quick shadows streaking across the white, sandy bottom.

Mattie had been here only once before, and she looked for Iolanda's house. She did not know how she would recognize it, only that she would—every house here was elaborate, and Mattie thought she would spot Iolanda's taste with ease.

She spent a long time wandering between the houses, studying the ornate ironwork on the gates, looking for any sign of Iolanda's presence. Most of the residences stood empty since their inhabitants had left the city, but a few harbored signs of life—soft music and laughter wafted through the air, along with a light clinking of dishes and glasses. But the gates were locked, and no matter how hard she looked, she saw no sign of Iolanda.

She was ready to give up, and turned back, now lost in the maze of the wide, quiet streets. She felt even more alien in this eerie, luxurious place, and she hurried along, suddenly afraid. And then she saw people in the streets.

They did not belong here either. Dressed in cheap, rough clothes covered with coal dust, their faces gaunt and peppered with coal particles absorbed into their skin so that no soap could get them out. They moved in a silent, tight formation, their eyes unnaturally light in their darkened faces. Several of them carried torches, and they cast a troubled orange light over the trees and the streets.

Mattie got out of the way, flattening against an iron fence. The bars felt reassuring against the metal of her back as she watched the silent and somber procession pass by. The tide of miners did not stem—they filled the street, and Mattie tasted coal and hot metal in the air.

There were others too—not as stained as the rest, but just as gaunt and silent. For a moment, Mattie thought that these people were ghosts vomited up by the Soul-Smoker and given flesh through some perversion of nature, through the foul magic of smoke and clanging metal that filled the city, rendering flesh more and more obsolete each day, and this unwanted flesh now walked the streets, lost.

At first, they didn't even look at Mattie, intent and determined. But as more and more men walked by, she noticed that a few glanced in her direction; when the end of the column was moving past her, they stared.

"Hey," one of them called, breaking the silence. "Shouldn't we do something about the clunker here?"

She was too scared to take offense as several men left their place in the column, creating a little eddy of people, and walked up to her.

"I've done nothing to you," Mattie said.

"It talks," one of them said, perplexed. "When did you learn to talk?"

"I always could," Mattie said. "I'm not like the other machines. I'm emancipated."

The man studied her, his narrow face unshaven and impenetrable. "We heard about the intelligent machine," he said, finally.

"The one who tells the government what to do with us," one of his fellows added. "Is it you? Is it you who took away our land and stuffed us into mines?"

"Their kind took our fields, too," another one said.

Mattie shook her head and folded her hands. "No," she said. "It's not me, I swear. I'm just an alchemist, I make ointments. You want the Calculator by the Grackle Pond."

"We'll get to it in due time," the first man said. "Now the question is, what to do with you?"

Mattie sensed restrained violence in the tense set of his

shoulders, in the subtle tightening of his fists, knobby and disproportionately large on his thin forearms.

A shout from somewhere at the head of the procession tore at the silence, and there was a sound of smashed glass and whooping. More shouting, more noises, and a thin wisp of dirty smoke curled into the sky like a curlicue. Mattie's interlocutors were compelled to look away, stretching their necks to see better.

Mattie bolted. The man closest to her gave a surprised gasp as she pushed him away, and reflexively his fist caught her on the cheek; she felt cracks opening in her face, blooming into stars, but already she ran, the wind hissing in the fissures of her porcelain mask.

The crowd had grown sparser and she had no trouble weaving her way between them. She was faster than any of them, and they seemed too preoccupied to pay her much mind. Her feet pounded the pavement, but instead of resonating loudly like before, her footfalls were nearly inaudible in the cacophony of destruction that erupted all around and behind her.

She heard a woman scream, and thought that the rioters had breached the gates somewhere and were destroying the houses. There was a smashing of glass, and a smell of burning wood and something else—hair? horn?—chased after her. Mattie tried not to think about Iolanda and Niobe, and yet she felt guilty that she was unable to find them— although what good would it have done? She felt a chip of porcelain detach from her cheek and heard it clink on the pavement.

Mattie slowed her steps only when she was certain that

the rioters had passed by; even then, she walked quickly, clinging close to the walls of the buildings. There was no one in the streets, and only occasionally she saw a worried face peer through the shutters—a sign that the rioters had passed this way. As she approached the palace district (she still thought of it this way, even though there was no palace anymore), she saw several of the enforcers' buggies, heading in the direction she came from. They swarmed by the Parliament, organizing, and she breathed a little easier. The riot would be over soon, and she only hoped that it would be stopped before Iolanda and Niobe were hurt. She felt guilty for her earlier resentment of them, as if her thoughts had brought them into danger.

They did not let her into the Parliament building, and she headed for Loharri's house—it was closer than hers, and she was not ready to face Sebastian just yet. Sebastian. She thought about telling Loharri where he was, about the missing medallion and explosives. Surely, it would be a reason enough? And yet, her entire being cried out against it. It didn't matter if he was the one who blew up the palace; it didn't matter if he was involved in the riots somehow. She just couldn't betray him. She had had enough of that for now. Instead, she wondered if perhaps Iolanda was visiting Loharri, and was thus spared the grisly fate Mattie tried really hard not to imagine.

THE DOOR WAS LOCKED, BUT MATTIE DECIDED TO WAIT. WITH the shrubbery so bold and unrestrained, she could sit on the front stoop, hidden by the glistening green wall studded with creamy and red roses, drinking in their sweet fragrance. She watched the sky turn deeper blue, and gingerly touched her face, exploring the new cracks. She extended her eyes to take a closer look, and her heart fell—there were so many, with whole chunks of porcelain missing, exposing the shining gears underneath. The corner of her lips was cracked horribly, and she thought that it almost mimicked Loharri's injury—now she too had half a face maimed. The difference was that he could replace hers.

Loharri came home when the shadows from the hedge grew long enough to touch the walls of the house, to lap at the foundation and to reach up to the windows, gradually consuming the wall from the ground up. The rose bushes looked black in the dimming light, and the night flowers' fragrance scented the breeze—Mattie smelled jasmine and gardenias, magnolias and lilacs in the thick night air, and almost missed the sound of familiar light footsteps on the path.

Loharri smiled at Mattie but his eyes remained tired. His clothes were rumpled as if he had slept in them, and the white collar and cuffs of his shirt bore long streaks of oil. His hands were stained, black semicircles of grime nestled under the fingernails of his usually clean hands. "Are you all right?" he asked. "Come on in; I'll get the fire going."

Loharri still signified home for Mattie, no matter how much she resented this fact. "You look tired," she said. "Did you see the riots?"

He smirked. "Yes, I did. They burned down a few houses and made a racket before the Parliament. But right now, I just want a bath, a sandwich and a nice drink. Come on in."

"I don't want to disturb you," Mattie said. Her words sounded perfunctory even to her; they both knew that Mattie's presence would neither tax nor disturb him.

She followed Loharri inside, and it felt as though they had just returned from one of their excursions—it felt like coming home after a long absence. The smells she hadn't noticed when she used to live here were obvious now—metal and oil, the weak scent of roses wafting through the open windows from the outside, an unfinished glass of tea left in the kitchen—and endearing in their familiarity.

"Go take your bath," she told Loharri. "I'll make you your tea and sandwich."

"I have an automaton for that."

She tilted her head. "I don't mind."

"Suit yourself." His footfalls retreated into the interior of the house, and she listened to the weak sounds as she rummaged through the ice chest looking for cheeses and cold meat. She heard the running water, the rustling of clothes shed to the floor, a splash and a tired sigh.

She thought that Loharri seemed unusually subdued, considering the events of the past weeks, and especially today. Perhaps the telegraph clerk was right; perhaps there came a time when the most reasonable response was to sigh and ignore everything, because the heart could not absorb all the misery of the world without breaking. Perhaps they should just stay in the kitchen, the kettle bubbling merrily on the woodstove, the flames of the fireplace casting a bright glow on the dark walls, and talk nonsense, and watch the elaborate dance of the fireflies outside.

Loharri was apparently of the same mind—when he came into the kitchen, his hair dripping water onto the collar of his clean shirt, he held up his hand. "I really don't want to talk about it."

"Neither do I," Mattie said. "I'm just worried about Iolanda—have you seen her today?"

He shook his head and gave her a sharp look. "Since when are the two of you best pals? She worries about you, you worry about her . . . "

"She bought some ointment for me," Mattie said, settling for a half-truth rather than an outright lie or a confession. "She seems nice. And you like her, don't you?"

He settled at the table and drank his tea. "It's complicated, Mattie."

She tilted her head. "Everything is complicated with you."

"It's a character flaw." He smiled, then squinted up at her. "Don't worry, she'll be fine. But what happened to your face? Did you fall again?"

"Yes," Mattie said. "No. I was watching the smoke over the city, and walked into a lamppost." It was just ridiculous enough for him to believe it.

He smiled. "Oh, Mattie. I don't have anything new for you, but maybe one of the prototypes will work for now."

"Prototypes?"

"You don't think I'd settle for a design without trying others, do you? Come on, I'll show you."

"Eat," she said. "I'm not going anywhere."

"Afraid of being home all by yourself?"

"No." *Afraid of being home with someone else*, she thought, but never said it out loud. "Eat your sandwich."

He obeyed, still smiling. "You don't hate me as much as you make out, do you, Mattie?"

"Don't talk with your mouth full," she said. "And I never said I hated you."

"You make a fairly good impression. No words needed, dear girl, and you know full well that I'm not entirely dim. Surely, you expected me to pick up on some of your mannerisms."

"I just don't want you touching me," she said. "And I want my key."

"I left it to you in my will," he said. "You won't kill me though, will you?"

"I'll consider it," she said.

He didn't think her dangerous—if he did, he wouldn't joke about it and pretend that her anger was indeed a concern to him. He occasionally enjoyed making a show out of capitulating to her, but only because they both knew he held more power. *Not any more*, Mattie thought. *I hope that Iolanda is all right.* She didn't mind feeling selfish just this once—of course, her concern for Iolanda was more about Iolanda and Niobe than it was about the blood homunculus; but she couldn't deny that the small bubbling creature figured in her thoughts prominently.

"This is nice," he said. He finished his meal and sat back in his chair, stretching his long legs with a drawn-out sigh. "Just like the old times."

Mattie inclined her head. "There was something you wanted to show me?"

He led her to his workshop, which seemed to grow more

cluttered by the day. Under the piles of scrap metal and gear trains, racks and pinions, he found a large crate, uncharacteristically well-kept and neatly covered with straw. In it, there were several faces, and Mattie was surprised to discover that they were all different from the one she had worn until then. There were faces with thin noses and upturned noses, plump and narrow lips, high and low foreheads, and a wide variety of cheekbones. "This one sort of looks like you," Loharri said and picked up a mask that indeed bore some resemblance to the face Mattie had grown accustomed to and recognized as her own—a face with rounded childish cheeks and wide eyes, with a small mouth smiling at some untold secret.

"I like this one better." The face Mattie picked was unpainted and plain, with features that suggested neither youth nor wisdom of experience. It was a very average face, and Mattie suspected that Loharri considered it a failure and only kept it because he could rarely bear to throw anything away, on the off chance that he might decide that he needed it after all.

Loharri grimaced. "I'm usually not the man to criticize my own work, but I regret to say that you lack artistic taste, Mattie."

"Can I have it?"

He shrugged. "Why not? It's only temporary." He helped her to put it on, and gave her a long appraising look. "Not terrible. But tell me something, my sweet machine, tell me—last time I visited, your face was already off. How'd you managed that?"

"I don't remember," Mattie lied. "I don't remember much of that day—only that Niobe was there to help me."

"And she's not a mechanic."

"Not that I know of," Mattie answered cautiously. "Does one need to be a mechanic to take my face off?"

"It certainly helps." Loharri watched her still, with a calm curiosity in his eyes that Mattie found unsettling. "If there was a mechanic who had stopped by, you would tell me, wouldn't you?"

"Of course." She made her voice as steady as she could manage. "Why wouldn't I?"

"This is exactly what I'm trying to figure out," Loharri said, smiling.

WE FEEL A STRANGE SENSE OF KINSHIP TO THE PEOPLE WHO *are burning the city down—not to their actions, but they have come from the stone, like us—the ground opened and disgorged them, a whole throng, torches and gaunt faces, as if they were born from the rock and appeared on the surface by magic, already sullen and dissatisfied with the world as it was.*

And then we see the deformed spiderlike men crawling out, their long weak arms grabbing onto the rocks as they struggle to exit narrow passages where diamonds and emeralds and rubies hide, where only small bodies and long fingers can reach; they haul themselves out, with little help from their deformed spindly legs, weak from constant crouching. Their red-rimmed eyes blink even though the sun is setting and the shadows are long and velvet-soft. We wonder if these children of stone are to succeed us and if they are the reason for our decline, if the stone has planned it like this, all these centuries ago—that we are to return where we came from and others would come in our stead.

But they look weak, and we know that they have been shaped by human hands—the hands that stuffed them into cages where their bodies could not grow; we know that they find it difficult to breathe and can easily suffocate in their sleep—every night is a gamble for them. Like it is for us, we suppose.

We follow them as they crawl, and more emerge from the earth, so pale, so blind, so helpless on the surface. They come in the wake of the first riots, and they watch the orange light tinting the horizon, streaked with black smoke. It's not like they remember it from last night, but last night was different, too—they did not enter the city but instead crawled to their hovels outside the city wall, to sleep and dream of death. Tonight, they pass through the gates, and we follow them, curious now.

They notice us—we do not know how, but they do, and their red eyes linger as we cling to the city wall, to the buildings.

"Don't be afraid," they croak and coo and call us in strangled voices. In their hands they have gems—blue and green and red, the stone that gave birth to them still clinging to their rough uneven edges. They offer the gemstones to us, and we cannot resist—we have been hungry for so long. We descend to the ground, to their level, and we eat the stones out of their hands. Their slender fingers touch our faces in wonder and apprehension, they slide off the abrupt precipices of our cheekbones and noses. The stones taste of cool subterranean depths, and we suddenly miss home.

"Come with us," they call and coo. "Come with us, help us like you haven't helped us before."

"But what can we do?" we say, the shards of emeralds and rubies grating on our worn teeth. "We can only watch."

"*Come with us,*" *they say and beckon.* "*There's stone down in these tunnels, and great twisting passages; there are crystals growing from the low roofs, and there's fluorescent moss covering the walls.*"

"*We can't,*" *we say, and we move away, the crumbs of gemstones dropping from our lips.*

We climb the walls again, and we follow them around the city on their slow, exploratory crawl. They pay us no attention, pretending that they have forgotten about us. But we know better. They are afraid of us, afraid that we will protect our city, and they want to lure us to the tunnels, where we will be out of the way, in the soft cradling embrace of our home. But we cannot go. The city is our responsibility—even though we can only watch.

They crawl toward the fires, drawn to them like all creatures living in the dark. There are men with torches everywhere, and they are not burning but fleeing now—we hear the distant clanging of the buggies and the shouts of their passengers, and musket shots ringing through the streets.

The windows are shuttered, and even the shopkeepers do not leave the safety when they hear the sounds of broken glass. The smells of smoke and jasmine make the air sing, make the darkness so much deeper, so much bluer. The buildings to our east are hidden by the darkness, but the ones to our west are outlined in black against the orange sky which grows brighter, then dims, pulsing, like a living heart.

We find that we are drawn to flames too, and we follow the crawling procession toward it. We taste soot in the air, and we almost weep when we see the scorched gardens, the blackened limbs of the dead trees still exhaling the heat of the recent fire, and we watch an occasional spark crackling and running along the fissures of the burned wood.

The broken windows gape, and there's no laughter or music; the shots and shouts are far away now, and silence hangs over the formerly beautiful place like a shroud. We wonder where all the people who used to live here went, and then we turn away because we cannot come up with an answer.

But the crawling, seething mass of people below is not deterred—we watch them crawling over the hot cinders and rubble, we hear their soft, strained voices calling to each other. And then they turn back.

They crawl through the silent streets, circumventing the sounds of fighting, distant now, they crawl to the gates as the city around them remains mute but awake—there's tension in the air, the tension that usually disappears when people sleep, but tonight, they are all watching through the shutters, their eyes glinting occasionally through the narrow slots. They watch and they pray, and just like us, they do not know what to do—they remain inside because once they venture out, they would be compelled to do something. Instead, they choose the dubious safety of the night vigil—even children are not crying—and they watch like we do, somber and quiet, as the gem miners explore the city they had left as children in small cages, as they talk to each other in tones of hushed wonder.

And we think the same thing the people in the locked houses think—or at least, we like to think that they do think about that, we like to think that as they look at the human spiders and their quick but uncertain crawl, they silently whisper to themselves, what have we done?

Chapter 14

————

MATTIE WAITED FOR LOHARRI TO WAKE UP, AND IDLY PICKED through the icebox. He appeared to have gone to the market the day before, and she inhaled the smells of foods she could not consume—figs and pomegranates, fresh berries and coconut milk. She was satisfied with the smell alone.

She thought that the figs—dark-red, almost purple— looked like tiny hearts, and the juice of the pomegranates was the color of human blood. She had no instruments, but in the kitchen she mashed the fig pulp awkwardly with her fingers, whispering the secret words she had learned from Ogdela—the words, Ogdela insisted, that could heal the heart of the world if only said right and with enough conviction. She poured the pomegranate juice over the red pulp when Loharri, still half-asleep, stumbled into the kitchen.

"Something smells good," he said, his voice still hoarse from sleep.

Mattie nodded. She liked the smell of people right after they slept—it was a warm, musky smell that made her feel at home and at peace. "How much damage did they do?"

Loharri shrugged and scooped a blob of fig and pomegranate mix with his fingers. "Mmmm," he said. "Delicious. As for the damage, I truly do not know. I don't want to know, frankly. I don't think the city treasury has enough money for a decent rebuilding effort."

"You're thinking of rebuilding?" Mattie watched him eat. Not the heart of the world, but if she could fix his heart it would be enough. "How do you know they won't come back?"

He stopped eating. "You think they will."

"I think they might. The enforcers kicked them out of the city this time, but . . . "

"I see your point." Loharri finished his meal, stretched, and paced. "What is it they want?"

Mattie told him about the men who attacked her yesterday. "They don't like being replaced in the fields by machines. They don't like being forced into the mines. I can't say I blame them."

"We all have a role to play. Otherwise, society couldn't function."

"I never hear it from people with miserable roles," Mattie said.

"Not everyone can be a mechanic. Or an alchemist for that matter, or a courtier."

"They don't want that," Mattie answered. "They just want to be peasants again. Just that."

Loharri sighed. "I better go and check on the Calculator. It was pretty well guarded, but still . . . "

Mattie shook her head. It surprised her how little affected by the riots Loharri appeared—he seemed to see them as a minor inconvenience; he was not able to grasp that the order of the world—or at least the city—had changed fundamentally. To him, the mechanics were still in charge and business continued as usual, and the riots were nothing but a minor wrinkle in the fabric of life, easily shrugged off, smoothed out, and forgotten.

"I don't think you understand," she said. "They will return, in greater numbers. They will take the city over."

Loharri laughed. "You're over-dramatizing, Mattie. Your imagination is running away with you."

"Look through the window," she said. "Then tell me that everything is unchanged."

He obeyed, nonchalant. He stared out of the window, over the rose bushes and into the streets clogged with traffic—caterpillars, lizards, men and women and children, in vehicles and on foot, most of them carrying or carting hastily assembled parcels of their belongings. Despite the commotion, the people remained curiously quiet—even children didn't cry but remained serious and subdued. The caterpillars ground, metal on metal, and the lizards gave an occasional troubled bark—the only sounds in the street.

"Everyone has lost their minds," Loharri observed. "They are dimmer than cattle."

"They are not stupid. They are afraid. Maybe you should be, too."

He stared into the street, his hand resting on the window trim. Mattie wished she could see his face when he said, "Do you suggest I run, too?"

"No," Mattie said. "But you might want to start taking this seriously. Maybe stop scapegoating people and look for real culprits. Or listen to their demands and reach an agreement. Or maybe just find out what happened to the courtiers."

"Who cares about them?"

"I do. Iolanda was there too."

He shook his head without turning. "She wasn't. I went there yesterday, but her automatons told me that she had left. I assumed she moved to the seaside with the rest of them, grew bored . . . but maybe she knew it was coming."

"What about Niobe?"

"That alchemist friend of yours?" He turned around, grinning. "What, did she ditch you for Iolanda?"

Mattie nodded.

"Hm," he said. "Apparently, there is an entire female conspiracy behind my back. What was it exactly you were doing for Io? And what does that girl have to do with it?"

"Iolanda bought perfume from both of us," Mattie said.

He made a face. "Dear girl, you can't possibly believe I'm dense enough to believe this foolishness?"

"But it is true," Mattie insisted.

"I'm sure. You're a bad liar, Mattie, and you know as well as I do that even if she did indeed buy some fragrant nonsense from you, it doesn't form the basis of your association. Although I do appreciate your effort at at least partial veracity." He laughed. "But you're not going to tell me, are you?"

Mattie shook her head. He couldn't really punish her, she thought; the days when he had enough power over her to take away her eyes so that she stumbled through the house blindly were gone now. Still, she worried that he would find another way to punish her disobedience.

Instead, he said, "Let me get dressed, and I'll go see what is going on at the Parliament. You're welcome to come along, of course—especially if you have any idea as to who the real culprit is."

"I don't," Mattie said.

"No matter. Your leader Bokker just might."

Mattie waited for him to get ready, listening for the soft stockinged footsteps and the rustling of clothes. Of course Bokker knew about Sebastian—of course he would tell the mechanics, to drive suspicion from the alchemists if nothing else. And they will look for him; she only hoped they wouldn't search her house—even if he wasn't there.

She felt a forceful pang of guilt when she thought about the last time she saw Sebastian. She had gained enough distance from the event to think about it now, but the shame and turmoil remained strong. She told herself that she had done nothing wrong, that this was what people were supposed to do when in love—and yet, he was the only one besides Loharri who had touched her secret place. She imagined what it would be like to give him her key, to let him wind her—and instead, she recoiled at the thought. If she were to get her key back, she thought, no one but her would ever touch it. She would wind herself well in advance so that she would never need to rely on another to keep herself alive.

THEY HAD TO PUSH THROUGH THE CROWD ALL THE WAY TO the ducal district, where the temple and the Parliament still stood but felt separate from the teeming life around them, like relics of a bygone era. They did not belong, Mattie thought, just like the gargoyles on the roof did not belong to the world around them. For the first time, she doubted her assignment—

perhaps, she thought, she shouldn't interfere with the natural order of things, perhaps it would be better to let the gargoyles pass into the realm of legends entirely. Perhaps they were turning to stone simply because there was no place for them.

Yet, it wasn't true, Mattie told herself. There would always be nooks and fissures where ancient things born of stone could survive. There was no reason to let them go simply because the world was changing; ushering in the new did not have to mean discarding the old. Did it?

"What are you thinking about?" Loharri said. They were approaching the Parliament, deserted in contrast to the rest of the city save for a few enforcers guarding it—it seemed that everyone was eager to get away, and Mattie doubted that the Parliament building would be open.

To her surprise, once they stepped inside they were ushered along by several enforcers. "Emergency meeting," they informed Loharri. "Would you like to leave your automaton here?"

"No, I want her along," Loharri said.

They didn't argue—apparently, they had more important things to worry about, and Mattie followed Loharri to the second floor, into a darkened and plush room dominated by a large oak table. Almost the entire parliament and a few other mechanics and alchemists sat around it. Loharri took a seat, and Mattie remained standing behind his chair, close to the wall, in the shadows where she betrayed her presence with only occasional glinting of metal and quiet ticking.

She listened to the men talk, and the same sense of disbelief and dread as she felt in Loharri's kitchen descended upon her—they talked as if the destruction outside was a temporary event, a tornado, disruptive but fleeting. They talked about containment and rebuilding, they talked about reforms as if the city itself hadn't turned on them; Bokker babbled about the missing medallions and the necessity to find Sebastian—or whoever he could've given his medallion to. The mechanics confirmed that his medallion was never surrendered upon his expulsion, and that they knew he was up to no good.

At this point, Loharri turned to look at her. Mattie remained motionless, her new face as mercifully blank as her old one. "What?" she whispered. "Do you need something?"

He shook his head and turned back.

Mattie listened to Bokker and Bergen argue about the measures that had to be taken—how they would look for Sebastian, and what they would have to do to stem the riots. "Cut the head off and the body will die," Bokker said, and the rest nodded sagely.

Mattie wanted to scream at them that it wasn't that simple—it wasn't just Sebastian, there were others. Thousands of miners and peasants, the workers in the automaton factories and those who cleaned the garbage off the streets— they probably didn't even know about Sebastian, and they wouldn't miss him.

She left the meeting quietly, her steps muted by the thick carpet, her skirts whispering against the wall as she exited.

She pushed through the crowd, heading for the gates—she wanted to make sure that Ilmarekh wasn't harmed by the violence, defenseless as he was alone in his this house, blind and weak.

The gates were guarded now—the enforcers swarmed like flies, their caterpillars staining the air with acrid black smoke. Those leaving the city were not detained, and she slid past the enforcers and their eyes hidden under the faceplates of their helms.

She ran up the hill and knocked on the Soul-Smoker's door. He was there, thankfully whole and in high spirits. He sat by the fireplace where the last flames still guttered and smoldered, his pipe in his pale hand. He smiled when he heard her wooden footfalls, and waved his pipe festively.

"I'm glad that you are all right," he said.

"I'm glad they didn't harm you," she replied.

He smiled a bit, his thin fingers fiddling with the buttons on his waistcoat. "Why would they? I am sympathetic."

"It doesn't matter," Mattie replied. "It doesn't matter to them."

She had realized something last night, and the terror of the understanding weighed heavily on her mind. It didn't matter what one thought or did—once perceived as an enemy by a malignant, blind force, one would be treated as such. Those who prided themselves in their intelligence and ability to rule and those who rebelled against them were just like the mindless automatons collecting the dead bodies and limbs amidst the carnage, like the enforcers that moved through the eastern district arresting whoever they saw fit and handing them over to the Soul-Smoker. There was no difference whatsoever; Mattie had been mistaken to think that there was, that they would listen to her.

"I don't think you know what you are talking about,"

Ilmarekh answered with a slight frown. "I can be useful to them—I am useful to anyone. You're just afraid of change."

"Of course I am!" Mattie stomped her foot, and the entire house shook. "Everyone should be afraid of change—people die in such times."

"It has to get worse before it gets better."

"Maybe." Mattie paced across the narrow room. At least he recognized that the change was happening, unlike the old men at the Parliament. "I saw the mechanics and the alchemists today . . . they are talking about repressing the riots. Defusing the situation, as they call it. The miners will get better wages—they will promise them, at least. I don't think they have enough money to do that, but they'll promise, and they think it'll be enough. Do you think it'll be enough?"

"I'm afraid it just might be," Ilmarekh answered with a sigh. "They are just people, Mattie. They don't want to burn buildings and kill people. Even when it is called for."

Mattie was not assured of the alleged docility of the men who almost killed her yesterday, but she did not argue. "Just be careful," she said.

Ilmarekh nodded and slouched by the fireplace, groping for a cinder that could be coaxed into lighting his pipe. Mattie found one for him and held it close to the pipe as he puffed on the stem, his brow wrinkled. The opium, resinous and moist, caught fire reluctantly, and Mattie smelled the sweet, cloying smoke. The spirits stirred as soon as the twin serpentine wisps of smoke curled from Ilmarekh's flared nostrils—the souls pried his mouth open and babbled, their voices mingling into an indistinct cacophony of word fragments and pained exclamations.

Mattie waited for them to calm down and sort out the speaking order among themselves; they always seemed so talkative when Mattie was around, and she thought that they probably disliked talking to each other—if they even could talk to each other—and resented Ilmarekh . . . they didn't need words to haunt his every waking moment.

"Do they leave you alone when you sleep?" Mattie asked.

Ilmarekh shook his head, struggling for control over his mouth and voice. "I haven't had a dream of my own in ages."

"You deserve it," one of the ghosts shouted.

"Leave him be," another interrupted. "He's not his own man."

His voice garbled again under the assault of many souls pressing from behind, filling his mouth, his eyes with their ethereal shapes. They cried and pleaded in turns, one after the other—the unfairness of it all, the unfinished business. Each seemed to have something to say to Mattie, because she was the only one who could listen to them, without any fear of her soul being sucked out of her.

But perhaps not—she thought of the gargoyles, and almost cried out once she realized that the gargoyles would be capable of listening to the wrath and pleading of the spirits without any risk. Would the soul of a dead person sever their bond with the stone? Mattie did not know, but she thought that this was an avenue worth investigating. She filed it away, for the next time she would speak to them. Now, she needed to listen.

"What do you know about Sebastian?" she asked. "What do you know about the explosives?"

Ilmarekh and his ghosts grew curiously silent then.

"I promise I won't tell anyone," Mattie said. "I need to know . . . for myself."

"They won't tell you," Ilmarekh said. "You've found him, haven't you?"

"Yes," Mattie said. "But I want to know what does he have to do with all of this. I want to help him, but I need to know."

"Why?" Ilmarekh's voice changed to a higher pitch, and Mattie guessed that it was Beresta, worried about the fate of her offspring.

"Because his mechanic's medallion was used to buy explosives," Mattie said. "The mechanics and the alchemists both know about it, they know he is in the city. He was only banished before, but now all the enforcers will be looking for him. I want to help, but I need to know what sort of risk I am taking."

Another soul pushed Beresta aside—Mattie thought she could've imagined it, but she got a distinct impression of two transparent shapeless ghosts engaging in a bit of tug of war—and spoke, with a strong eastern accent. "I know the man," the soul said. "I've done nothing wrong, but I was killed because I was a foreigner. You don't treat us well, this city doesn't. You don't treat anyone well, not even your own. Many are unhappy—is it a surprise that they are coming together to stop your injustice?"

"So the easterners were involved?" Mattie said.

Ilmarekh shrugged. "Some were, some weren't. I wasn't and now I regret it. I blamed those who brought it on us, but now I realize that it wasn't those who plotted, it wasn't those who rebelled who were at fault."

Ilmarekh sighed and spoke in his own voice. "I asked you about your friends in high places. Did you talk to them?"

Mattie shook her head, ashamed. "I never had a chance. I . . . " She didn't say it out loud, but she had been too preoccupied with plotting Loharri's downfall to talk to Iolanda when she could. And now, how would she find Iolanda and Niobe?

"I can help you," another ghost spoke. "I can tell you about a place they gather—but you'll go at your own risk. If they don't trust you, you are dead."

Mattie inclined her head, agreeing. "Just tell me when and where."

"Not far," the ghost said. "No one comes to this blasted hill, and if you go down the northern slope at midnight, you'll see the entrance to an abandoned mine. It's closed during the day, but the spiders open it at night. Can you see in the dark?"

"Yes."

"It won't help you," the ghost said. "It's dark there, so dark, not even a torch will help you."

MATTIE WAITED FOR NIGHTFALL, LISTENING TO THE RISING wind outside. The Soul-Smoker's pipe had been extinguished, and the spirits, exhausted, quieted down and only occasionally whispered dark warnings and petty complaints. Ilmarekh appeared to have fallen asleep in front of the cold fireplace, and Mattie found the sudden movements of his lips and fierce, abruptly whispered words disconcerting, and looked at the window, waiting for the moon to rise and the constellations to arrange themselves in the proper order for the middle of the night.

Beresta, the shy ghost, used the lull to surprise Mattie. "My son is a good boy," she whispered, as if not to wake the others. "A good man. He wouldn't do anything to hurt others."

He almost killed me when I first met him, Mattie thought. She didn't utter those words out loud—she was well familiar with the usual arguments people gave her. You do not count, you are a machine. You are made of metal, you have no soul. As if any of it mattered.

Beresta understood her silence. "You disagree."

"I don't think he is bad," Mattie said. "I think I might even love him."

"But you . . . " Beresta choked down the reflexive protest.

"I was made to feel pain."

The ghost recoiled, her translucent form shrinking close to Ilmarekh's lips, coating them like water. "What sort of a man would build a machine who feels pain?"

Mattie saw no need to answer—they both knew it. It took a specific brand of cruelty, cruelty masquerading as concern. *It will help you learn better. This way you won't damage yourself. It's for your own good.*

And yet, Mattie could not quite bring herself to blame him—she knew how he had learned these words. "I can also feel pleasure," Mattie said.

"That seems even more cruel," Beresta whispered.

"And why is that?"

"You know," the ghost said. "Machines break. Always, all of them, no matter what the mechanics say."

"People die," Mattie countered. And added, "Even the ghosts."

"And yet you work on reversing death."

"Don't we all?" The words came out of her mouth of their own volition, but she immediately felt the truth of them deep in her metal bones. What else did they all do if not try to stave off disappearance? Alchemists cured the sick and made concoctions to brighten existence; the mechanics built, pouring their cold passion into things more durable than their own flesh; even the gargoyles grew stone to leave a trace in the world—something besides their lithified bodies.

"These are idle thoughts," Beresta said. "You better get going, or you'll daydream until morning."

Mattie looked at the sky, at the constellation of the Lizard almost aligned with the Carriage, and hurried out of the door without saying goodbye. She walked down the slope, the wind shoving her in the back and buffeting her skirts as if they were a sail. It was dark, and she had to extend the stalks of her eyes and force the diaphragms open, to let in whatever little light scattered over the battered slopes of the Ram's Head.

She saw the opening of the shaft—black on black, its square outline only hinted at—at the same time as she heard human voices. She stood still, listening, her heartbeat almost inaudible under the shifting of gravel under the clumsy footfalls and the lowered voices. Two men rounded the hill and came into her view, black and orange in the flames of their torches flailing in the wind. She wondered at first why they hadn't brought lamps, but guessed that they were either poor or didn't want to attract attention of their households.

There was nowhere to hide, and she stood motionless, even after the light of the torches snatched her out of the darkness and she had no doubt that the men could see her. Both were dressed in rough, unbleached linen shirts and no overcoats despite the chill in the air. They had dark faces, colored not by nature but by years in the shaft.

"Where are you going?" one of them asked. They did not look friendly.

"I'm looking for Sebastian," she said. "I'm a friend of his."

"Who's Sebastian?" the first man asked, and his companion whispered in his ear. "Oh," the first man said. "Did he tell you to come here then?"

"Yes," Mattie said. "At least he didn't say not to." She hoped that an imperfect excuse would have the appearance of the truth.

"All right," the second man said. "Come along then. But if you're a spy . . . "

"Look at her," the first one interrupted. "If they sent a spy, wouldn't they choose someone less obvious?"

Mattie followed them down into the shaft, down the rough wooden ladder into a tunnel where the air grew suddenly warm and still, as if it had been breathed in and out of human lungs over and over again, until it was drained of life and succor. She tried to think of something to say to these men, so aloof and alien, so different from anyone she ever knew, but the usual chitchat about the weather seemed frivolous, and questions about their occupation—extraneous.

After they traveled a short while down the tunnel, the flames of the torches smoldered as if suffocated by lack of sustenance in the air, but the men did not seem perturbed. They came upon a large niche carved into the stone wall, behind the wooden supports and scaffolds that kept the tunnel from collapsing, and her guides reached into the niche, the sounds of shifting stone and gravel disturbed by their hands muffled. The man nearest Mattie pulled out a strange contraption—a short belt of cured leather with its ends stitched together, and a small round apparatus mounted on the belt; Mattie recognized it for a miniature bronze lamp ensconced in porcelain. His companion helped him light the lamp from the torch, and it blazed with a bright white light. He affixed the belt to his head, and the lamplight cut a swath of light through the dank blackness of the tunnel.

"I was wondering how you worked there, in the darkness," Mattie said and retracted her eyes back into her face, narrowing the aperture of the diaphragms. "It's a clever contraption."

"If you were wondering so much why didn't you find out?" the man with the lamp on his head said as they continued along the tunnel.

Mattie faltered for words.

"I guess you weren't really wondering then," the man continued. There was no anger in his voice, just the habitual bitterness of an unhappy person. "You just thought of it now, making conversation."

"Yes," Mattie admitted. "I don't know anyone like you."

"Anyone who works for a living, you mean," the second man said and spat.

"I work," Mattie said. "I'm an alchemist."

"You're in the elite then." The man chuckled, making the beam of light jump up and down. "It's all right though. There are quite a few of you helping us. I won't say no to a helping hand, although it beats me what your types see in it."

Mattie was starting to wonder about the same question—even if a few alchemists or mechanics or courtiers weren't happy with the way things were, they had so little in common with these crude men that she doubted that any alliance was meaningful. "Are there any other mines like these?" she asked instead.

The men laughed. "Sure," the second one said. "The ground here, it's riddled with mines like a honeycomb. You in the city, you think you walk on solid ground, and you don't know what's beneath you."

"They extend under the city?"

The men nodded. "No exits there, so as not to bother the pretty ladies and the merchants, but there are mines there."

"I meant other mines where people meet," she said.

"Sure," the first man said. "There are meeting places aplenty, only I'm not telling you where."

"I wasn't asking."

"Good, 'cause I'm not telling."

They fell silent, but now there were other people and other light beams—they came from behind and from the side tunnels, and soon Mattie found herself walking in a small crowd. She looked over the faces, hoping to glimpse someone familiar, but they were all the same, the same men who attacked her the day before. But now they seemed different, as if the laws of the surface failed to apply to them and Mattie here.

She whirred and clunked along, feeling trapped and out of place. What if they decided to turn on her? What if Sebastian denied ever knowing her? Who would miss her, who would even know she was gone? She did not like to think of the answer.

Chapter 15

WE CANNOT HELP BUT THINK OF THE SHAFTS NOW, WINDING *deep in the stone below, looping through and running up and down; we cannot help but think of all the people underneath. They seem to like it lately, and we watch the furtive figures down below, certain that they are invisible in the darkness, dash through the streets snaking beneath us. The city smells of smoke and trouble, and we think that this smell is more appropriate for fall than spring, this tang of burning leaves and bitterness. It reminds us of the underground, of its suffocating air and the bite of brimstone and magma, boiling not too far underneath.*

We did not understand why they had to change the city we've built, just like we do not understand now why they must destroy it—befuddled and distraught, we huddle closer together on the roofs, wing brushing against wing, our mouths mute, heavy with unborn words, the taste of gemstones still fresh in their crevices.

We do not like the metal girl going underground; we fear that the stone that gave us birth will lead her away from us, just like the books, just like the books. We feel selfish and undeserving as we consider our impending death and her reluctance to help us, her preoccupation with other concerns. But we suppose she cannot help herself, and we just try to maintain our faith, and we hold onto each other, as if a touch of hands will prevent our rough flesh from becoming stone, as if we won't have to wake up with our arms wrapped around yet another one of our number cold and unresponsive and dead.

THE MEETING PLACE FELT AS IF IT WERE IN THE VERY BOWELS of the earth—hot and stuffy, filled with the smell of pipe tobacco and opium, its cloying sweetness reminding Mattie of Ilmarekh. She expected something reminiscent of the meetings the mechanics and the alchemists held—if not actual long tables with interminable rows of chairs surrounding them in concentric circles, like waves after a stone tossed into the Grackle Pond.

Instead it felt like the telegraph or the offices of the Parliament—people came and went, and the telegraph chittered; she wondered at first where the telegraph apparatus came from, but then remembered that the one in Ilmarekh's hovel seemed to be missing when she last visited. The widening of the tunnel lit by the hanging lanterns felt almost mundane, despite the blackness of two tunnels—two circles of nothingness—framing it. There were chairs and tables, a peeling chaise, a jumble of furniture and papers and pillows; it felt like a trash heap, and Mattie thought that most things here must've been salvaged from the trash.

People came in, and others left, and all this activity seemed directed at something by the back wall of the cave, next to the hungry, gaping mouth of the tunnel. Mattie approached meekly, apologetic in advance.

There were several chairs pushed against the stone wall and

the lattice of scaffolding hugging it, and a few makeshift desks constructed out of roughly hewn boards and wicker shipping crates such as one usually found broken and empty behind the marketplace, after the market was over. They smelled weakly of peaches and scorched wood. People crowded around the tables, speaking in low voices; the new arrivals came up to say hello, and some of them were given parcels and papers.

Two men appeared from the tunnel, dragging a large wicker crate between them, and without even looking, Mattie guessed what was in it. They stacked the crate against the wall, and turned around to go back into the tunnel when one of them noticed Mattie. He squinted at her. "What are you doing here?"

"Looking for Sebastian," she said.

"He's coming," the man said, and disappeared back into the tunnel.

Mattie looked around, by habit searching for familiar faces, but could not find any. She passed the time studying the crowd; to her surprise, a few of those present did not look like either miners or peasants—their fine clothes and clean hands, their affectations clearly indicated a higher station in life than of the rest of those present. They segregated in their own little group and talked in hushed voices, occasionally stealing glances at the people around them. Mattie noticed that they were all quite young and well-groomed—adult children who hadn't come into their inheritance yet, Mattie guessed. Social butterflies with too much free time on their hands. She should've guessed that they would be involved in something like this.

They looked like people Mattie was used to, and she took a step closer to them.

"Hey," said a young man with hair so light that he had an appearance of missing eyebrows. "I know you; you're that automaton who used to come to Bergen's parties a lot."

"Mattie," she said. "My name is Mattie."

The man smiled. "That's right. I'm Aerin. Nice to meet you; I've seen you many times, but I don't think we've been properly introduced."

"Charmed," Mattie said, and shook the proffered hand. She felt suddenly at home, and she thought it odd that those who despised her and never saw her as anything deserving of consideration made her feel most at ease. "I'm surprised to see you here."

The man shrugged, laughed, and gestured at his friends. "We all are here because we were concerned about the plight of the common man."

"Was it you who blew up the palace?" Mattie said.

"You're quite blunt," a woman standing to Mattie's right said. She had heavily lined eyes and an overall air of languor Loharri would've found appealing.

"Of course she is," one of the courtiers murmured. "She's an instrument."

A few of the others snickered.

"That's not what I meant, Cedrik," the woman said, without even looking at Mattie's detractor. She smiled at Mattie. "Don't pay attention to him, dear. He's daft. Now, to answer your question—yes, our group was a part of it. Actually, the initial explosion was meant to show people that we are on their side—after this, they had to believe that we have categorically cut ourselves off from the city's government and its aims. We have disowned our parents and the advantages our birthright has conferred upon us."

Mattie thought that apparently the disowned advantages did not include clothes, but nodded politely. "It is very noble of you." Her mind boiled with questions, and finally she chose the most pressing one. "Is Iolanda all right?"

"Why?" the woman said. "Do you know her?"

Mattie nodded. "Is she all right? I was so worried when they . . . when the houses were burned."

"She's fine," the woman answered. "Never better. She and that new servant of hers were not there—they are safe and well."

"Niobe is not a servant," Mattie said. "She is my friend. Where are they? Here?"

"No," the man named Cedrik said. "We have many safe houses . . . but of course you will forgive me for not divulging their location."

"Of course." Mattie glanced toward the mouth of the tunnel, anxious to see Sebastian. "And this place here?"

"One of many," he answered. "It's just one cell, but there are plenty of others. It's a good place to meet and distribute supplies and catch up on the news for those who can't show their faces in the city proper."

Mattie wondered if Ilmarekh had given them his telegraph apparatus voluntarily—but of course he had to. Mattie kept forgetting that his frail appearance concealed a remarkable weapon—people were afraid of him, in danger from his mere proximity. Of course he had to leave it outside, to be found or collected, the ghosts calling to those they had left behind.

She remembered something Ilmarekh told her on their first meeting. *The spirits*, he said, *the souls. They are not angry at the living, they just want to help. Helping others is the only way we can prove we still matter.* She looked at the apparatus with new respect—it wasn't just a cast-off; it was an expression of support from those who were dead.

Mattie heard a familiar voice at the mouth of the tunnel, and focused her eyes to look at the face behind the blinding light beam. Her heart faltered and ticked louder as she recalled these eyes half-closed in ecstasy, this smiling mouth pressed against her chest . . . she suppressed the rising wave of shame and stepped forward to greet him.

His smile faded and his eyes widened for just a moment, but Mattie noticed. "Mattie," he said. "How did you find me?"

She shrugged. "It wasn't difficult. I need to know something."

"Ask then," he said, with just a hint of irritation giving an edge to his voice. "I've a few things I need to do."

"Was it you?" she said. "Was it you who bought the explosives?"

He shook his head. "No. I did let them use my medallion, so there you have it. Anything else you want to know?"

Do you love me? she wanted to ask, but there were people and their faces, their eyes watching her askance, as if too embarrassed to admit that they were indeed looking. Instead, she looked at her hands when she said, "The mechanics and the alchemists know it was your medallion. They will be looking for you—and this time really looking for you. You can't go into the city anymore."

"They were bound to find out sooner or later," he said with a shrug of his large shoulders. "But thank you for telling me. I'll be careful." He shifted from one foot to another and raked his hand through his hair. "Perhaps you should get going—there's much to do, and for you there's no point in getting involved and endangering yourself like that."

Mattie realized that he was embarrassed of her—not just of what they had done earlier, but of her mere presence here. He did not want his friends to know that he was friendly with a machine. "When will I see you again?" she said. She did not know why it was important to her to make him admit that he knew her, that he was her friend.

"I don't know, Mattie," he answered. "But you're welcome here any time—please come and visit."

There was nothing left for Mattie to do but to say her goodbyes and head out. The way back through the tunnel, alone and in the dark so thick that even her eyes barely penetrated it, seemed longer than before, when there were people surrounding her. She wished she could've waited for someone else to leave, just so she wouldn't have to travel alone, but Sebastian seemed eager to see her go.

She imagined things hiding in the darkness, terrible things that could rend her to pieces, limb by limb, gear by toothed gear, nothing left of her but a pile of spare parts, just like the one that occupied most of Loharri's workshop. Her thoughts turned to him—was he mad at her that she had left so abruptly earlier? Would he be happy to see her back unharmed?

The walls, gray stone behind the scaffolding, reminded her of the color of the gargoyles—it was sleek and cold like their skins, and Mattie couldn't help but think that this was the stone they came from, the solid mass of rock that gave them birth. It was not so solid anymore, shot through with shafts and tunnels and mines. Maybe this is why the gargoyles are losing their strength, their power, Mattie thought. People are destroying the stone the city is built on, and what could one expect but a collapse? She felt the floor by the walls blindly, until she found a few stone slivers, and put them in her pocket. She would work and find out how this stone was different from any other, and why it held the gargoyles in such thrall. Work offered the comfort of familiarity and preoccupation with matters she could control, and which did not hurt so much.

IN HER LABORATORY, MATTIE CRUSHED THE GRAY STONES almost vengefully, and listened to the smallest crystals sigh and squeal under the slow twists of her pestle. She poured solvents over the crumbs and set them ablaze, carefully noting the blue and green color of the flames and the tiny salamanders that frolicked inside, playful and mischievous like puppies.

Mattie watched them for a while. She remembered Ogdela giving her a funny look when she had first seen the salamanders. "What are you staring at?" Ogdela had asked her then.

"Salamanders," Mattie answered. "The fire denizens."

Ogdela snorted. "Silly girl, you can't see them, so there's no point in looking for them."

"But I do see them," Mattie said. "Look!"

Ogdela shook her head. "Your eyes are better than mine then. Better than anyone's."

When Mattie questioned Loharri about her eyes, he grinned with the undamaged half of his face, and said something about polarized light and varying light sensitivity. Mattie did not understand the exact meaning, but figured that it meant that her eyes were special—something she suspected ever since he took them away from her. He did it again on a few occasions—sometimes as a punishment, sometimes for mere tinkering and improving.

"They are good enough," Mattie had begged on many occasions when he wanted to work on her eyes just once more. "Please, don't do this again."

"They could be better," he always answered. "You could see things no one else could see."

"I already can," she told him. "And I don't like it when you take my eyes—I can see nothing at all then."

The flames went out and the salamanders disappeared, and Mattie shifted idly through the charred remnants of the rock, its essence burned away in the blue and green flames, leaving behind only the most simple and most basic constituents.

She dribbled some sheep's blood over them, added the herbs and the elements, and a small crystal of her eye to animate it, to make it listen to her. The homunculus took form, and Mattie put it in the same jar as the previous one, made from regular stone before Sebastian's appearance interrupted her work.

The homunculi bubbled and seemed to size each other up, and Mattie quickly poured the mineral essence into the jar to feed them, and tightened the lid. She watched as the two creatures lapped up her offering and then locked arms. They struggled and wrestled with each other, and for a while it looked like neither was gaining the upper hand, until Mattie realized that their hands and arms had fused together.

Their shoulders touched and stuck, then their stomachs. Mattie thought that soon she would be in possession of a much larger homunculus, when the one made with gargoyle stone opened its mouth with slow hissing and bubbling of drying blood, and engulfed the head of its adversary. The other homunculus, headless now, thrashed, and Mattie wondered if it was capable of feeling pain.

The homunculus made of gargoyle stone devoured its fallen opponent, wrapping itself around the lifeless body and engulfing it, bit by bit.

"Hm," Mattie said. "I wonder what that means."

The homunculus burbled and tittered, and banged its shapeless fists on the glass surrounding it. Pink bubbles formed on its lipless mouth as the homunculus closed and opened it, as if trying to speak. Mattie hesitated—she wanted to hear what the thing had to say, but she felt disturbed by its behavior; Niobe hasn't warned her about the possibility of homuncular cannibalism. She also didn't tell Mattie that these things could talk, or at least attempt to; or maybe Niobe did not know. Mattie felt an electric tingling in her fingers such as she usually experienced when something special happened.

She turned away from the jar and paced along the bench, her heart ticking like a cricket on July night. She was not prepared to have created something so unexpected—and, she guessed, horrible. For a moment she fought the temptation to just destroy the creature, fling it with its tightly locked jar into the fireplace and flee from the apartment; toss it onto the streets below and let the lizards' claws and the segmented legs of the mechanical caterpillars tear it to pieces and smear it into a long bloody streak on the cobbled pavement; destroy it forever so it never got a chance to whisper its terrible secrets to her with its mutable, liquid mouth.

She stared out of the window, distraught, until she realized that the streets below were unnaturally silent. She hung out of the window, to see as far as she could, but there seemed to be no signs of disturbance. She was about to pull the shutters closed when she heard a distant but unmistakable crackling of musket shots—a fast rattle at first, getting more disorganized and scattered soon after.

Mattie wanted to worry, to run to the Parliament to see if everything was all right, to check on the unfinished Calculator to make sure it still stood. She could picture it in her mind, towering and clanging and belching, like a miniature foundry surrounded by a phalanx of grim and determined mechanics . . . Loharri would be there for sure, she thought, ready to defend the Calculator.

The sound of breaking glass startled her from her reverie, and Mattie whipped around, the joints of her waist whining with the sudden movement, the springs of her back taut and stretched to their limit.

The jar lay shattered on the floor—the homunculus inside must've wrestled it to the edge of the bench and flung it over, and now it gathered itself into a human form again, moving toward Mattie on its soft, boneless legs. It hissed and burbled, and Mattie stepped back, only to feel the hard ledge of the windowsill behind her back.

The homunculus, almost knee-high, reached for her, and its small, fingerless hands left dark smears on her skirt. Its hissing and bubbling grew louder, and it tugged in her skirt, demanding.

Mattie kneeled next to the creature, repulsed and intrigued. Its disgusting mouth formed another pink bubble, and it hissed—boiling of blood, susurrus of waves reaching the sandy shore—strange words. Mattie bent lower.

"Lissssen," the homunculus whispered, its lips next to her ear.

THE CHILDREN OF STONE CLAMBER TO THE SURFACE IN BROAD daylight, and we watch them with a measure of surprise. The spiders and the miners, the ones who smell of soft earth and grain (and we think, they shouldn't even be here, underground)— they all are there, afraid yet exhilarated. They carry weapons— heavy axes and hoes, mostly, but there are a few muskets, the silver filigree on their stocks glittering.

We want to ask them to be gentle, but the very thought is ridiculous; their eyes, squinted in the sun glare, dream only of burning, we can see it plainly. They do not want to be underground, and we cannot blame them.

They emerge like cicadas, in great numbers and all over. We know the tunnels and the shafts under the city where they and others like them had burrowed for centuries—like cicadas— until one day they realized that instead of digging sideways they should go up, up, toward the sun, where they can become what they always dreamed of. We did the same before them—at least, we assume we did; we cannot remember our lives before the stone shuddered and vomited us into the pool of sunlight, harsh and beautiful, where only the basalt under our feet felt familiar.

The children of the city—our children—run at the sight of them, except the ones encased in metal, glittering like large iridescent beetles. They advance, on foot and on their small mechanized monstrosities that carry them around on their backs, metal heaped upon metal, and we wonder if there is any flesh in them at all.

One of the miners fires the first shot, and the metal man jerks backwards, an almost comical fountain of blood springs forth from where the metal of his head doesn't quite meet the metal of his chest, and we guess that the flesh underneath was not just our imagination.

The metal men fire into the crowd, and many fall. And then other people come—they come from behind the houses, from the alleys, many on lizard back and dressed in expensive clothes; there are also the children of red earth, dark-skinned traders and artisans that tried to make their homes here, and we cannot watch anymore.

We flee from the carnage, aware of disregarding our duty of eternal watching, but our eyes refuse to look and close or turn away, and our legs carry us against our will across the roofs. In other streets, other places we see the same scene—we see blood and gutted lizards, the metal monsters devoid of their riders bumping mindlessly into the walls of the buildings, the sizzling metal buckles, the coal spills, the houses catch fire. We do not recognize the city anymore and flee to our only hope, to the girl who can help us.

We look through her window, suddenly worried that she might be dead and dismembered somewhere, the ticking of her heart silenced, the window in her chest broken. But she is alive and at home, and we sigh with relief, and wonder why is she kneeling next to the creature who smells of blood and stone, the creature who is whispering into the pink perfect shell of her ear. She is so absorbed in its words that she does not hear the door opening behind her, and we do not think of warning her.

Chapter 16

———

Mattie startled when someone tapped her on the shoulder, and jumped to her feet, her fists balling.

Loharri smiled. "Easy there," she said. His eyes watched the homunculus with keen interest. "What is this, Mattie? Did you make that?"

"Yes," she said.

"What does it do?"

"I'm trying to make it obey me," Mattie said. "I made it from the stone of the gargoyles, and now I want to compel it to release them . . . but I want to find something else to attach them to, first."

"Fascinating," Loharri said, and looked away from the homunculus. His long eyes seemed cold now, and Mattie felt another wave of creeping terror. Had he guessed that she made one for Iolanda? Did he suspect that Mattie had the power to bind him? She thought back to the very first time she had met Ogdela, and saw Loharri afraid; how she envied that power then! And yet now she wished he didn't know what she was capable of, that he wouldn't look at her like that—as if sizing up the enemy. "You're not safe here," he said. "They've taken the northern district, everything there. The enforcers are holding them off, but they are advancing on the east. Best you come with me. Bring that thing along."

"But . . . "

"I'm not asking," he said. "I'm telling you. You are coming with me. Bring it with you."

Numb, Mattie obeyed. It was just like before, and no matter what had happened to her since, no matter how powerful or emancipated, she still did as she was told—because she could not do otherwise, because he was the one that made her. Just like the gargoyles obeyed the stone—or was it the other way around? she could not remember—she obeyed Loharri, and mutely gathered the homunculus into the cradling hammock of her skirt. It wobbled and hissed and stained the dark brown fabric a darker red; Mattie did not complain and followed Loharri out of the house, past the boarded-up entrance of the apothecary downstairs.

He did not say a word, and Mattie felt a dark foreboding. The city matched her mood—the traffic was sparse, and there seemed to be fewer people in the streets. She heard occasional musket shots coming from the east and smelled the smoke and gunpowder in the air. But that did not preoccupy Mattie—at least, not as much as Loharri did. His brisk, angry steps, his tight-lipped demeanor of disappointment all indicated the inevitable punishment. *He can't take my eyes away*, Mattie thought. *He can't do this.* And yet, when she asked herself who would prevent him, there was no answer. The enforcers were too busy fighting, and even if they weren't, would they ever interfere with a high-station mechanic taking apart his creation?

She wished she could cry. Her freedom was just an illusion—she was emancipated because Loharri let her, and therefore she had no power at all. Everything she had was either given or allowed by him. Mattie wondered if it were possible to hate anyone more than she hated Loharri that moment, to be more afraid.

And where was Iolanda? Probably busy with other things, probably safe away and underground, with Niobe at her side, both of them real women who shared a bond Mattie neither understood nor could ever hope to partake in. Iolanda would defend her, of course—if she were here to defend, and if it didn't interfere with her plans. Protecting Mattie, helping her get her key back was not a high priority, and she bided her time before she would attempt to control Loharri—bided it until it was needed. It was not about love, Mattie realized; it was about gaining access to the mechanics' secrets. When her co-conspirators would take the city, then she would use her influence to build an alliance with the mechanics, to tame them.

"Bokker is a good alchemist," Loharri said without looking at her.

Eager to maintain whatever illusion of amicability she could get from him, Mattie nodded. "He is. Why, were you working with him on the city defenses?"

"No," Loharri said. "He finished the project I needed finished—the one you were working on before you started with the gargoyles. Remember? You asked my permission to take a break, but I didn't expect you to abandon it completely."

"I'm sorry," Mattie said. Despite her better judgment, a feeling of relief filled her—if it was just about that silly project, then he would forgive her soon enough. How important was it, now? Just a game, a curiosity. "I remember—you wanted a chemical that would capture images for you. Too cheap to pay the painters."

He smiled at that. "Indeed. But Bokker, he did well—thanks to your list. And I worked out how to record not just pictures but also sounds; I can watch people as they move, as they talk, without ever being there. Very entertaining."

"I thought you were preoccupied with the Calculator."

"So I was; but you've had your distractions too, haven't you?"

Mattie nodded and hung her head pensively. "I'm sorry."

"We do what we must," he said with a shrug.

They remained silent until they reached the western district and his house. He stopped in front of it, patting his pockets for his keys. He unlocked the door and Mattie followed him meekly inside.

"I have a new face for you," Loharri said, and locked the door behind him. "Come to the workshop, and I'll fit it on."

"I like this one," Mattie said.

"I don't." He took Mattie's elbow and dragged her to the workshop. The homunculus, sleeping peacefully until then in the folds of her skirt, woke up and hissed.

"And shut that thing up," Loharri said, and shrugged off his overcoat, letting it drop to the floor. "I'm really not in the mood for this, Mattie. Tell it that if it doesn't become quiet, I'll smear it on the walls."

The homunculus apparently did not need intermediaries, and fell silent at once.

"Put it down and sit," Loharri said as soon as they entered the dark cluttered space of the workshop.

Mattie obeyed, and the homunculus stood on its liquid legs but did not leave Mattie's side, holding onto her skirts as if afraid to let go. Loharri did not look overly bothered by its presence—he merely made a peevish face and made a show of circumventing the creature in a wide arc. He dug around in the pile of junk.

Mattie watched him extract another face—an exact replica of her previous one—and wanted to be able to cry. No other response seemed fitting as she realized that she was about to be forced back into the mold she was working so hard to escape. "You are not going to take my eyes, are you?"

"Of course not." He dug under her jaw and popped off her face. Instead of putting the new one immediately on, he tinkered with something in Mattie's head. She heard the faint click of a tumbler, and lost sensation in her limbs. She tried to move, but her arms hung by her sides, limp, and her legs, heavy now, straightened against her will in front of her. "What did you do?" she whispered.

"It's only a temporary disabling switch," he said. "You won't feel any pain—in fact, you shouldn't feel anything at all. And you won't be tempted to run."

He dug again, and Mattie cringed as she felt the contents of her head, the delicate gears, beveled and plain, grate against each other as Loharri's fingers moved around. "Don't let it bother you," he said, and turned her chair to face the wall—a plain white wall with nothing interesting painted on it. He shifted more tumblers, and Mattie's eyes emitted two light beams that met on the wall, creating two partially overlapping spotlights. She whined in fear.

"It's all right," he said. "It's nifty, really—Bokker's chemical captures images onto a rotating copper roll, and the same roll records the sound. And everything you see is written on it—it's like your memory, but now I can see it, too."

"How long has it been there?" Mattie whispered.

"Since you were last . . . broken," he answered. "I'm not a fool, Mattie, and I notice things. I notice it when you lie, when Iolanda lies—she thinks she is so clever not to hide her feelings but make them sound like jokes. But now we will see what really happened."

The light coming from her eyes blinded Mattie, but still she could see through the haze the vague shapes moving, the cobbles of the city streets jumping up and down in rhythm with her steps. Iolanda's frizzed hair, her pitying look as she leaned closer, her face taking up most of Mattie's vision. Niobe standing by the window, watching them, her arms crossed.

Sebastian's face appeared, by turns kind and mocking—Mattie was surprised to see it so clearly now. His face leaning closer, his lips smiling . . . Then the image became dark, and Mattie recalled with embarrassment that her eyes were retracted then, blind, the rest of her oblivious to everything but the pleasure of Sebastian's hands on her chest.

Loharri made a small sound, of surprise or annoyance, Mattie could not tell. He touched something in Mattie's head, and the image blurred. Loharri swore through his teeth but fell silent when the pale face of the Soul-Smoker took up the entire wall and the shouts and whispers of the dead poured from his lips. And then there was darkness of the tunnels, the faces of the courtiers . . . Mattie's voice asking about Iolanda.

"Interesting," Loharri said. His face remained composed, but she could see the vein swelling on his mangled cheek. "I knew you were hiding something, but this, Mattie, this . . . I have to go now and talk to Bergen. You stay here and we will talk when I get back."

He picked up his overcoat and put it on, his movements slow and measured. Mattie wanted to plead with him, to remind him that he loved her. But the ice in his eyes told her that he was beyond pleading and entreaties, that she was beyond forgiveness—perhaps, even beyond the consideration that one gives to the most insignificant creatures. She could even hope to live through this, because now she was even beyond vengeful dismantling.

He turned to leave, but stopped abruptly. "Oh, I almost forgot: I'll need these to show to my peers." His fingers, cold and accurate, prized her left eye out of her head, then her right. She cried out, but her only answer was the sound of the slamming door, the turn of a key, and a quick rattle of footfalls on the steps outside.

MATTIE DID NOT KNOW HOW MUCH TIME HAD PASSED. SHE had counted her heartbeats at first, but given up after two thousand. She wished she could see the sun, and if she tried hard enough she could imagine how it would look out of Loharri's workshop window—large and molten, with a tang of copper, enclosed in the delicate cage of black rose branches, still like cast iron.

It was always so peaceful here, so quiet—Loharri had often said that he enjoyed the stillness of the air, the absence of sound, which made it easy to imagine that this house was the only place that existed, surrounded by an infinite bubble of luminous and empty space. And now Mattie realized that even if she screamed for help, her cries would be muffled by the dense hedge, and in any case, people were used to screams by now and hid and ran rather than rushed to help.

Something touched her lips—a wet, cold, and unpleasant touch tasting of blood and sulfur—and Mattie started. The familiar hissing reassured her; the homunculus clambered up her senseless form and now whispered in her ear, its voice indistinct and blurred by the gargling quality of its speech. "I can help," it said. "Help?"

"Do you know which switch he has turned?" Mattie asked, her disgust for the creature tempered somewhat by hope.

"Yessss," it hissed. "I see everything."

"Can you turn it?"

The slurping sounds indicated the homunculus's progress; there was a shifting of metal, and a sudden jolt shot through her arms and legs. She doubled over in pain, sending the homunculus splashing to the floor. "Are you all right?" she asked. "I'm sorry."

"Yessss," it said and burbled. "Would you like me to find you new eyes?"

"Yes please," Mattie said. "You are a clever little fellow."

"Of course," it answered. "I am earth. I am stone."

The homunculus slurped across the workshop floor, and even though Mattie could not see it she imagined the black blood trail it was leaving on its wake. She heard the sounds of rummaging, slow and laborious, and she thought that it took such a little thing an enormous effort to shift the pile of parts and rejected machines; the limitations of its size posed an almost comical contradiction to its grandiose claims, but Mattie was disinclined to find humor in anything just now. It was earth, or at the very least its essence. She wondered if the gnomi, the earth elementals, looked just like the homunculus; she wondered if it was somehow one of them, a creature that could move through solid stone with the same ease as she moved through the air. She discarded the thought as unlikely, and carefully stretched her arms and legs, awakening to life with tingling and electric jolts.

She felt around with her fingers; the layout of the workshop was familiar to her and after a few minutes investigating her immediate surroundings, she remembered how she used to navigate these rooms by touch. Often even touch was superfluous—after a day of darkness she developed new senses, which allowed her to feel when the walls were too close, and to circumvent the obstacles.

Mattie felt her way to the pile of parts and rooted through it, the shape of her eyes familiar to her—long cool cylinders with latches in the end that locked into her eye stalks. Her fingers felt gears, faces, metal plates, bits of armor, coils, valves, engine parts, and flywheels. She recognized them all and was momentarily delighted before discarding yet another disappointment.

The homunculus labored by her side, its quiet boiling and hissing always present. She imagined the mess they were making—strewn-about parts, some smeared with pungent sheep's blood, and she felt a small pang of dark satisfaction.

Let him clean up after her, for once. When he gets back, she would be gone, hidden, on her way to find Iolanda and to beg her to speed up Loharri's binding. And to warn Sebastian, of course.

"Is this it?" the homunculus whispered and put something in her hands. She was used enough to him to not recoil at the touch of his hands, wet like a kiss.

She wrapped her fingers around a small heavy cylinder. "Yes, this is it. Thank you. Is there another one?"

"No," the homunculus answered.

Mattie fitted the cylinder into its socket. It was an old eye, discarded years ago, and Mattie tried to accept the dullness of her vision, the gray shroud of dust that seemed to cling to everything. "No matter," she said. "One is fine for now, but we better get moving."

She gathered the creature into her skirt and smoothed the white petticoat underneath—she wanted to look at least somewhat presentable, not as a crazed one-eyed automaton smeared in sheep's blood with her skirts bundled about her waist, exposing her long, metal legs.

"Go easssst," the homunculus said, and nestled deeper into the hammock of Mattie's skirt. "He won't look for you there."

"No," Mattie said. "North. We have to see the Soul-Smoker and warn Sebastian."

The homunculus gave no other advice and asked no more questions, and seemed to have fallen asleep, lulled by the sound of her steps.

———

We WALK IN SMALL NUMBERS; WE CAN COUNT OURSELVES NOW with what fingers a creature has on two hands and two feet. We don't bother, unwilling (afraid) to dwell on our diminishment. Instead, we watch the city crumble. There is fighting, and it feels like it has been going on forever—or at least long enough for us to forget what the city used to look like, before the smoke and fire, before the growing ruins and gutted buildings, before the Grackle Pond was cluttered with scorched, mutilated metal and bits of steam engines and the gears of an automaton brain large enough to make decisions but too small to predict their consequences. We forget so quickly now, our memory so dependent on our numbers; the more of us do the remembering the better the memories are.

The lizards do not drag carts behind them anymore; a few of them have broken loose and stomp the streets in blind panic. Automatons are few and far in between, most of them smashed to pieces or sent away to the farms. The paper factory, as well as all other ones, has stopped, soon after the caravans of coal stopped coming through the city gates. The air has a different quality to it—woodsmoke and clay and stone instead of metal and burning coal; we are trying to decide whether it is an improvement.

We watch the enforcers, their buggies abandoned, their armor nowhere to be seen (too heavy to walk in) head toward the city gates. They cannot possibly hope to retake the farms or the mines; they lead a prisoner among them, and we realize that they want the Soul-Smoker—one always brings a decoy, a sacrifice on such outings. Or perhaps they want to bargain with the rebels and the man walking with his head low, his clothes soaked with the rain, is their bargaining chip. We cannot be sure, but we worry about the blind boy, all alone in his cabin.

The telegraphs all over the city chatter and thrash and spew forth endless ribbons of paper covered in messages no one reads—no one has to anymore. Soon they will run out of paper, and we imagine them straining and chittering, and punching the empty air with their beaks that will have run out of ink too. We wonder how long the water will keep flowing.

The markets are quiet now, and there is little left to buy besides last year's corn and turnips. We see hollow-eyed women cowering—how fast they learned to move in quick dashes between the buildings!—and keeping close to the corners and houses. The merchants leave the centers of the markets free too, their stands leaning sparsely against the protective walls.

The children are gone, as if they had all disappeared over-night—we know it is not true, we know that some are locked inside and others were taken by their parents out of the city; yet others were sent away to relatives in other cities, where they could be children and carefree, while the adults wait out the awfulness that befell them. But it feels to us that they ran away, abandoning the city that disappointed them, and we try and imagine what it would be like, to run away forever, turning our ridged, winged backs on this city. We imagine the sounds of the sea and the smell of red, kind earth, the smells of different spices and the taste of unfamiliar rocks, made of lime-stone born by the sea and not the cruel hot compressions of the earth underneath. We contemplate joining the circus, like we *imagine everyone does—idly, not seriously, but wistfully. There is such temptation, such forbidden joy in abandonment.*

And then the rain starts falling, black rain tainted with soot; it weeps from the ledges and mourns in the gutters, it roars as it runs through the streets, like organ pipes, like a song. We look into each other's faces and wipe away the black rain that weeps from our hardened eyes, leaving black tracks down our cheeks. And we are suddenly not sure whether it is the sky or us who is crying.

We look around us, and we mourn ourselves, we mourn the fact that even after the city and we are gone, the rock will remain. We mourn the ruined city, the unfinished construction, the demolished palace, the gutted houses. Even if it is right for it to be ruined, we can still feel sadness at its passing, can't we? Can't we? And the rain falls.

We watch a lone figure stagger through the streets, holding a parcel to its chest. We recognize our metal girl, our friend, and we creep closer. She does not look good with her one eye and her blood homunculus, which she cradles to her chest, protecting it from rain. The homunculus wails as if water hurts it. The girl lurches onward, determined and half-blind, but heading steadily north. We imagine her walking like that, broken but unbreakable, forever, the homunculus at her chest crying in its gurgling incessant whine.

We eye it with suspicion—we are not of blood and bone, we are not of plant magic, and yet we feel a strange kinship to the pathetic creature, so soft it is almost liquid. And yet somehow it smells of stone, of the gray-limned stone that bore us—when we close our eyes, we see its layers and hair-thin ridges, the minus-

cule inclusions of black granite and crystal-bright quartz. Somehow, the creature is related to us, and we don't know if it is good or bad, but we try to like it, as one would an obnoxious relative.

And the girl herself is not well—we can see it in her staggering, lurching step, in the dull green (where is the iridescent blue of a dragonfly's wings?) glow of her single eye that reflects only the rain back at us.

She sees us only when descend into the street and stand like a wall in front of her, a wall of sour gray bodies streaked with black.

"I know how to help you," she whispers.

"Shhh," we answer. "It can wait." (It cannot.) "Let us take care of you first. Where are you going?"

"The Soul-Smoker," she answers.

We tell her about the soldiers.

Her fingers tighten on the soaked fabric of her skirt, and she cradles the bundle with the homunculus—a monstrous child—closer to her metal bosom. "We have to hurry then. Do you know a quick way there?"

We nod, and we pick her and her bundle up, we gather her into a protective embrace and cradle her close. She falls silent, so tired now.

And then we fly.

Chapter 17

MATTIE WAS TIRED FOR THE FIRST TIME IN HER LIFE. SHE WAS not built to feel fatigue, to experience exhaustion—the whale-bone and metal and the springs that held them together were tireless, for as long as she was wound up properly. But now, lying in the supporting net of the intertwined gargoyle arms, she felt her sole eye retracting into her head, and her mind screaming for permission to just rest, to shut down and not have to whir along anymore. Her heart beat with an irregular tick-tock, and after every click, Mattie feared that the next one would not come.

Loharri's digging around in her head, wrenching out the hidden device and her eyes, damaged something—something important, she feared. Even after the homunculus threw the switch, her extremities felt wrong and awkward, as if wrapped in wool. Her thoughts turned around and around, sluggish and blind, running like trapped animals in the same compulsive circle.

She was broken, she thought; and the time had come when Loharri would not fix her, no matter how she pleaded and folded her hands, how she tilted her head to look up at him shyly. He was the one who broke her, with intentional care-lessness. *Iolanda*, she thought. Iolanda would make him do what she wants—she would make him fix Mattie and give her the key, she would make him be nice to her and forgive her betrayal. It mattered that he would.

But before she could tell Iolanda all that, she needed to make sure that the Soul-Smoker was all right. Why it felt so important, she wasn't sure. Perhaps because he housed the spirit of Beresta, Sebastian's mother, or perhaps because she felt responsible because it was her—no matter how inadvertently—who gave away the treasonous spirits that he housed, told the mechanics that the telegraph they gave him was used to intercept their messages, that he kept secrets from them.

The enforcers would do away with him—from a distance, so as not to endanger their own spirits, using the decoy they brought with them—and they would continue on, to the mouth of the shaft by the slope of the Ram's Head, down into the passage that burrowed under the city . . . Mattie did not want to continue this thought, for the truth was too bitter for even her diminished capacity. "It's all my fault," she whispered, like a spell, without letting the meaning of the words reach her mind.

The gargoyles heard, and their arms swayed, calming, lulling. "Shhh," they whispered as if to a child. "Shhh."

Mattie did not dare to look down, at the streets below, and watched the low tendrils of the clouds streaking across the sky. It was so gray now, yet clear—the transparent bluish gray of a dove's underside, the blue shine of well-polished metal. She had never seen a sky like this, unobscured by smoke and everyday city emanations.

"It is always like this," the gargoyles whispered, barely

audible above the whistling of the wind. "Up here, it is always clear and beautiful. This is why we rarely fly anymore."

It made sense to Mattie—sometimes, one was better off not seeing, not knowing. The wind tore at her hair, the hair that used to belong to someone else, and her eye watched the clear skies above.

THE GARGOYLES HAD LANDED DOWNSLOPE, AND MATTIE FELT wobbly on her feet. She held the homunculus tighter as it grew agitated and babbled and gurgled, and pointed toward the Soul-Smoker's shack; Mattie doubted they would be able to approach it undetected. Even the elusive gargoyles were exposed on this slope, out of their element and somehow smaller.

The enforcers surrounded Ilmarekh's shack, their decoy still between them. His crestfallen look indicated that he was well aware of his impending fate, and did not relish it. The enforcers looked strangely vulnerable relieved of the bulk of their armor, and Mattie found it hard to believe that she used to feel kinship with them at the sight of their metal carapaces.

The homunculus in her arms struggled and heaved, straining against the confines of her binding skirt. She unwrapped the terrible bloody bundle. "What?" she whispered.

"Let me go," it said. "I can help you, help you."

Mattie considered. The homunculus was perhaps small enough to sneak by the enforcers undetected, if only it would cease its burbling. "What will you do?" she asked it.

"What I was made to do," the homunculus answered, and struggled free of her arms.

The gargoyles huddled close to the ground, their wings

fanned low, and they seemed like stones on the hillside. Mattie crouched close to them, watching the homunculus' progress up the hill.

The enforcers shouted, and one of them discharged his musket. The wind carried away their words, but Mattie surmised that they were calling for Ilmarekh to step outside. Then they left the prisoner by the door and retreated a few steps away, their muskets trained on the door.

"We must help him," Mattie told to the gargoyles. "You can do something—they won't shoot at you. Save him like you saved me."

"What can we do?" the gargoyles whispered mournfully, but straightened and fanned their wings.

"Stop!" Mattie shouted at the enforcers.

A few of them turned and lowered their weapons in awe as they saw the flock of gargoyles bounding up the hill, a mechanical girl stumbling at their heels. They never saw the homunculus.

The door swung open, and Ilmarekh, dressed as if he were going out, stood on the threshold, his cane tapping a slow rhythm. He was dressed in his usual black coat with a very white shirt underneath, his face and hands only a shade darker than his white hair.

Mattie's legs buckled under her, as if the joints went loose, and she hobbled after the gargoyles, aware of the growing distance between them and her, unable to look away from Ilmarekh—a black-and-white drawing framed by the doorway, with just a splash of color as the homunculus clambered up the step and to his feet.

"Stay away!" one of the enforcers shouted at the approaching gargoyles. "This does not concern you!"

The gargoyles hesitated, falling easily into the habit of meekness. The enforcers lifted their muskets, mistaking, as people usually did, mild spirit for surrender. The prisoner, the dark-skinned and forgotten man, gasped and heaved, and Mattie realized that his soul was straining to join its brethren. With her inferior new eye, she could not see the shape of the soul, and she regretted it—she wanted to see it detach from the man's lips, transparent yet iridescent like a soap bubble, and bound toward Ilmarekh, joyfully shedding its fears as its former owner buckled and fell to his knees and then to his stomach and lay still.

The enforcers could wait no longer, and they turned the muskets away from the gargoyles. There was no time for the gargoyles to do anything, as several shots rang out. Ilmarekh, still reeling from the absorption of a new soul, sputtered forth a mouthful of blood. It spilled over Mattie's homunculus, and the homunculus absorbed the new offering of blood eagerly, greedily, and only then did the enforcers notice it.

Mattie watched too—the souls, the wisps of smoke, poured out of Ilmarekh's prostrate body sprawled in the rapidly spreading puddle of blood. Judging by their gasps and muttered curses, the enforcers could see them too. The tendrils of souls reached out, and everyone, including Mattie, took an involuntary step back, away from the hissing and writhing wisps. Only the homunculus stood its ground.

The souls found it and reached into it; for a moment, the homunculus looked like a skinned sheep carcass—red, shot through with white strands of marbling; it bubbled and hissed, boiling, yet remaining standing. The air erupted through its sides and face, sending forth small clouds of red mist. Gradually, the violent eruptions subsided, and the homunculus stopped seething and bubbling—it seemed bigger now, as big as a three-year-old child, and more solid, as if the souls had given it a semblance of flesh and independent life.

Mattie watched the unfolding of the strange event, forgetting about her pain and fatigue, unable to look away. Understanding took a while to take hold, but when it did, it bloomed forth with radiant certainty, and Mattie laughed—a sudden, too-screeching sound that broke the enforcers out of their reverie.

They all spoke at once, asking each other questions and pointing at the homunculus—the silent, calm center of the violent events. They discussed destroying it and wondered where it came from; they asked each other what had just happened, unable to comprehend the transition.

It is stone, Mattie wanted to say. The homunculus is the essence of the stone, now infused with the spirits of the dead. Now, every stone in the city, every old building was alive with countless spirits, all whispering their tedious and mournful tales.

And now, it was time to fulfill her promise to the gargoyles. She turned toward them. "Now," she said. "Now it is yours. The essence of the stone and the spirits of the dead are alive within this creature, and it will break the bond that ties you to your fate. Take it, and accept the spirits of the dead people, and carry them with you. The stone cannot touch you now."

The enforcers must have realized that they were witnesses to a momentous event. They lowered their weapons and let the gargoyles pass between them, they let the gargoyles pick up the homunculus, which stained their hands and visibly diminished with every touch. The gargoyles passed it from one to the next, and as the homunculus grew smaller and their hands stained a deeper red, a change came over them.

Their hides changed their color from gray to the faintest blue, like clay on the riverbanks, and a slight color infused their faces with a glow the likes of which Mattie had never seen. Their features softened, and they no longer seemed carved of stone, but mere creatures of flesh. Flesh that did not last, but Mattie decided not to think about it now. They asked her for freedom, not immortality, and this is what she gave them.

She wished she could talk to Beresta just one more time, a quiet shy ghost of the woman who was the first alchemist to walk down this road. Mattie imagined that Beresta would be proud that her work was concluded, would be happy with Mattie's achievement. She wished Ilmarekh had not needed to die to release the souls he had consumed; she wondered what he would be like if he were not so haunted. She missed the friend she did not even know—the friend she could've had.

WE LACK THE WORDS TO DESCRIBE WHAT IS HAPPENING TO us. We know that we are supposed to do something, to help the girl who has helped us, but we feel dazed, awash in the new experience of being separate from the stone. We feel floating, uprooted, like the clouds. Weightless. The city looms behind us, and for the first time we feel separate from it; we float, disembodied, while it remains substantial and stationary and alien.

We look around us with new eyes—like the girl who is now sitting on the ground for some reason; we do not think we have ever seen her sitting down. The enforcers do not know what to do with us, and we feel sorry for them because we understand what it was like, to shed one's hard protective carapace and to stand on the hillside, exposed, with two dead men lying on the ground, mere objects, just like the city and the hill. We smell the salty marine smell of blood on our hands and in the air, we inhale with full chest absorbing the stench of burning—the Soul-Smoker's shack is starting to smoke; did he leave a flame inside unattended? But it is salt we smell most of all, and it stirs memories within us, memories we have no right to possess.

We remember the voyage across the sea, smooth as glass, the ship becalmed for days on this green surface; we remember it wrinkling like silk under the first breath of wind; we remember the waves and the terrible precipitous valleys that open between them; we remember the sensation of our stomach leaping to our throat as the ship poses on the crest of a wave, hesitant, and then plummets downwards, accompanied by cries of terror and exhilaration.

We remember the cities we have never visited, the lives we have not lived—children and grandchildren, and the inevitable aging of the parents; we remember smells of cardamom and moist tropical heat; we remember the soft, red earth which gave so generously when it was not compelled to do so, and was so barren when farmed. We remember the dances in the city squares—open squares fringed with low buildings, which were much more about air than they were about stone; we remember the bright paints children use to decorate themselves and to throw at each other, laughing.

And then our vision doubles as we see our city but through the eyes of the outsiders—the imposing edifice, carved of stone; we see ourselves as others used to see us—perched on the steepled roofs, our wings a sharp silhouette against the fading sky. We see the gray severity and the stern beauty, which does not invite appreciation but rather demands it. We grow dizzy, and we shake our heads, bedazzled and entranced.

And then the other voices awaken inside us, the souls of the people who were ripped away from the dead man who is cooling on the ground before us. We hear a multitude of voices whispering to us, insistent. "Listen," they say. "Just listen."

MATTIE FORCED HERSELF TO STAND ON HER WOBBLING LEGS. The right knee joint kept alternately locking up and buckling under her, but she paid it no mind.

She felt no satisfaction from her accomplishment but rather an emptiness she did not know how to fill—there was nothing left to do. The thoughts shifted sluggishly in her mind, as the gears turned and clicked with unusual hesitation. There was Sebastian and Iolanda and Niobe, none of whom wanted her. There was Loharri, who did not want her anymore either. Then there was the key—her key, the key that would spark her back to life. When she would be her own mistress, she would find a mechanic to fix whatever was wrong with her. And yet none of this seemed important next to the gargoyles, transformed by her alchemy.

They nudged her, gentle, still in awe of their new hands. "Shouldn't we go after them?"

She looked after the pointing fingers, flushed gloriously golden, a real life pulsing within them. "Go after who?"

"Them."

Then she forced her eye to move from the gargoyles to the object of their attention—the enforcers trudging dutifully toward the mouth of the mine. There were enough of them to open the hidden entrance, Mattie thought. There were too many of them to follow. "No," she said. "They have muskets. They will kill us—even you. You are not what you used to be, remember that. You are mortal now. You can be killed."

The gargoyle faces turned fearful, and she hurried to reassure them. "They won't do anything unless you provoke them. And following them now would be provoking. Come on, you must know of other ways to get underground."

The gargoyles nodded, all together, like they always did. "There is a secret place inside the city, near the district that burned first."

"Can you take me there?"

They did not answer but swept her up again, holding her securely aloft, and flew.

The time of inactivity let Mattie think in ways she wasn't able to while walking—she could force her thoughts into an organized pattern, to stack them against each other, to decide on priorities. Ilmarekh was dead, and she was done looking after the others. She needed her key so that she could take care of herself, not needing anyone's condescending help or grudging friendship. And to get her key, she needed Iolanda.

But not just as a friend; Mattie could call on a promised favor. And after that, the sting of their indifference would be tempered by Mattie's knowledge that she did not need them. Perhaps then Sebastian would love her back.

The gargoyles landed just inside the northern gates. Mattie's legs still felt wobbly, but she steadied herself, and bent them a few times, making sure that sensation and flexibility were still present. "Where to?" Mattie asked. The ruins of the orphanage towered above her.

The gargoyles pointed at what appeared as a small hollow in the ground—overgrown with sun-scorched grass, and quite unremarkable in itself. When she looked closer, she discovered an uneven patch of ground, with only a thin gap outlining its irregular shape.

The gargoyles gathered around it and fitted their fingers into the gap. They lifted the thin slab of stone, with grass still clinging to it, and Mattie felt the wet, dark exhale of the shaft mouth, with its familiar scent of stale air and deep underground wet and warm stone.

"Will you come?" she asked the gargoyles.

They shook their heads in unison. "We must go now, but we will see you again."

Mattie descended underground, not looking back. There was no point in watching the luminous, winged figures soar over the still-beautiful city when one was about to descend into a dark place.

HER NEW EYE COULD NOT SEE IN THE DARKNESS, AND SHE kept one hand on the wall of the tunnel, feeling her way with one foot. Her progress was slow and laborious, and Mattie worried that she had taken a wrong turn somewhere and was now heading down an abandoned dead end, where she would never be discovered, and would be unable to find her way back. She took mental notes of the bumps on the wall, of any distinguishing features she felt on the ground—an abandoned axe handle, a bundle of rags.

When Mattie saw a weak glint on the walls of the tunnel, she did not dare to believe that she was nearing the end of her journey. It could be the faulty eye or some underground fluorescent life; it could be anything. She did not let the hope take hold until the glint became a steady glimmer, an inviting white dot of light with thin rays radiating from it, and the stale, warm breath of the tunnel brought with it smells of burning lamp oil and sounds of human voices.

She emerged into the light and space with the walls receding at a distance, so suddenly large and free, and she cried out in relief and anguish. Her eye took a long time adjusting to light in the cave, and people around her appeared as blurs. They asked her questions, but their words all buzzed together, like the sound of flies that now swarmed in the streets, and instead she spoke. She told them about the enforcers who went down the other tunnel. She told them that the mechanics knew.

She felt arms wrapping around her, and for a moment she thought that they belonged to the gargoyles, that somehow the transformed creatures had found her in the darkest underground. She squinted and recognized Niobe's face close to her, with Iolanda just behind. Both women looked changed—

their features had grown gaunter, sharper, and their eyes seemed more knowing than before.

"Loharri," Mattie said to Iolanda. "He knows about the tunnels, and he knows about you and the other courtiers. Don't let him get to you, don't let him take your spell away."

Iolanda shook her head. "Don't worry about that now, Mattie. What happened to you?"

Mattie's legs wobbled.

"We need a mechanic here," Niobe shouted into the interior of the cave. "This woman is ill."

It was nice to be attended to, Mattie thought. Niobe and Iolanda made a fuss, insisting that she sit down by the wall, on a stack of empty crates. Everything in the cave seemed scavenged from the surface, and the smell of mold and rotten fruit clung to the crates as Mattie sank into them.

"What happened to you?" Niobe asked. And added, in a small whisper, "I'm sorry."

Mattie told her—she told her about how worried she was, wandering through the burning district; she told her about the assault and Loharri's betrayal, about the death of the Soul-Smoker and the gargoyles' transformation.

"That was very clever of you," Niobe interrupted her story. "I'm glad that you've succeeded."

"Thank you for your aid," Mattie said. "The things you taught me were beneficial."

Niobe nodded. "I have to say the same to you. I've been caring for the wounded, and I couldn't have done it without the knowledge of plants. Thank you for teaching me."

"I hope we will be able to teach each other again soon,"

Mattie said. She felt vulnerable now, and clung to the warmth in Niobe's voice despite her earlier resolutions. "It is so much nicer than . . . this." Her arm traced an arc in the air.

Niobe smiled at her vague gesture. "Indeed," she said. "I think everyone is eager for the fighting to end. But I suppose it will be different."

"They will always need alchemists," Mattie said. "As long as people get hurt they'll need us."

Iolanda listened to their conversation with the impatient expression which she seemed to acquire whenever she was not talking. "This is all well and good," she said. "But I can't believe what this bastard had done to you."

Mattie nodded and cringed at the clicking sound in her neck and the difficulty of such a simple movement. "I'm sure he feels the same way about me. I've betrayed him."

Iolanda shrugged. "You had a better reason."

Mattie did not feel certain that reasons mattered more than deeds themselves, but felt too exhausted to argue. After her initial burst of verbosity she seemed to have run out of words, and so she listened mutely as Niobe and Iolanda called for a mechanic again and busied themselves with rearranging the crates. Mattie's heart groaned in laborious beats that seemed to fall farther and farther away from each other. And what did it matter? she thought. If her heart stopped, no one but Loharri would be able to revive her. And maybe as time went on he would forgive her. She could last like this, immobile, awaiting the gentle scraping of the key as it entered the keyhole, a slow turn and a click that would bring her back. Perhaps it would be better to wait until she was forgiven and things had sorted themselves out, so she could awake to a semblance of normalcy. It would be nice just to sleep the chaos away, and wake up in the world where Loharri did not hate her. Even in her pitiful state Mattie realized that it was not likely.

"Iolanda," she said. "Please use the homunculus soon."

"It's not my decision . . . " Iolanda started.

Mattie held up her hand. "I know. You want to wait until you have control of the city. But I cannot wait that long. Get my key for me, please. Even if my heart stops. You can wind me again. Just get my key, I beg of you."

Iolanda nodded. "I will, I promise. Don't worry about a thing." She looked over her shoulder and threw her hands into the air. "Finally!" she said. "About time a mechanic showed up."

As Mattie had hoped, it was Sebastian. He nudged Mattie to her feet. "Come on," he said gently. "Come to my workshop, and we will get you fixed up."

"My key," Mattie whispered.

"Shhh," Sebastian said. "Don't worry about a thing—we'll get you back on your feet yet."

Mattie nodded and tried not to worry as she followed him through a wide, short corridor to another cave that smelled of metal, machine oil, and explosives.

Chapter 18

WE LOOK AT EVERYTHING WITH OUR NEW EYES, EYES ATTUNED *to noticing flesh before stone. No longer are we paying attention to the buildings, but rather to the buzzing of the slow, overfed flies that seem to be everywhere. They smell our sweat and land on our lips and eyes, their buzzing loud and somehow unclean. We wince and wave them off our faces, but we still feel the greasy touch of their tiny claws.*

And the smell . . . the mindless automatons are clearing the streets, but too few of them had survived the riots. Even those that did are in a poor shape—they stumble about, and some of their limbs are missing. And they collect the bodies of the dead miners the enforcers do not bother to pick up anymore. They still carry off their own after skirmishes, but we see the fatigue in their eyes, and we guess that soon they will abandon their bodies too.

There is a smell of rotting garbage everywhere, and it takes us a while to realize that it is coming from the dead bodies, stripped of their poor clothing and crude weapons by the scavengers. We recognize the scavengers too, hiding in the shadows—the light-eyed feral children let loose after the Stone Monks left the city.

We suddenly feel fearful and apprehensive, naked in our perishable flesh, and for just a moment we wish we could go back to being stone—crumbling in death rather than rotting, trapped inside an immobile prison of stone rather than reduced to immaterial souls like those that now rattled within our skulls. The moment passes. There is no point in regretting irreversible decisions—one has to live with them, and we try.

We move toward the building of the Parliament—the windows are yellow with light, even though it is morning, and we know that they have been in there all night, too preoccupied to remember to conserve oil, which is going to run out soon, just like everything else in the city.

We climb up the walls and crouch on the windowsills. They don't see us, too preoccupied with peering inward and at each other. They seem worn now, ragged—their eyes are red and swollen, and their soft cheeks are peppered with steel-gray and dark stubble. And as we cling to the narrow windowsills, we feel the taut muscles in our legs cramping, we feel our fingers relax their grip on the window frames, fatigued, and suddenly we understand—in our bones!—how tired these people are, how vulnerable and hurt. Just like the ones fighting in the streets below, just like the ones waiting in the tunnels, just like the merchants in the market square and their skittish customers.

An explosion rocks the air, and a blast of warm and almost solid wind knocks us off our perch. We recover mid-air and spread our wings to buffet the fall, to let us land softly, with dignity and grace.

We look around, to locate the source of the explosion, but we cannot see if any buildings are missing: we would need to be higher, away from the ground. We hear a soft tinkling, and *we look up, to see the shards of glass raining down from the destroyed windows of the Parliament, falling like jagged ice crystals; it is a miracle that we are not harmed.*

We climb up the wall, pressing closely against it, so that the men who are now looking out of the windows—the unshaven and red-eyed alchemists and mechanics—can't see us, but they are not even looking in our direction. They are pointing west, to the districts where the destruction has been the greatest.

We run through the layout of the city in our minds—there are houses there mostly, and the barracks of the enforcers not far from the western gate; there are telegraphs and the markets, there are factories. All of them seem like equally likely targets, and none of them matter.

It was the second time that Mattie found herself naked in Sebastian's presence, and from his pretend lightheartedness and joking manner she surmised that he was thinking about it too. She wanted to ask him now, why did he go along with it? Why did he make love to her—was it a fetish of a mechanic enamored with intricate devices and easily prompted to express his affection the moment a device resembled a girl, or was it something else? She did not know how to ask, and her sluggish mind refused to do any more work than was strictly necessary—another self-preservation mode Loharri built into her, undoubtedly passing along the ridiculous desire to live despite one's inevitable mortality.

Sebastian checked her joints, oiling and adjusting fiddly little parts in her knees. It hurt only a little.

"Pity," Sebastian said. "I wish you didn't feel it, like other automatons." He still regretted their encounter, he still wished she hadn't shown up to remind him.

"There's a module in my head that disconnects the sensation," Mattie said. "Only I don't really know where it is exactly. And I didn't like the last time it was used—I think this is why I'm so poorly now."

"I won't touch it," Sebastian promised. "But I'll have to check inside your head, to make sure there's nothing broken there."

"Last time you said you didn't know how I worked," Mattie said.

"I don't. But I can still see if the gears are misaligned or if the connectors are missing or detached. Now that I've seen how it's supposed to look."

"I think I will need winding soon," Mattie whispered, her voice giving out and then coming back again. "I need my key—make sure Iolanda gets it for me."

"I will," Sebastian said. His voice sounded so earnest that Mattie believed him. "I promise you I will." He thought a bit, his hand clasping his chin absent-mindedly. "Maybe I could take a cast of the keyhole and machine you a new one. I have the equipment here."

Of course, Mattie thought. They machined keys—Iolanda and the rest had access to every important keyhole in the city. That was why they could place the explosives wherever they wanted. In her muddled state, the walls of the cave—dimly lit, just bare hints of solid matter under the gauze of shadows—reminded her of the dark paneling of Loharri's workshop. It smelled the same, and was just as cluttered, and Sebastian became Loharri in her mind and then himself again. Perhaps that was why the thought of a second key in another mechanic's hands scared her.

"No," she whispered. "Just let Iolanda or Niobe get my only key—I do not want more than one, I do not want anyone but me to have it. And I don't want anyone but them touching it."

Sebastian smiled. "Not even me?"

"Especially not you," Mattie said. "No offense meant."

"None taken," he replied. "Maybe just a temporary one? I'll give it to you right away."

The vexing survival module let itself known again. "Yes," Mattie whispered, and the shadows grew darker around her. "Just a temporary one then."

"I will need to take a print," Sebastian said.

Mattie nodded her consent and watched him take the glass bubble off the lamp, and heat a metal tin over the flames. When it started crackling and smelling of hot metal, he dropped a lump of wax into the tin, letting it soften but not melt. He tossed the tin down and blew on his fingers. The lump of wax had grown transparent around the edges, and Sebastian rolled in his hands, letting it cool a bit, stretching it between his fingers.

When the warm, fragrant wax touched her skin, Mattie gasped. This touch felt so alive, so gentle. The pliable wax pushed into the opening of the keyhole, and Mattie tensed, waiting for the turn of a key. None came, of course—it was silly to expect one, and yet she was so attuned to being wound that she could not completely extinguish her anticipation and excitement.

"Stay still," Sebastian whispered. He pressed on the wax lump with his hand, and Mattie looked away. Not because she felt awkward (although she did), but because he was so mechanic-like now—his lips pursed in concentration, his eyes narrowed, he thought only about the task at hand, forgetting everything about Mattie. It struck her, in the slow, grating way her thoughts had acquired, how much like Loharri he was. She found it neither comforting nor disturbing, just odd.

Sebastian extracted the wax and squinted at it. "Son of a bitch," he muttered.

"What?"

Sebastian shook his head. "Look."

The wax looked like a simple narrow cylinder, devoid of any marks. "It doesn't look like my key," Mattie said.

"Of course it doesn't. It's protected, see—the outer opening is more narrow than the internal mechanism."

"I think he told me once that it's a complex key."

"That's an understatement," Sebastian agreed. "It opens up once it's inside and fits into the grooves. But I can't make a print of it."

Mattie lowered her eyes. "He didn't want me to be able to get a copy. Even if I had thought of it earlier, I couldn't have done it."

Sebastian stared. "You never thought of it before?"

Mattie shook her head, and the joints in her neck whined. "I always thought of it as the only key. If there were more, it would be . . . disconcerting." She thought a while, straining after some thought that kept flickering at the edges of her mind. Finally, she remembered. "Did Iolanda tell you about the thing in my head?" she murmured.

"No," he said. "What thing in your head?"

She told him about Loharri and about her unwilling betrayal.

He listened, his hands clasped behind his back, his face carefully composed. But she could tell that he was upset: from the tendons in his neck, from the way they stood out under his skin. "You sure he took it out?" he said.

Mattie nodded.

"No matter," Sebastian said, and reached for her face. "I'm going to take a look inside anyway. Let's see what's in there, hm?"

Mattie did not protest—it was just another punishment, she thought, her punishment for having done something wrong. She submitted to Sebastian's hands taking off her face and popping out her eye, to his strong fingers digging with such cool nonchalance in her head. She felt him flipping switches and adjusting gears, and sometimes she blacked out, just for a moment, but she always came to. He found the switch that rendered her immobile. "I'm sorry," he said. "I have to turn you off for a little while. I promise you will feel better."

WHEN MATTIE CAME TO, THE QUALITY OF LIGHT IN THE CAVE remained the same—why would it change, after all, underground so deep that time did not dare to penetrate it. But it felt like time had passed—the oil in the lamps seemed lower, and Sebastian looked older, a dark shadow of stubble appearing on his face.

Mattie was relieved to have woken up, and to be able to see. She felt better too—her neck turned without grinding, and her thoughts flowed quicker and smoother, without the annoying snags of forgotten words or memories. He had managed to fix her, at least partially. "Thank you," Mattie said. "I feel much better."

He nodded. "Don't mention it."

Mattie hesitated. "What do I do now?"

He shrugged. "Whatever you want. I don't advise going to the surface, though—there's still fighting there." He raked his hands through his hair. "I don't know what they are hoping for—we are right under them! And still they build fortifications. They have a machine that detects vibrations now, so every one of the last raids to the surface was anticipated. Explosives seem to be the way to go, but . . . " He stopped talking abruptly, and waved his hand in the air. "Go, Mattie. Find your friends. I have things to do."

Her heart still whined occasionally, and the beats remained irregular. But there was no point in sulking or wishing that he didn't treat her as an inconvenience. Mattie found one of the lamps that people underground wore on their heads, and she went exploring. The underground tunnels branched and multiplied and widened into caves, the intricate network rife with startling surprises—Mattie wandered through the labyrinth, occasionally finding hidden caches of explosives or food or clothes or equipment; sometimes she found secret groups of people; a few of them were spiders, and they watched Mattie silently out of their dark, sunken eyes. In the dusk, their eyes glistened deep within their sockets like the gems which the spiders often carried in their long hands—as reminders, Mattie guessed, or mementos. Or perhaps they were just entranced with their soft glow. The spiders rarely talked—Mattie supposed it was difficult for them, with their wheezing, whistling breaths. They made Mattie feel uneasy.

When she passed people in the tunnels, she tried not to look at the crates they carried, and she did not ask what part of the city they were going to. She did not ask about what happened to the enforcers who had gone underground before her eyes, and whether they found anything but the abandoned tunnels.

Other times, she helped Niobe to care for the wounded—there were few of them, and the two alchemists had no trouble mixing enough potions and unguents. They talked only of alchemy—Mattie shared her little secrets and contrivances about the use of aloe leaves or chamomile flowers; she taught Niobe to make a strong, tart-smelling brew of green blackberry branches and to apply it to the bandages for stopping bleeding. She talked about her concoctions with a sense of urgency; she never said it out loud, but with a fear that her heart might give out at any moment, she wanted to pass on as much of her knowledge as she could. Niobe did not talk about it either, but she remained alert and attentive.

Mattie grew anxious—there was no sign of changes, and she worried that her body, although ably patched up by Sebastian, would run out before she could see the homunculus work its dark bloody alchemy on Loharri. She needed her key, and she began to feel its absence as a dull ache in her chest.

MATTIE DID NOT KNOW WHETHER IT WAS MORNING OR NIGHT. She left Niobe to care for the sick and went to wander through the tunnels, but her heart was not in it. Instead, she went to Sebastian's workshop. He was gone, but she found the smell of metal and oil reassuring in its familiarity. She sat on a crate and waited for the time when she would be able to go to the surface and see the gargoyles again.

There was a rustling of cloth, and Iolanda entered the workshop. Mattie smiled, and Iolanda sat next to her and rubbed her shoulder gently. She seemed so subdued now, her countenance sad, her flesh not galling anymore but merely soft and tired. Mattie wondered where her glee went, her bouncing joyfulness; she wondered if Iolanda had grown disappointed.

Iolanda smiled and sighed, and pulled Mattie's head into her lap. Mattie resisted at first, but Iolanda took a brush with short dense bristles and a long handle out of her sleeve. "Let me brush your hair," she said. "You will feel better."

Mattie carefully rested her head on the soft flesh of Iolanda's thigh and closed her eye. The brush whispered through the strands of Mattie's hair—not really hers; she thought of the dead boy the gargoyles had told her about. She thought about Loharri, and what possessed him to save these locks for such a long time, what made him painstakingly attach them to Mattie's metal scalp. The same thing, she supposed, that compelled the Soul-Smoker to engulf the dead boy's soul—compassion and desire to remember. Could they really be so similar?

Soon, the repetitive strokes of the brush lulled her and

she stopped wondering. Instead, she imagined the things she would say to Loharri if she saw him again—when she saw him again, she corrected herself. If nothing else, she had to see him subjected to another's will—maybe then he would finally understand what it was like, and would stop being angry with her.

"By all rights he should be down here, with us," Iolanda said.

"You mean Loharri?"

Iolanda put the brush away and stroked Mattie's hair. "Yes. He has as many reasons to hate this city as any of us."

"I don't hate it," Mattie said. "I'm here by accident."

Iolanda did not seem to hear her. "I just don't understand him. He told me he had been in the orphanage; he should be happy to see it blown up. But instead, he goes and converts the caterpillars into barricades and mounts weapons on them."

"Is this why we're still here?" Mattie asked. "There's still fighting?"

"There's fighting," Iolanda answered. "And he, of all people, is acting like resisting the natural course of progress is the right thing to do. What do you make of that, Mattie?"

Disappointment stirred weakly—every time she thought Iolanda was growing interested in her, it was just a pretext for asking Mattie questions of interest to Iolanda. She just shrugged, her metal shoulder butting against Iolanda's thigh. But in her mind, she thought that Loharri's behavior was only reasonable. She knew how hard it was to achieve something, to reach a position of some influence; to give it all away would be unbearable. And unlike her, Loharri could not possibly hope to retain his power—the mechanics were the enemy, and he was too prominent to escape notice. He was not defending the city, he was defending himself. She felt close to him now that she knew what the desire to survive just a little bit longer made one do. After all, she had agreed to a duplicate key, and she was disappointed that she could not have it.

Iolanda's fingers played with Mattie's hair absent-mindedly. "I wonder sometimes, Mattie," she said. "I wonder at the things we do—I wonder at myself. Have you ever done things that you didn't expect to? Things that just . . . happened?"

"Yes," Mattie said. "Lately, I've been feeling that I've been doing nothing but."

Iolanda laughed.

Mattie sat upright. "Don't forget about my key," she pleaded.

"I won't. I know it's important to you."

Mattie grasped her hand. "It's not just important. It is everything to me, and I hate leaving it in someone else's hands, even yours. Please try and understand."

Iolanda shook her head. "I understand. I think maybe this is what we have in common, the desire to take one's life into one's own hands, even if it doesn't work out and one is worse off in the end."

Mattie nodded in agreement. She would be better off if she stayed with Loharri and never angered him.

Iolanda rose from her seat, smoothing her skirts. "In any case," she said, "I cannot wait to see the sun. I hope we will get to the surface soon."

Mattie agreed that it would be not a moment too soon.

———

AND SOON IT WAS TIME TO GO. IOLANDA WAS BOTH EXCITED and fearful, and Niobe only frowned, her lips pressed together in an expression of determination.

"We're going to the surface," Iolanda informed Mattie.

She did not need to bother—Mattie already had guessed it from the feverish movement that started in the morning and the endless chain of the miners and the spiders dragging out the crates with explosives and the few muskets that they possessed along with boxes of bullets. She was not sure whether the resistance of the city had been subdued, or if the miners were getting ready for their last assault.

"Did you see it yet?" Iolanda asked.

"See what?"

"If you need to ask then you haven't," Niobe said, smiling. "Come on, I'll show you. Sebastian is getting it ready."

Mattie followed Niobe through the tunnels, marveling at the ease with which Niobe navigated the maze. The beam of her lantern snatched the sparkling veins of ore on the rough surface of the walls from the darkness.

Mattie had never been this far in the tunnels—it felt different. The air grew cold and sharp, and condensation trickled down the walls. The supporting scaffolding was scarce, and Mattie guessed that these were little-used tunnels.

"Can you smell the river?" Niobe asked.

"Yes," Mattie answered. "We're under the city, aren't we?"

"Not far from the paper factory," Niobe confirmed. "The mines come close to the sewers here—this is why they were abandoned. They couldn't dig farther without the risk of damaging the sewers or flooding the mines if they got too close to the river."

"Can we get to the city from here?"

Niobe shrugged. "It's possible. But first, look at this."

She led Mattie to a large cavern where water stood ankle-deep and dripped down along the walls, through tiny channels shaped over many years. There were human voices there too, and clanging of metal, and the acrid smell of smoke. As they moved carefully, their feet uncertain on the silty slippery floor, something big started to take shape in the darkness, and Mattie gasped the moment she discerned the true dimensions of the contraption.

It was as tall as two men, broad and squat, furnished with a multitude of jointed legs, like a giant crab. The rivets of the creature's carapace were mismatched, some dull and gray, others shining copper. In the center of the machine there was a small tower, and through its glass Mattie saw a man within. The contraption groaned and shuddered, and the gears ground heavily within it.

"What is it?" Mattie said.

"A weapon," Niobe answered. "Sebastian built it—others helped, of course. I suspect that this is why miners tolerated our presence. They don't like the mechanics or the machines, but if any can be used to their advantage . . . "

Mattie circumvented the machine and found herself staring down the barrel of a short and broad cannon. She had no doubt that the contraption would be a fitting match for the mechanics' barricades on the surface as well as the enforcers' muskets.

"Impressed?" Niobe asked.

Mattie nodded wordlessly. She was impressed although perhaps not in the way her friend meant. Along with her fear at the machine's formidable proportions and its obvious destructive capabilities, Mattie felt relief—there was a finality about the thing, sitting so calmly and yet boiling and shuddering with the hidden workings of its mechanism. It would be capable of ending the fighting, and it would be capable of overcoming the city's resistance. Mattie was ashamed to realize that she did not truly care who won—all she wanted was for this to end, so she could go home and resume the making of her unguents, not before getting her key of course, but otherwise she wanted things to go back to the way they were. And it didn't really matter who was governing the city—as long as they kept building such machines, people would bleed, and there would be work for an alchemist. Mattie proudly thought that she was a good one—after all, she was the one to free the gargoyles from their bondage, the only one to accomplish such a difficult task among those who had tried. And that had to count for something.

Chapter 19

———

The surface world assaulted Mattie with bright light and acrid smoke. She emerged from the newly blasted exit, climbing awkwardly up a ladder improvised from bits of scaffolding, following Niobe, Iolanda close behind. Mattie hoped that by now the fighting would be over, and she would have to witness just the consequences but not the actual bloodshed. She was surrounded by people—mostly the courtiers, but Niobe and a few miners remained nearby, reassuring.

"The city is ours now," one of the miners said.

"Not quite," the light-haired courtier answered. "We still need the fighting to cease and power to be transferred in an orderly fashion. We need the mechanics to formally surrender. Otherwise, the resistance will fester."

They walked through the streets, silent and empty at the moment. There were no dead bodies and no lizards, but a low cloud of ash hung over the city, and the air smelled of gunpowder. A thin layer of dust seemed to have settled over everything—the cobbled pavements, the awnings of the still-standing buildings, the twisted remains of the abandoned caterpillars stacked in the streets.

The rumor was, the fighting was continuing by the western district still, where the enforcers and the mechanics occupied a defensive position between the Grackle Pond and the paper mill, barricaded by caterpillars and what remained of the Calculator. Mattie could appreciate the defensive quality of so much metal, and she was apprehensive when they turned west.

Iolanda carried the jar with the homunculus—she fed it well, and the creature swelled with blood, barely fitting into its jar. Iolanda frowned, worried. "I wonder if my influence will last enough time to have him do what he must."

"Let you into the Parliament, you mean," Mattie said. "You could've used explosives."

Iolanda shook her head. "Too many valuable documents in there," she said. "Besides, if we want people to turn to our side, we will have to take the seat of legitimate power, not destroy it."

Mattie suspected that Iolanda was not exactly lying, but simply not telling the whole truth. The rebels wanted the support of the ruling party, however fleeting and limited. Legitimizing one in the eyes of the populace was a familiar concern—the mechanics always talked about it at their meetings, as did the alchemists, but usually such talks happened before the election. Mattie was surprised to learn that a violent overthrow was not free of such considerations either.

They did not dare to approach the Grackle Pond, where musket shots resonated among the gutted buildings, abandoned by their wealthy owners. Mattie thought that everyone who was able to had moved on by now, and only the poor and the stubborn remained behind. This is why it was so quiet— what few people still remained in the city were not venturing into the streets without acute necessity. The winners would have an empty, mutilated city to govern, and Mattie could not imagine why anyone would want that.

They stopped in the street not far from the pond, and Iolanda crouched down and shook the homunculus out of its vitreous prison. It landed on a pavement with a wet thwack, and stood on its soft boneless legs and burbled. "Go," Iolanda commanded. "Go and bring him to me."

The homunculus departed toward the sound of the shots and the hulking gray structure standing in the distance, on the far shore of the pond, the outlines of which Mattie could not quite make out due to dust and smoke in the air. She only tasted warm metal and tired flesh, gunpowder and crumbling stone. "What do we do now?" she asked Iolanda.

"We wait for your master," Iolanda answered. "Our troops were instructed to let him pass through unharmed."

The people settled on the steps of the buildings and on the pavement. As much as Mattie missed the habitual bustle of the city, she only wished to see Loharri for the last time, to get her key, and to go home. She pictured in her mind her small apartment nestled under the roof that got so hot in the summer. She missed the long bench with all of her painstakingly collected equipment, and she worried that the sheep's eyes, pickled as they were, would go bad in the heat. She missed the constant slamming of the door in the apothecary downstairs, the squeaking of the steps announcing a client. She missed having no other concerns but missing a deadline on a potion for an important client, or hunting down an obscure recipe. There was simplicity in her life as it used to be, and she longed for its return.

———

WE WATCH THE SPIDERS AS THEY CRAWL THROUGH THE streets, endlessly fascinating and pitiful. We follow them, trying to reconcile the vision of the children as they used to be with the deformed creatures down below, sifting through the piles of garbage and dead bodies. With most of the automatons destroyed, they took on their jobs—sorting and cleaning, collecting what could be saved and piling the rest into heaps and burning it. Fires smolder low, bringing with them a surprising, gentle reminder of autumnal leaves and bitter fall air.

We fear that they will be forgotten and cast aside soon— they are not as useful as the able-bodied men with dark faces and pale eyes who came from the mines, their stained clothes overlaying bulging shoulders and thick arms. We fear that the spiders will forever sift through refuse, unable to do much else, and we resolve to protect them as much as we can.

We follow them through the streets that were recently abandoned by the fighters, where bodies can still be found, lying face down or face up; we prefer the former as do the spiders—they always roll the dead on their stomachs before going through their pockets and collecting things the dead don't really need. Then they drag them to the heaps that will become bonfires soon.

The surface of the Grackle Pond is sleek and gray, just like the sky above it, just like the fortifications erected on its distal shore. It is quiet now, and it looks deserted—we almost believe the illusion, even though we know there are people crouching behind the barricades, some looking for the enemy through slits carved in metal, their hands tight on musket barrels, while *others crawl away for supplies and come back with food or bullets. We know too that there are men hiding in the buildings, in every doorway along the street, waiting for an opportunity to take aim.*

We notice a strange creature—similar to the one that had turned us, and yet different, for it does not smell of stone— toddle around the pond. We take positions to watch its progress, and we feel protective of it. We wonder if the mechanical girl is nearby then, if she's among those hidden, waiting to storm the barricades. We wonder if the creature is carrying an important message, and we decide to guard it.

But it is only little, and men at the barricades do not see or pay attention to it. It climbs and flows over the barricades, and we follow. Here in the open, it is hard to hide but we slide through the shadows and the sparse bushes fringing the pond, we hover hidden by the low veil of smoke. We see behind the barricades, into a maze of fortifications and crates, people and automatons. We hover in the ash-filled fog and watch—we are not afraid that we will be seen; everyone is looking into the streets, not to the sky.

The homunculus is heading for the man lying on the ground, sleeping or resting or dead. No, not dead—he raises his head and he sees the creature. He sits up, slowly, sluggishly, and we recognize him by his twisted face. He holds his right arm to his chest with his left hand, and we see the dark right sleeve grown darker with blood. He looks at the homunculus as if he recognizes it, and he smiles.

"Come here, little fellow," he says, and extends his injured arm. "Come here, I'll feed you."

The homunculus totters closer and drinks fat lazy drops falling from the man's fingertips.

"There you go," the man says, and he smiles with one side of his mouth. His motions are languid, as if he had just awakened—even when his eyes flicker upward to meet ours, he does not look startled or hurried. He doesn't look away from us, but speaks to the creature. "You'll be my friend now, yes?"

The thing burbles in the affirmative, and laps at the pool of blood collected on the ground, and it swells up, up, like a rising loaf of bread.

The homunculus swells almost to bursting as it sops up the wounded man's blood—not beautiful anymore, we whisper to ourselves. Never again, because there is just no going back with those things.

The wounded man rises to his knees, then to his feet, pushing himself off the ground with his good arm. The injured one only gets in the way and bleeds more. The people by the barricades look up—their faces so similar now, all hollow-cheeked and half-hidden in the thatches of ungroomed beards.

"Where are you going, Loharri?" one of them says, an older man with a generous sprinkling of gray in his beard and long hair. "The alchemists are coming to take care of the wounded, they will have something to stem the bleeding."

"Look around you," he says. "No one is coming."

"You're not going to forget your mechanic's oath, are you?" the older man says.

Loharri shakes his head. "I'm not forgetting anything. But I will go, and I will talk to them, and if you want to shoot me in the back then help yourself."

"You have no authority to negotiate," the older man says.

Loharri smiles and looks down at the homunculus, which is pooling around his feet, just a fat blood smear. "I have as much authority as you do," he says. "That is, not much. But enough to see what can be saved." He looks at the pile of metal with sadness in his eyes, the same sadness we feel when we look down at all the children of our city whom we cannot help.

And then he walks between the twisted metal bars as tall as a man, and climbs over the corrugated sheets piled on top of each other. Once he reaches the top, he stops and thinks, crouching down for stability, but we can see that it takes him a lot of effort to remain upright.

He searches through his pockets and extracts a handkerchief—it used to be white at some point of its existence, but now it is crusted with blood and dirt. He waves it in the air; his opponents are invisible, but he and we know that they have him in the sights of their muskets.

He waves the handkerchief, stiff as a board, in the air to signal his peaceful intentions, and starts his slow descent onto the embankment of the pond below.

MATTIE WATCHED IOLANDA BITING HER LIPS AND PACING back and forth. They made a post of sorts in one of the abandoned houses, and judging by the smell of urine and burned rags, they were not the first ones to have done so. It had once been a nice dwelling—the wallpaper, white with delicate blue flowers, spoke of taste and wealth, and the remnants of the wooden floors, now wrenched free and dragged away somewhere to build fires, were well-polished and clean. There was no furniture remaining, and the small party camped out on the floors, apparently just happy to be anywhere but an underground mineshaft. There were maybe twenty people here, mostly courtiers and a few miners armed with axes and a couple of muskets. The crates with explosives were stacked in the kitchen, well out of sight. The men with weapons guarded the entrance, even though no danger was apparent. Mattie felt quite sure that the men at the barricade by the pond were not going to launch an offensive raid.

She listened to the distant sounds of carnage wrought by Sebastian's war machine, and wondered if the Parliament building survived. Everyone talked excitedly about how all but a few pockets of resistance had been extinguished, and that soon they could start rebuilding. They talked about returning the land to the peasants, and improving conditions in the mines. She overheard a few of Iolanda's friends arguing in fierce whispers whether the miners and the peasants would be fit to govern, and whether they should establish a temporary council consisting of the courtiers who had abandoned their position, and what to do about the enforcers—after all, they've been just following orders, and once the power changes hands, they would have no qualms about serving the new government, would they? And a new Soul-Smoker would have to be appointed—too bad the monks had left, but surely they could find one. Maybe among the spiders who really couldn't hope for anything better.

For some reason, the conversation made Mattie feel sad—she thought that things always happened around her, but without letting her touch them directly. Life flowed around her, like a stream flows around a solitary rock, which, no matter how much it wanted to, was unable to see anything upstream or downstream from it.

Mattie shook her head. After all, she wouldn't want it any other way—she was happy to retire into a quiet corner, where she did not have to look at Sebastian's machine attacking the barricades, crushing metal and flesh with its massive legs and shooting fire from its cannon.

One of the sentries posted by the door came inside. "He's coming," he whispered to Iolanda, and Mattie felt a small flutter in her chest at the thought of facing Loharri again. "He's wounded," the sentry continued. "You better come outside, it is safe on this side of the pond."

Iolanda nodded and headed for the door; Niobe and Mattie followed, neither willing to miss Loharri's surrender. Mattie was anxious now that her goal was so close. She could imagine the weight of the key in her hand, she could almost feel it sliding in and clicking into place, tugging at the spring of her heart, making it well again.

She saw Loharri right away, and the way he walked, stiffly and yet unsteadily, reminded her of the first time she met the Soul-Smoker. She whipped around, to look at the front of the house, and the trampled flowerbeds. There was no doubt—it was the same house where she watched Ilmarekh consume a restless spirit, the same porch from which she first saw him approach. She had a vertiginous feeling of time spinning her around and throwing her into the point where it all began; and yet, Ilmarekh was dead and the gargoyles were flesh. Loharri stumbled along, his feet slurping in the dripping pool of blood that seemed to move along with him—Mattie guessed it for the homunculus, leading him toward his bondage.

Iolanda walked up to him, and they stopped at the embankment, just a few steps away from the house. Mattie watched his face for any sign of recognition, but his gaze slid off her as if she were a fragment of an empty sky, a stone in an unremarkable wall. He looked at Iolanda only, his lips pressed together as if he was trying not to speak.

"Loharri," Iolanda said. "I need you to do something for me. Talk to Bergen, to the other mechanics. Tell them that they have nothing to be afraid of; tell them that we are willing to make truce."

Loharri nodded, slowly, his gaze still lingering on Iolanda's face, a distracted smile forming on his lips.

Mattie grabbed Niobe's hand. "Something is not right," she whispered. It was just a vague feeling, an irrational sense of dread that descended upon her out of nowhere but refused to leave.

Niobe smiled. "What do you mean, Mattie?"

"I don't know," she whispered. "But let's go."

Iolanda shot Mattie a reassuring look, and spoke to Loharri. "Tell them that they will be spared. Convince them that they need to help us. Do what you must, but ensure the mechanics' surrender, even if you have to kill Bergen to take his place. Now, give me Mattie's key, and then go."

His left hand, pale and awkward, reached for the chain. Mattie felt a wrenching anxiety as he slowly pulled the chain from under his shirt, a bright sparkling of the key sending a sense of relief. Her hands reached out without her meaning to do so.

Iolanda reached for the key, just as Loharri lost his balance and stumbled forward. His lips brushed against Iolanda's hair, and he had to grab her shoulder to regain his feet. He straightened, slowly, and pressed the key into Iolanda's waiting hand.

"Go now," Iolanda said, and wriggled from under his hand.

Loharri looked at Mattie, just for a moment, but she felt her unease return as she noticed the slow smile she knew so well twisting his mouth. "Mattie," he said. "Help me. I'm weak, and it is difficult to walk. I need you to help me along."

"I'll come too," Niobe said.

Loharri acknowledged her kindness with a nod, and Niobe grabbed his uninjured arm, letting Mattie prop him on the other side. Iolanda turned toward the house, and the homunculus finally detached itself from Loharri and followed Iolanda instead, its mission completed.

They started down the embankment, toward the towering remains of several caterpillars and what Mattie presumed used to be the Calculator. But she could not help stealing glances over her shoulder. She saw Iolanda, Mattie's key still in her hand, enter the house, and she regretted not taking it with her. Just a few yards more, she told herself, and then we can go back, and she would have her key, never to leave her person.

They were almost halfway to the barricade, when Mattie heard a commotion behind her. She and Niobe turned simultaneously, to see a blast of fire shoot through the door; a pillar of flames engulfed the house instantaneously, before the blast of solid air knocked Mattie off her feet. She clanked on the pavement and felt her fingers give under her weight, unable to withstand the force of the blow. Her face hit the suddenly close stones and shattered into a thousand pieces; she had been too stunned to cover it. She struggled to prop herself up, to see behind her a solid cylinder of fire where the house used to be. She became aware of a clinking of debris as it rained onto the stones.

"Mattie," Niobe gasped beside her. Her face was bruised, and a long scratch on her cheekbone swelled with blood. "Are you all right?"

She nodded. "What happened?"

Niobe's eyes flicked to Loharri. He sprawled on the pavement, face down, not struggling to get up. Mattie knew that he was alive when she heard his quiet laughter.

Niobe crawled over to the prostrate mechanic, and shook his shoulder violently. "What did you do?"

He laughed still, and did not resist Niobe's shaking, his arm flopping like that of a rag doll in her hands. He did not have to explain—Mattie replayed in her mind his stumbling, his lips so close to Iolanda's ear. Dead Iolanda, she realized. Dead because the man Mattie used to call her master whispered a word of command in her ear, and she obeyed, commanded by strands of her hair braided into the homuncular heart.

"How did you know?" Niobe screamed at Loharri. "How did you turn the homunculus?"

Loharri's uninjured arm fluttered, jerking his hand up. His

fingers were broken like Mattie's, but there was no mistaking the fact that he pointed at her.

"It was the device in my head," Mattie whispered. "I'm sorry. I did not know he had seen it."

Niobe let go. "It's not your fault," she said, not looking at Mattie but at the burning house instead.

Loharri stopped laughing. "Yes it is," he said.

Mattie's broken fingers curled into misshapen fists. "How dare you," she said, momentarily forgetting the burning building and the people inside it, overcome by rage. "I'll . . ." Her voice gave out.

Loharri did not answer; he was not laughing anymore, but lay quietly in the spreading dark puddle—blood gushed out of his torn sleeve. It took Mattie a moment to realize what had happened.

"He's dead," Niobe said. She rose to her feet and prodded the inert form with the tip of her shoe. "He bled out."

Mattie grabbed the dead man's shoulders. "Wake up." She gave him a forceful shake. "Wake up, you bastard! You have to make me a new key. You have to!"

He remained silent and still, and Mattie's fists struck the pavement, chipping stone but unable to wake a dead man.

There would be time to grieve later, and Mattie would mourn Iolanda and others, whose names she could not remember and felt bad about it. Maybe some day she would be able to mourn Loharri too—if she survived long enough, that is. But for now her heartbreak was for herself, keyless and doomed. "My key was in there," Mattie said. "It was in that house."

Niobe looked at her with irritation. Blood trickled from her ears, drying on the skin of her neck in a beaded serpentine trail. "Come on," she said. "Get up."

Mattie did; she was not sure whether it was the shock from the loss of her key—forever irretrievable—or a real sensation, but her heartbeat slowed, and the image of the smoldering, charred walls swam in and out of her field of vision. She wondered if Loharri had led her away from the house to show kindness or malice, sparing her the immediate disintegration in favor of a slow, lingering demise; if his last thought was not to avenge the destruction of the city but to punish Mattie for disobeying him. It did not matter now, she told herself. There was no reason for the dead man to have such a hold on her. She should try and help, she should live out the time she had left as well as she could. Her legs wobbled, but she took Niobe by the elbow, steadying her. "It'll be all right," Mattie whispered, even though she knew that it wouldn't be.

She looked up, searching for the gargoyles—she was certain that they were following her, crawling in the rain gutters along the roofs, hovering in the thick clouds of greasy smoke. "Funny," she said, addressing the low clouds and empty air. "Now it is my turn to become immobile, and no one can stop it."

Great wings dispersed the smoke as several gargoyles descended into the street around her. "Can we help?" They spoke in one voice.

"No, but it doesn't matter," Mattie said. "I'm going home. You're welcome to come along if you wish."

She gave one last look at the smoldering ruins and the lone

figure of Niobe, to the prostrate form of Loharri, and walked east. The gargoyles followed her in their usual way, along the gutters, crawling along the facades—a habit really, since there were no passersby to see them. They clung to the faces of the walls with their clawed fingers and toes, their presence a mute consolation.

The house still stood, although the apothecary in the first floor was gutted and burned out, all the salves and bandages long gone, and only a weak smell of aloe still lingered over the stench of charred wood and paint.

The stairs were missing the lowest step, and Mattie had to pick up her skirts to swing her foot high. She could smell her bitter herbs and spoiling sheep's eyes upstairs, a familiar, embracing aroma that brought to mind her long workbench and the rustling of pages in her books. She only wanted to touch them again, but instead of hurrying, she lingered.

Mattie looked over her shoulder, at the winged shapes splayed in the shadows and crouched in narrow places. She thought of how still she would soon be, how quiet her heart. The slow rising of feathered wings outside made up for it—or at least, it had to.

Epilogue

AND SO THE CITY STAYS, CHANGED BUT ETERNAL. EVERYONE has to adjust, to carve a new niche in the mutable landscape, find a fitting fissure to wedge oneself into. Some of the former residents have returned, but others never will—not the deceased Duke, not his family. But there are voices of the dead whispering to us every day, and we learn to live with the constant ebb and flow of their memories and regrets.

We hide in the rain gutters and on the rooftops, we slide through the shadows; we overnight in the abandoned buildings and the remains of the Calculator. Parts of it still clack and whir, and exhale the ghostly remnants of pungent steam. It comforts us; this is also where we keep her.

The mechanical girl is broken, but we put her together the best we could. Still, she would not wake up and the hole in her chest gapes at us, pleading and longing. We know what it wants, and we search for it—we search through the debris and the refuse of the markets, through the burned-out houses; we dive to the bottom of the Grackle Pond, our wings silvery with the powder of air bubbles, and we look in the clouds.

Sometimes the mechanic—a child of red earth, of the world that is not so distant to us anymore—comes to the ruins of the Calculator, its metal insides mysterious and inviting. He sits by the girl for a while and then leaves; we let him come and go as he pleases, because he seems so different now. Even his smell has changed—he now smells of dusty paper and ink, and we suspect that it is the cause of his sadness.

We never tell him about our search, of our moonlit flights over the rooftops, of our bargaining with the spiders who spend almost as much time searching for something in the city's filth as we do. But we do not let him touch her because it is our duty to fix her, and it is our task to find the key.

Some days we despair and think that it has melted in the fire, into a shapeless lump fused to the cinderblocks of the foundation; sometimes we think that it was vaporized by the first blast of the explosion, like the woman who had been holding it in her soft hand. But we chase away such thoughts. It's out there somewhere, and if anyone can find it, it is us—and we will keep looking as long as we live.

AN EXCERPT FROM
THE SECRET HISTORY
OF MOSCOW

*Every city contains secret places. Moscow in the tumultuous
1990s is no different, its citizens seeking safety in a world below
the streets—a dark, cavernous world of magic, weeping trees,
and albino jackdaws, where exiled pagan deities and faerytale
creatures whisper strange tales to those who would listen.*

*Galina is a young woman caught, like her contemporaries, in the
seeming lawlessness of the new Russia. In the midst of this chaos,
her sister Maria turns into a jackdaw and flies away—prompting
Galina to join Yakov, a policeman investigating a rash of recent
disappearances.*

*Their search will take them to the underground realm of hidden
truths and archetypes, to find themselves caught between reality
and myth, past and present, honor and betrayal . . . the secret
history of Moscow.*

1: *Galina*

SHE HAD LONG PALE FINGERS, TAPERED LIKE CANDLES AT the church. She swiped them through the flame of a match carefully at first, feeling nothing. Then she held them there longer, expecting them to drip and melt. Instead they turned red and blistered, and she withdrew carefully, watching the skin peel and stand in tiny transparent tents on her fingertips. She was already thinking of a lie to tell her coworkers to explain the blisters. Iron. Sizzling, spitting oil in the skillet. Napalm. She laughed at the thought. Napalm is never reassuring, and only reassuring things made for good lies—food, ironing, domesticity.

There was a knock on the bathroom door. "Galka, are you asleep in there?" Masha asked. "Come on, I have to go."

She blew out the match. "Will be right out."

"Are you smoking in there?"

"No," she said, and opened the door.

Masha, pink and sweating, bustled past her, brushing her enormous pregnant belly against Galina, already hiking up her housecoat.

Galina exited hastily. Masha's pregnancy bothered her—not just because she was only eighteen and not because Masha's husband-to-be was still in the army, serving the last of his two draft years. The impending arrival of the squalling pink thing that would steal the remnants of her sister's affection away from her hurt more than she would dare to admit—their mother and grandmother were so excited about the baby. Galina pretended that she was, too, and burned herself with matches when nobody was watching as a punishment for being so selfish. She hoped she wouldn't get into trouble again.

She blew on her fingers and headed for the room she shared with her mother and grandmother; Masha now had a room of her own, all the more reason for resentment and consequent weeping at her own monstrosity. The grandmother was away, at the hospital again and perhaps not ever coming back home, and the mother was on the phone in the hallway. Galina relished the moments of solitude. She stretched on her bed and listened to the familiar noises of the railroad outside, and to the mumbling of her mother's voice in the hallway. Quite despite her intentions, she listened to her mother's words.

Of course she's too young, the mother said. *But better too early than too late, and you know Galina: she's an old maid and I doubt there would be any grandchildren out of her, and really, I wish she would just have one out of wedlock, nowadays who really cares. I know she won't find a husband and I've resigned to that. But if she would just have a baby . . . Oh, I know, I told her a million times. But she's stubborn like you wouldn't believe, and I doubt any man would put up with that for long.*

There was nothing there Galina hadn't heard before—to her mother, men were rare and precious prey that had to be snared with cunning and artifice. Galina couldn't remember when last their conversation hadn't turned into a lesson in making herself attractive—how she should dress nicer, and mouth off less and smile more. Maybe this way she would hold someone's attention long enough to get knocked up. Neither mentioned the premise of these speeches—that Galina was unlovable without artifice and deception. She tried to avoid talking to her mother lately. But the voice in the hallway continued:

I just don't want her to turn into a bitter man-hater, her mother said. *Last time when she came home from the hospital* (she could never bring herself to say 'mental institution') *I had hope for a while. But now—I don't know if she should just go back or if there's nothing they can do to fix her.*

Galina remembered that day, when she had returned home, still swollen from the sulfazine-and-neuroleptics cocktails they had plied her with. The injection sites still hurt, and she resolved then to never do anything that would cause her to go back. She never told anyone about the things that flickered in the edges of her vision—strange creatures, awful sights. The mental institution was an extension of her mother, punishing her every time she disappointed. She chose her mother's dull torment over the acute pain of needles and the semiconscious nightmare of neuroleptics. She still felt guilty about her lies.

She pushed her face deeper into the pillow and pulled the pillow corners over her ears to block out the voice from the hallway. But it was too late—the fear had already kicked in, urging her to run, run far away, to protect herself. Like when she was a child (the only child), and there was a driving fear that the life she saw around her was all that awaited her in the future, and she wanted to run to avoid being trapped in the soul-killing routine of home and work, of TV, of acquiring things for the sake of it. How she longed to escape then; now, the desire was given a special urgency by her adult awareness that there wasn't anywhere to run to. The books she loved, the promises of secret worlds turned out to be lies.

And then there was a scream—she thought it was a cat at first, a neighbor's cat with a stepped-on tail complaining loudly of its bitter injury, and Galina wrapped the pillow tighter around her head. Then she realized that the cry was not feline at all but human. A baby.

She tossed the pillow aside and ran, her socks sliding on the smooth surface of hardwood floors. The cry was coming out of the bathroom, and Galina pounded on the locked door. No answer came.

Her mother, the phone abandoned dangling from the little table in the hallway, banged on the door too. A small woman, her fists struck the door with enough force to shake it. Galina stepped back.

"Don't just stand here," her mother snapped.

Galina ran into the kitchen. There was an old chest of tools their father left before he departed for environs unknown, and she searched for it, slamming the cupboard doors, her panic growing with every little door opened and slammed shut in disappointment. She finally found the chest on top of the china cabinet, and grabbed the largest screwdriver there was. Armed, she rushed back to the bathroom door, where her mother was still banging and the baby still cried inside.

She pushed her mother out of the way and struck the door by the handle, chipping away long slivers of wood over the lock. When the lock was exposed, she pried it open.

The baby, umbilical cord still attached, lay on the floor. A squirming purple thing her mother rushed to pick up and rubbed with a towel. Galina's gaze cast about, between the white porcelain of the toilet and the chipped rim of the tub. Vanity. Mirror. Window. The window is open. But no Masha.

Her mother was too preoccupied with the baby to notice her youngest daughter's disappearance. Galina looked out of the window, as if expecting to see Masha hovering by some miracle eight stories above the ground. The air in front of her was empty, save for a lone jackdaw that circled and circled.

She stood on tiptoes, half-hanging out of the window to see the ground below her, afraid to see it. Through vertigo and the waves of nascent nausea she saw the asphalt below—empty, save for a couple of stray cats and a clump of old ladies on the bench by the entrance. The jackdaw cawed and flapped its wings. It circled over Galina's head, demanding attention; it landed on the windowsill and cocked its head, looking at Galina with a shiny black eye, its beak half-open as if it were trying to talk. Its dull feathers looked like iron.

Galina felt the world careen under her feet, and the incessant crying of the baby and her mother's plaintive voice fell away, the jackdaw's eye trapping her in a bubble of silence and awe. "Masha?" she whispered with cold lips. "Is that really you?"

The jackdaw hopped closer and nodded its head as if saying, *yes it is me. It is me.*

"No," Galina said. "It cannot be. I don't believe you."

The bird cawed once and hopped off the window ledge. It fell like a stone until it almost hit the dead asphalt below; then it took wing and soared higher, obscuring the sun in the pale September sky.

The sounds intruded back, and Galina winced and pressed her fingers—blistered on her left hand but untouched on the right—to her ears, and turned around.

Her mother sat on the floor, the wailing baby cradled in the sagging folds of her housecoat, and cried. Her voice rose to a high-pitched scream, oddly matching that of the newborn infant, as the realization of her loss enveloped her. "Masha, Masha!" she cried, and the birds outside answered in angry shouts and caws.

"She's gone, Mom," Galina said. She never mentioned the jackdaw. She didn't want to go back to the hospital.